IN THE WINTER OF HER SEASON

by Joan Robertson

PublishAmerica
Baltimore

First printing

ISBN: 1-4137-6086-4
PUBLISHED BY PUBLISHAMERICA, LLLP
www.publishamerica.com
Baltimore

Printed in the United States of America

In Memory of
Mildred Robertson

(1923-1990)

ACKNOWLEDGMENTS

I am grateful to Amanda Materne, who has been with me from the beginning of this project. I am thankful for her valuable critique as well as for pushing me beyond what I had perceived to be my emotional limit. To the women at work—Debra Wood, Julie Delgado, Carol Mullings, and Monique Dennis—thank you for your enthusiastic reading of the early draft and providing much support. I give thanks to God for giving me the gift of imagination.

-PART ONE-

PROLOGUE

She resolved to walk into her father's bedroom, fling open the window, wait, watch. His hollow eyes would fly open, acknowledging the horror. Her hand pressed against the doorknob. Oh, how she'd waited for this moment, hoping the event would be as satisfying as she'd imagined. The yellow glow of the nightlight crept from the bottom of the entryway. She opened the door, pushing forward on the balls of her feet, a creak underfoot. She stopped, listened, moved forward again—no turning back, not even if she wanted to. Then, the voice came.

Sandra knew the morning was unusually blustery, yet she hadn't stepped outside to witness violence against bare branches or the awful whipping the trash bin endured the night before. Truth was, Sandra hadn't stepped outside in months, but she heard the wind slap its palms against the windowpane, trying its best to come in—then the voice. The voice called her name, so soft and soothing, soothing as the sight of a steeple to a man who'd strayed from faith too long. This voice made Sandra think about her father, Reverend Dr. Trevor Hamilton Jr., and love and hatred overwhelmed her.

The wind died down, as did the voice. But Sandra was certain she would hear it again the next morning; she heard it *every* morning. No one else knew. Sandra would have told her brother if he'd been alive. Certainly, she could have told Lilly, but the admission would probably prove the strain of the past few years had been far too great.

Sandra released the curtains and slipped back into bed, her kinky hair flattened from sleep and neglect, ears now glued to different sounds: the solemn tick of the grandfather clock in the downstairs hall, Lilly's hum in the next room, the hiss of the radiator. Then the spongy thud of rubber-soled footsteps on carpeted stairs—a new nurse who'd come to work the day shift to care for her father. The nurse was a constant tug on Sandra's shoulder that he'd outlived her mother and brother, and heavy sorrow settled beside her beneath the patchwork quilt. Her bleary eyes slowly closed again. Drowsy. Still.

Her mother's face appeared behind her eyelids: dainty nose turned upward, thin pink lips, skin almost devoid of color. Sandra's face: dark, sturdy, mighty brow, high chiseled cheekbones. As early as Sandra could remember, people made a distinction between her and her mother. Even first grade classmates—yellow-haired little girls with plaid pleated skirts and crisp white blouses and already preoccupied with color—asked, "Why don't you look like your mother?" As always, Sandra would reply, "Just don't."

The heat in the room became stifling and the cottony fuzz of her flannel gown stuck to her sweaty neck. She kicked back the sheets, quilt, and the scent of herself suddenly sprung to her nostrils. She thought to wash, but the thought was as heavy as the malaise descending upon her like a shadow, a shadow not produced by light. So Sandra relaxed against the dampness, content with small things. It was effortless, like listening to the sound of the wind that began to stir again, stirring Sandra to think of the events that led her captive to this house in Cambridge. Her mind searched for an opening, navigating her to the night when she'd received that phone call in January 1990.

"Sandy," her mother said, "they think your father has non-Hodgkins lymphoma!"

"Lymphoma?"

"Cancer in the lymph nodes." Her voice broke, followed by sobs and incoherent words—something about a biopsy. "What are we going to do? Oh God!"

Then Sandra heard a distant voice, and identified it as Lilly's. "Now, now, now. You done gone and upset yourself." Her voice suddenly amplified: "Sandy, your mama has to get some rest. I'll call you tomorrow."

The dial tone. Deafening.

Sandra stared at the receiver with her hand over her mouth and then quickly dialed her brother's number. It was busy. Damn! A few minutes later, she dialed his number again...

CHAPTER 1
JIMMY

"And this is why you call me? Listen! You know I don't care about the reverend. Let the cancer eat him up. And when he dies, let him stand before his God and be held accountable for all the pain he caused me, you, Mama, and the woman who bore his illegitimate child—the one in his own congregation!"

Sandra pressed the receiver to her chest, closed her eyes, and counted to three. She placed it back to her ear.

". . . and then he had the nerve to accuse Mama of adultery when it was him spreading his seed across the country. I never forget the time I caught that woman before him—on her knees, Sandy! On her—"

"Jimmy! I'm not the only child here. When Mama had her stroke, who took care of her? I did. You came to see her twice. That's it. I'm not going through the same thing with Daddy."

"For your information, I didn't come to see Mama much because I didn't want to see him. That's why!"

"That's always your excuse!"

"It's not an excuse! It's true. I was only thirteen when I caught him with that woman. Thirteen years old! And it changed me forever. That's when I told Mama I no longer wanted my name to be Trevor, and why I changed it to Jimmy later on. Hell! Jimi Hendrix was more of a daddy to me than he was! And then it hit me. My own father was a hypocrite! My own father! I didn't want anything to do with him anymore!"

Sandra wanted to hang up the phone. "You know, Jimmy, sometimes you act like Daddy only gave you hell. He gave me hell too, especially after you left home. You have no idea!"

"Well, tell me then…always so hush-hush about it. Constantly throwing it up in my face, 'after I left home.' Like it's my fault!"

Silence.

Sandra took a deep breath. "Listen. All I'm saying is, we should both go home and pay Daddy a visit. That's all."

"I'm not going to Cambridge!"

"Jimmy, whether you like it or not, he's our father."

Gee snatched the phone from Jimmy. "Listen, Sandy, Jimmy will be there."

Sandra heard Jimmy protesting in the background. "What? What do you mean, it's time to get over this? This is different…I'm not going to Massa—"

Gee covered the receiver.

Sandra heard muffled sounds.

Then, clear as a bell, she heard Gee say, "Listen, we're due for vacation. We'll come to New York to visit you and Les. Then we'll all drive to Massachusetts to see your parents. How's that?"

"Fine."

Sandra didn't hear Jimmy's voice at all, and she knew Gee had once again cast her spell. Gee was Jimmy's wife and comrade in battle. She had helped him kick his cocaine addiction fifteen years before, and had given him two beautiful children, Laurence and Rita. Sandra recalled how Gee and Jimmy had met on Venice Beach. Jimmy, strung out, strumming his electric guitar for a few bucks, a sandwich, anything. How he'd wound up in California, Jimmy had said he didn't know. He only knew he had left home one early Sunday morning, with nothing but pocket change, his electric guitar, the clothes on his back, stoned. Sandra still waited for Jimmy's rebuttal, but nothing. She grinned, now certain Gee persuaded him to change direction, like the sudden swerve of a car, the screech of rubber on asphalt.

The doorbell rang a week later. Sandra jumped up from her seat and shouted, "It's them!" Les remained calm until Sandra opened the front door.

"Hey, Jimmy! My man!"

"It's cold as a mother out there. This ain't Santa Monica, that's for sure!"

"Quit complaining and give me a hug," said Sandra, tugging on the sleeve of his pea coat.

"Hey! Where's Gee?" asked Les. Les really liked Gee. He always said she was the coolest white woman he'd ever met, plus she was just plain intriguing.

"Ta da!" Gee popped her head into the doorway. Her blonde, waist-length hair swung like a pendulum.

Later that evening, Gee prepared dinner for them all—a curried tofu dish and seaweed salad. She topped it off with a crisp white wine. Gee's eyes followed Jimmy around the living room while he looked at pieces of artwork Les and Sandra had brought back from their numerous trips to Africa.

"That comes from the Ashanti tribe," said Les, reclining on the hardwood floor, an elbow pressed against a large decorative pillow, a glass of wine in hand.

Jimmy knelt down to look at the intricately carved calabash. "Check this out, Gee."

Her long printed skirt swayed as she swept across the room toward her husband. Gee squatted on her haunches, rubbing the small of Jimmy's back in soft circular motions.

"Isn't this beautiful, baby?"

"Yes, it is," she said softly, "but not as beautiful as you." Gee removed Jimmy's shoulder-length dreadlocks from his face and lightly kissed his temples. Their eyes locked, their tongues met.

Les and Sandra looked blankly at each other, sitting on opposite sides of the room. And something in Sandra dropped, scattering shards of glass in the pit of her stomach. She'd remembered that, ten years ago, she'd loaded her car and headed for New York. Then Les was the epitome of New York, so full of life and excitement. She had met him through a friend of a friend. He was sitting on the edge of his seat in a dark, cramped corner at the Blue Note, entranced by McCoy Tyner's piano magic. His eyes were closed, head swaying back and forth, while playing an imaginary keyboard in the smoke-filled air. Beads of sweat glistened on his blue-black face. He was far, far away. Sandra liked Les immediately. He was a man different from her father, so free-spirited. When Les smiled, his strong white teeth lit up his face, making Sandra's insides dance, and his knowledge of the world fascinated her. Now Sandra turned her head away from Les, looking at the small patch of pale blue outside the window, yearning to see the sun again.

Gee and Jimmy were still kissing.

"Hey! Enough of that!" Les said jokingly. "Keep that for the bedroom. So, Gee, how's the practice?"

Gee and Jimmy sat down on the black leather sofa.

"Booming! People are looking for alternative ways to find their spiritual paths, to understand themselves. My father calls it New Age fluff. But little does he know that the techniques I use have been around for centuries." Gee smiled, placing her hair behind her ears.

And still, Sandra yearned to see the sun.

Gee took a sip of water from a cup on the glass coffee table, then propped her feet on her husband's lap. Born Geneva Gordon, Gee was a clinical hypnotherapist, drawing on the healing music traditions of ancient cultures.

"Gee, what are those things you were telling us about again?" asked Les, snapping his fingers. "Oh, man. Right on the tip of my tongue."

"Chakras."

"Right! *Chakras.*"

"Whirling physical, emotional, and spiritual energy existing in and around the body. The term chakras derives from the Sanskrit word meaning wheel." Gee's index fingers moved in circular motions. "There are seven main chakras, each associated with a specific color, frequency, body system and mantra. My patients balance and affect the connections between mind, body and spirit by visualizing these chakras while meditating or listening to specific sounds or music. It strengthens them. If you don't believe me, ask Jimmy." She squeezed Jimmy's hand.

Jimmy looked at her lovingly.

"Tell me," said Les, "what's the name of the chakra located here?" He pointed to his forehead.

"Oh, that's the Ajna chakra. It's associated with the pituitary gland, the color indigo and the sound 'om.' Here is the solar plexus chakra." Gee used Jimmy as a model. "It's located between the navel and chest, and it's associated with the adrenal gland, the color yellow and the sound 'ram.'" Gee sensuously rubbed Jimmy's chest. "Well. Enough about chakras." She plopped her upper body onto Jimmy's lap, stretching her arms above her head. A thin braid adorned with turquoise beads crossed her peach-colored face. "If you'll oblige, my dearest, I'd like to be ravished tonight."

Les looked disappointed. Sandra still looked outside for the sun. And no one spoke of Reverend Hamilton.

The next morning, Jimmy found Sandra already sitting at the kitchen table with a large cup of freshly brewed coffee. She was barefooted, dressed in an oversized t-shirt. "Good morning, sis." He kissed Sandra on the forehead.

"Ummm. I'm working on my second cup, want some?"

"Uh-uh. Coffee does a number to my stomach. I'll stick to the echinacea tea.

I brought some from my health food store. You should try some." Jimmy placed the chrome teakettle on the stove.

"No, thank you! Hey, I don't recall coffee ever upsetting your stomach. You used to drink lots of it."

"Yeah. Used to. That's when I was young." He pinched Sandra's cheek. "Remember, I'm thirty-six now." Jimmy sat down at the table and slouched in his seat, stretching his long legs. He absentmindedly played with his goatee before shoving both hands into the front pockets of his jeans. They were worn with holes at the knees. Jimmy was as fair-skinned as their mother. Underneath his translucent skin ran small blue veins. His face was sprinkled with a generous helping of freckles. He was bare-chested and barefooted. Sandra had forgotten Jimmy's age—not that thirty-six was old; she was thirty-two herself. But Jimmy looked good. He was still slim, and the torment of his earlier days had not etched itself upon his smooth face. Tufts of blondish-red hair covered his upper body.

Jimmy exhaled an exaggerated sigh. "Yeah, Sandy, your big brother is an old married man now, with two kids—one twelve, the other fourteen. Laurence is just as tall as I am. Swears he's a man! In many respects he is. He's a helluva lot more mature than I was at that age. Rita and Laurence are real good kids. They're staying with my in-laws now."

"Fourteen. Wow! Time flies."

"Yep."

For a moment, they both sat silent, the phrase "Time flies" nudged them into their own space, absorbing them in their own thoughts.

"Do...do...do you ever think about dying?" Sandra asked, breaking the silence. "Time is flying. Mama and Daddy won't be around forever, you know. It makes you wonder about your own mortality...things you haven't accomplished, doesn't it?"

Jimmy got up to prepare his cup of tea. He genuinely sighed this time. "I think about it from time to time, but, truthfully, if I were to die tomorrow, I would die a very happy man." He sat down and sipped his steaming tea. "Many people can't say that."

"I can't! Happy. Huh. I don't know what the word means. Happy." Sandra placed both hands on the top of her head and leaned back in her chair, staring at the space before her. "I'm talking about dying when it feels like I haven't lived. Like all along I've been living somebody else's life—" Sandra stopped and looked at Jimmy, realizing she had said too much.

"Well, to be happy is to be truthful with yourself and others." Jimmy looked at Sandra with raised eyebrows for a moment. "That's the reason why I'm

15

here—to be truthful. You know I've never gotten along with the reverend." A sound of disgust escaped Jimmy's lips and he shook his head. "But I'm a father now. I would hate to think my own children wouldn't want to see me if I were sick or dying. I have to see closure to this. Plus Gee's always talking about the inner child in every adult. You know how Gee gets when she thinks she's right. Claims my inner child is angry!" Jimmy paused and looked to the ceiling. "Huh, I guess she's right." He began stroking his goatee again.

"You're lucky that you met someone supportive like Gee. She helped you along the way, didn't tear you down."

"I know. It's Gee's support that convinced me to come here in the first place. She knows I've wrestled many demons in the past—drugs, alcohol, meaningless sex—but my hatred for the reverend was the source of all those demons. I have to put an end to this and continue my life." Jimmy drew closer to Sandra. "You see, what I have is what the reverend and Mama never had. Their marriage is built on a foundation of sand. Always has been. You know it's true. And the house they built together is near seashore. There's no solidity in that. Their so-called union is just a showcase for the neighbors, the community. We know the score. But what I have with Gee and the kids is real, Sandy. Real. Just as real as you and me." Jimmy flashed an angelic smile.

Sandra remembered how much she loved him. "Les and I are having problems," she said abruptly.

Jimmy looked at her and calmly said, "I sort of sensed it. Les has a restless soul, Sandy. He's still seeking something that he can't hold in his hands. What he's seeking he'll never find in a woman. A woman is made of flesh and blood. She's not an ideal." Jimmy traced the pattern of hair on Sandra's forearm. "Whatever happens, don't lose yourself in the process. You're a good woman, Sandy—which is not to say that Les is a bad man."

"Well, good morning!" It was Gee. She plopped onto Jimmy's lap and kissed him.

"It's a good thing you're a lightweight!"

Gee smiled, showing her pink gums and pearly white teeth. She looked like a little girl, although she was Jimmy's age. "What are you drinking, baby?" She peered into the cup. "Tea? I can use some of that."

Jimmy covered Gee's mouth and whispered to Sandra, "Morning breath." Gee slapped his hand. They kissed again. Sandra looked on with envy. Les stormed into the kitchen with a grin on his face, vigorously rubbing his hands as if standing around a campfire.

"Guess what, folks? We're going to have a party!"

"What's the occasion?" Sandra asked nonchalantly.

"Our beautiful guests."

"Where?" Gee looked under the table.

Les laughed, rubbing his stomach. He was the old man of the group at thirty-eight. He, too, had no shirt on, but unlike Jimmy, Les had a hairless chest, with nipples like raisins. There was a time when Sandra delighted in running her fingertips along Les's tight skin, his sleek, black, panther-like physique. There was not an ounce of fat on this man's body, just hills of tight muscle.

"So, who's game?"

"Why not?"

"Count me in."

"Great! My father may be dying, and you want to party," Sandra hissed.

"Listen, that don't mean we can't celebrate life!" Les replied, holding out his hands as if checking for rain.

"You've always hated him, anyway!"

"What?" It took two long strides for Les to reach Sandra. He bent forward, making eye-to-eye contact. His arm was on the back of her chair, grazing Sandra's shoulder blades. "Well, let me tell you something," he said slowly, deliberately, "so have you. But you'll never admit that! No, suh! Would destroy the loving daughter image you created for yourself, now woodnit?"

Gee tried to diffuse the situation. "So! I guess Sandra and I will have to do some cooking, huh?"

"That'll be nice," Les said, still glaring at Sandra. Les drew his face closer to Sandra's face after saying "now woodnit?" And Sandra now felt the air coming from his nostrils, blasting her face. She knew Les had struck a chord, a chord not far from the truth. He was in one of those vicious moods, and she thought it best to leave him alone, especially when he threw in that slave talk, implying that she was a slave and prisoner to herself.

Jimmy sat frozen, his jaw tightened.

The oppressive air in the room suddenly lifted. Les turned toward Jimmy and spoke in a jovial voice, "You and I will have to get the liquor and other refreshments. I should call my man, Jake. Yeah! Man got some serious music! You'll like Jake. Real people. Hey, come on down the basement. I want you to listen to some of his stuff."

Gee jumped off Jimmy's lap, and she caught a glimpse of the perplexity in his eyes.

"Sure, man, sure," Jimmy said hesitantly. He was beginning to think that he was wrong about Les not being a bad man.

Sandra listened to Les's voice trail down the hallway.

Gee sat down. She waved her hands in front of Sandra's face. "Are you okay?"

Sandra snapped out of her trance, a little annoyed. "Yeah, yeah. I'm okay." Sandra knew she wasn't okay. Gee knew Sandra wasn't okay. But Sandra was not in the mood for one of Gee's touchy-feely discussions.

Les had the music blasting that evening, with John Coltrane's "A Love Supreme" coursing through the air. Sandra heard his fingers snapping all the way in the basement. He was in an exceptionally good mood that night, and Sandra couldn't understand why. Their relationship was shot. No! They didn't have a relationship to be shot. They weren't married, and she knew she would never marry him now, but they'd put in a lot of years together. They'd bought a brownstone in Clinton Hills together. Stupid. They'd brought a car together. Dumb. They'd brought an African clothes shop together. Fool. Sandra had invested her whole life with this man—even her friends were his friends. She suddenly remembered the conversation she had with her father long ago—her father's words after she had told him she was going to live with Lester Ricks:

"Do you have a ring on your finger?"

"Nope."

"And so you're all right living in sin?"

"Actually, Daddy, since we have sex, we've already been living in sin. You know what sex is, don't you?"

"Don't you get flippant with me! I don't know what you learned in New York, but I didn't raise you that way."

"Raise me? Yeah, you raised me holy and mighty, Daddy. So holy and mighty and sheltered and ignorant of the world, and so stifled that I had to get away from you!"

There was a heavy pause. Sandra knew she had thrust the knife in deep. First it was Jimmy who had wanted to get away from him, then his baby girl.

"Well! Lord have mercy on your soul when you burn in Hell!"

Sandra arranged the last bit of garnish on the hummus dip she made earlier. During the day, she and Gee prepared a variety of foods: salad, collard greens, curried chicken, fish, rice, black beans, an array of vegetables (made especially for Jimmy and Gee), fried plantains, potato salad, shrimp and fried calamari. She put the dip back into the refrigerator, as those words echoed in her mind again. "Well! Lord have mercy on your soul when you burn in Hell!" Now what will happen? Sandra thought. She remembered what Jimmy had said, "Whatever happens, don't lose yourself in the process."

Most people arrived at 11:00 PM. All the rooms were dimly lit. In the air, swirls of smoke from burning incense danced with clouds of smoke from burning pot. "Les's reefer-smoking friends!" Sandra mumbled. Gee quickly searched the room for Jimmy upon smelling its scent. Jimmy was apparently undisturbed by it, sitting with Les and Jake having a discussion about jazz. Les was gesticulating wildly. Jimmy caught sight of Gee, smiled and winked.

Gee was the perfect little helper to the host and hostess. She collected empty glasses, asked if anyone needed a refill, and kindly walked up to people and introduced herself. People were very receptive to Gee. In fact, they adored her. The greatest thing about Gee was that she knew her virtues, but wasn't distracted by them. No doubt she was physically beautiful. She wore a long white tunic, soft and billowy like the robe of Jesus. But Gee's most refreshing quality was the radiance within, which spoke for itself.

Sandra looked around the room. People were playing backgammon, chess, some were in dark corners having private conversations, but all were enjoying themselves. No one really danced at Les's parties. One may have tapped his or her feet or occasionally got up to bust a move, but in most cases it was a gathering hall to talk about personal and world events. Coltrane entertained them as usual. Many people complimented the food, and some said they wanted to take a plate home, prompting Les to say, "That's cullid folks for ya." Les thought that his slave talk was funny, while Sandra hated it. Sandra began to loosen up after the third glass of wine, mingling with the crowd. She wore a hip-hugging, African-print skirt and a black Danskin leotard, her head wrapped in cloth. One of Les's friends, Janice, was admiring one of Sandra's black-and-white photographs, a picture of a still pond in Central Park. It was hanging on a living room wall of brick exposure, and a track light shone on it. Sandra wanted to explain to Janice that sometimes she'd felt like that still pond—lonely, isolated. Sandra looked around the room again. She saw Jimmy looking calm and serene. A woman with a paper plate in her hand walked toward him. Sandra stood close enough to hear the conversation.

"It takes a lot of pain to possess that kind of serenity. My name is Jade, and yours?" She extended her free hand.

"Jimmy. The name is Jimmy."

"May I sit?"

"Sure." Jimmy scooted over to make room on the couch. Les and Jake continued to talk without noticing. But Jade was noticeable. She was very tall and thin, about six feet. The pencil-slim, black leather pants made her legs look extremely long. She wore a black leather bra to match. Her ebony skin contrasted with the closely cropped, platinum-colored hair. An earring was in her nose, another in her brow. She set the plate on the glass coffee table.

"So what evil have you seen, Jimmy? And when did you overcome it? You have that glow of peace in your beautiful eyes."

Jimmy smiled, not knowing how to respond. Jade was young, around twenty-four, twenty-five, and very forthright. It made Jimmy feel flattered and nervous. Times had changed since he'd last been on the scene. Jade reached for the plate, nibbling on a small block of cheese positioned on a toothpick.

"Where did you get a name like Jade?"

"Begging the questions. Not good." Jade made herself comfortable, spreading one arm across the back of the sofa. She sat like a man: legs wide open. She looked at Jimmy with a strong, clear gaze. "So what do you have there, Jimmy?" Her chin pointed to his drink.

"Club soda." He held up his glass. The ice rattled.

"Perhaps you're a recovering alcoholic, then?" Jade threw back her head and howled a dark laugh.

"Perhaps," Jimmy said, with a gallant nod. "I see you get the answers any way you can. Clever. Very clever."

"I'd like to think so. You know what else I like? I like you, Jimmy. Your aura is strong. It beckoned me from across the room. Your aura tells me you're on a mission, maybe some kind of quest. You look surprised. Am I onto something?"

"Well, yeah."

"What? Tell me." The block of cheese disappeared into Jade's mouth. She placed the toothpick on the plate and then pulled out a long tall cigarette from a gold-tone case. She held it between her long fingers without lighting it. "Just one of my vices I'm trying to conquer. So go on, baby, tell me what I'm onto."

Jimmy smiled, shifted in his seat, and looked to the floor.

Jade's eyes scanned his lean body.

"So what are your other vices?"

"Dodging the questions again. Okay, I'll let you have this one. My other vices are men…women. Love them both…had them both…don't know which one to choose. Many days I sit in my apartment distraught…out of my mind! My woman says I'm too cold…detached…but my men say I'm too clingy. So I was thinking about leaving it all, you know, like running away to the Himalayas—now, what brings you here, Jimmy?"

Jimmy stared at Jade.

"So?"

He cleared his throat. "My father's sick," he said softly. "We don't really get along, but I'm here to sort of iron out the differences, you know. There's a great big hole between us. I'm not sure if it can be filled." Jimmy had tears in his eyes. He couldn't understand why he felt so emotional.

Jade leaned forward, looking deeply into his moist eyes. She sat back. "You and your father will make amends, but your time on earth is limited," she whispered.

"What?" Jimmy yelled over the sudden din.

"I said that you and your father will make amends."

"And how would you know that?" Jimmy snickered.

"Because I know lots of things most people will never understand." Jade got up. "See you around, Jimmy. Remember me on the next journey." She walked away and disappeared into the crowd.

Jimmy was perplexed, scratching his head.

Within seconds, Jake's voice was in earshot. "Les, my man, I don't care what you say. I still think that 'Bitches' Brew' was Miles's best work ever!"

CHAPTER 2
DADDY

Roads trips usually made Sandra think of new possibilities, freedom. But now, on their way to Massachusetts, she sat quietly in the back seat of their black Jeep Cherokee. Her throat constricted, sensing that freedom had escaped through the small space in the opened window. Gee sat next to her. Jimmy sat in the front seat, with Les driving. Their luggage filled the back.

"Les, who's Jade?" Jimmy asked.

"Who?"

"Jade. The young girl at the party."

"Oh, you mean Jessica." He slapped the steering wheel. "She's the daughter of a friend of mine. A brother I'd met in Ghana. She goes by the name Jade. I don't know where she got that name. I remember when the girl was normal. But now, huh, Jade is in all kinds of mess, or so her father tells it."

"What kind of mess?"

"I don't know." Les shrugged. "Spiritualism…lesbianism…all kinds of isms. Now, look at this fool trying to cut me off!"

"Who's this, Les?" asked Gee. She leaned forward, resting her chin on the back of Jimmy's seat.

"This fool in the red Honda!"

Jimmy laughed. "Man, she means Jade."

"Oh! I thought Gee was talking 'bout—never mind. Nookey's kid. The one I introduced to you at the party. Babe, you know Nookey, right?" He glanced at Sandra through the rearview mirror.

Sandra did not respond.

Les frowned, pushing back his baseball cap.

"Oh, yeah," said Gee, shaking her head. "She looks like she's really out there."

"She is. I'm telling you. The girl was an angel, but now she's a witch…Obeah woman."

"You talk a lot of crap, Les."

"Jimmy, she says she can see the future, man! Huh, I say, the devil himself."

"Well, the devil was an angel before he became the devil," Jimmy said jokingly.

"Well, ex-cuse me! I forgets I'm sitting next to the son of a preacher man!"

Jimmy chuckled, smacking his palm on the dashboard.

"Hey! Watch it, man." Les grinned.

"You're right about being the son of a preacher. Sandra and I sat in church every Sunday morning knowing full well we were the reverend's children." Jimmy turned around, grinning. He tapped Sandra on the knee.

Sandra cracked a dry smile. Yeah. Those Sunday mornings. She remembered her father roaring behind the pulpit, "Now! The Bible says that God created many spirits similar to himself. And these spirits, I say these spirits, are called angels." Sweat dripped from his dark face. Sandra was small, sitting upright in the pew, but her daddy was larger than life. "And all these angels were perfect—not one of them was a devil or Satan! Now can someone in this congregation tell me what devil or Satan means? Well, I'll tell you! Devil, I saaay, devil means slanderer. Satan means opposer." Her father walked across the church platform. He stopped, looked at his congregation, hands before him as if forming a steeple.

"But the time came when one of these spirits made himself the devil, that hateful liar who speaks bad things about another! He also made himself Satan, that is, an opposer of God! He was not—" Her father slammed his hand on the pulpit. "I say he was not created that way, but later became that evil spirit. That angel who became the devil was present when God created the earth, and later, Adam and Eve. And that devil, that serpent, knew after a while the whole earth would be filled with righteous people worshiping God. That was God's purpose. We know it was his purpose! But you know what happened! I don't have to tell you because you read your Bible! I know you do." He nodded his head. "Yes, I know you do. Open your Bibles to Revelations, chapter twelve, verses seven through nine, then verse twelve.

". . . Waaar!" Her father's index finger stabbed the air. "War! Broke out in heaven. Michael and his angels battled with the dragon…the dragon and its angels battled…but did not prevail! Neither was a place found for them any longer in heaven! So down! down! down! the great dragon was hurled, that original serpent, that one called devil and Satan, who is misleading the entire inhabited earth. He was hurled down to the earth, and his angels were hurled down with him. Woe! For the earth and for the sea, for the devil has come down to you! Having great anger, knowing he has a short period of time. A very short period of time! Look around you, brothers and sisters of this congregation! The devil may be disguising himself as a beacon of light. He may be lurking in your own hearts! Beware! I tell you. Beware! Because he is the master of deceit!"

Lilly opened the front door. "Jimmy!" She hugged him hard. For a moment, she saw only Jimmy. It had been so long since he left Cambridge. She remembered Jimmy as a spirited young man, tough-minded, too. Lilly, who was Mrs. Johnson to most, was a long time member of Reverend Hamilton's congregation. Sandra hired her when their mother, Hyacinth, had her first stroke. Lilly was a black-as-coal woman, with a plump, pleasant face. Despite years of living up North, she had never lost her down-home Southern ways.

"Hey, Lilly!" Jimmy hugged her for a good while.

"You sure looking good, Jimmy. Mighty fine! The Lord is taking good care of you. And how you doing, Miss Sandy?"

"I'm fine, Lilly."

They hugged.

"Well, you fine folks just come on in."

"Lilly, I'd like you to meet my wife, Geneva. You can call her Gee."

"Nice to meet you," Gee said reverently, extending her hand.

"My pleasure." Lilly's hands enveloped Gee's. She quickly turned around. "Why you so quiet, Lester?"

"Tired."

"And I guess you folks are hungry, too. Come on in and take off your coats, and head toward the kitchen. I've been waiting for you. Your mama's in there."

Everyone followed Lilly except Jimmy.

"Are you coming?" Gee asked.

"You go right ahead. I'm going to hang back for a while."

Emotions overwhelmed Jimmy. He thought he was prepared for this moment, but wasn't. Now he wanted to walk—run—out the front door, back to Santa Monica. He heard his mother's voice. She sounded happy. A brief moment of happiness, Jimmy supposed. He looked up the long winding staircase. As a boy, he had slid down its banister. He placed his foot on the first step, hesitantly, then boldly climbed several more steps.

Jimmy stopped to look at the black-and-white photographs on the wall. He heard a cough from upstairs, knowing it was his father. The cough sounded strong, not feeble as he'd imagined. His heart pounded as his feet involuntarily continued up the stairs, stopping at the landing. He wanted to walk into the study with the hunter-green walls and mahogany furniture, but his feet would not allow him to go any further. It was early afternoon and the sun's rays streamed outside the doorway. Jimmy smelled rich cherry tobacco. He can still smoke? But…but…he's sick, isn't he? Jimmy stood there, not knowing what to do, when he heard footsteps. A huge shadow appeared at the doorway. It was his father, full strength.

"Who's there? Trevor?" His father squinted. "Is that you? I thought I heard a noise."

"Yeah, it's me." Jimmy walked toward his father. He hadn't shrunk either, he thought. Reverend Hamilton still stood six feet four. His shoulders were as wide as a football field. Jimmy shook his father's hand.

"Come on in," his father said in a deep baritone. When Reverend Hamilton spoke, it sounded like a clap of thunder.

Jimmy walked into his father's study and sat in a chair opposite the desk. The room hadn't changed a bit. Jimmy looked at his father in the sunlight. He looked healthy. His silver-gray hair was stylishly cut and his matching gray mustache was properly trimmed. He wore a camel-colored cardigan, a white shirt, and khaki trousers. Exquisite, brown leather slippers were on his feet. Reverend Hamilton held a pipe firmly in his hand as he sat behind the desk in a leather swivel chair. His glasses were perched on an opened book. Many plaques and degrees hung on the walls, a testimony to a life dedicated to education, community involvement, and leadership.

He'd earned a Bachelor of Divinity Degree from Talbot Theological Seminary, a Master's and Doctorate of Theology from Andover Newton Theological Seminary. He was also a life member of the NAACP, a leader in the National Baptist Congress of Christian Education, a religious editor for a community journal, Community Relations Specialist for Police Commission, and pastor of Mount Baptist Church for nearly forty years. Jimmy looked at his father in all his glory.

"How are you doing?" Jimmy asked, rubbing his lap.

"Fine, as expected." Reverend Hamilton never gave too many details about how he felt, at least not to Jimmy. "You look like Samson," he said, pointing to Jimmy's hair.

Jimmy touched his dreadlocks. "Oh! Yeah."

They laughed.

"When I was a kid, I always liked that story," Jimmy mused. "All one's strength in one's hair."

"You look good. Taking care of yourself, I see."

"Thanks. You look good, too. I was expecting for you to look—"

"What? Dead!"

"Well, no. I was going to say—"

"So how are the kids? They must be big now. Your mother showed me the last set of pictures." Reverend Hamilton put the pipe to his mouth. Its stem clicked against his teeth.

"Yeah, they're growing fast." Jimmy sat back in his chair. "They're staying with Gee's parents until we get back. I miss them already. Kids are great. Fatherhood is great."

"How old is Laurence now?"

"Fourteen. I can't believe it!"

"Thinks he's a man, huh?"

"Yep. Yep." Jimmy stroked his goatee.

"So has he challenged you yet?"

Jimmy looked directly at his father. It was happening, and so soon. His blood began to boil. "Laurence is assertive, if that's what you mean."

"Then he hasn't challenged you yet. The word assertive is too passive for what I'm talking about. What I'm talking about is war between father and son." Reverend Hamilton tightened his grip on the pipe.

"Listen, just because we have our differences, doesn't mean we're at war, Dad!"

Reverend Hamilton stiffened, staring at Jimmy, shocked. Jimmy called him Dad. Jimmy was surprised, too. The voice came from his mouth, but it sounded like somebody else's. He was thirteen years old the last time he called his father Dad. His father's frozen emotions began to break up and flow, but Jimmy couldn't tell. He still looked as stern as an old-time schoolteacher.

"Well, perhaps you're right. Maybe war is too severe. How about some Scotch?"

"I haven't touched a drink in years."

"Well, that's good. As for myself, a little for the stomach's sake." Reverend Hamilton placed his pipe on the edge of an ashtray. He got up and grabbed a glass from a bookcase. He reached for the decanter, poured himself a drink, sat back down.

"Should you be drinking?"

"I'm not dead yet! I don't know how long I have before I meet the Lord. But for now, I'd like to enjoy a little indulgence. Moderation being the key." Truth was, Reverend Hamilton couldn't handle the emotion. He needed a drink to calm himself.

Someone was coming upstairs. It was Sandra.

"Hi, Daddy!" She bent over to hug him.

He held on to her tightly. Oh, how he loved his baby girl. "You look beautiful."

"Thanks. Look, I brought you something." She presented a small package.

"What is it?"

"Open it, Daddy."

Her father put down his drink and opened the package. It was a picture of a lovely sunrise in the Bahamas. A note was attached to it. It read: "I thought of you when I took this picture. The sunrise is God's splendor to the world. So are you. Love, Sandy." Her father wanted to cry. He stood up and hugged Sandra a long time. Jimmy looked on. There was a time when he hugged his father, but now he couldn't.

Sandra turned to Jimmy. "Jimmy, Mama is dying to see you. Since she's in a wheelchair, you know she can't climb the stairs."

"Don't let your mother fool you, Sandy. She could climb a mountaintop if she wanted to. She just likes all the fuss and attention." Their father wrinkled his nose, then laughed, sounding like a giant. "Let's go downstairs to see your mother."

Reverend Hamilton grabbed his pipe and walked toward the door. At that moment, Sandra and Jimmy could see a difference in their father. He walked a little slower, somewhat carefully, as if he were made of china. They followed him. It took a while before their father reached the bottom step. He seemed embarrassed, believing his sickness was a weakness in some way. Neither Sandra nor Jimmy tried to help him for fear of insulting him. Reverend Hamilton was a very proud man who, in spite of his illness, carried himself with nobility. When he walked, one could hear the trumpets sound.

They entered the kitchen. It smelled of freshly baked bread and roasted chicken. Everyone sat around the rustic pine table, enjoying the meal. Jimmy's eyes landed on his mother. She looked like a First Lady. She wore a smart navy-blue dress with a white collar, a strand of pearls around her neck. Years of good living had preserved her looks. Jimmy walked over to kiss her.

"Did you get all dressed up for me, Mama?"

"Certainly. To me, this is a great big homecoming." She stroked his face. Her nails were beautifully manicured, her shiny wedding ring on her finger. "Sit next to me, son. The Lord is certainly good. Yes, he is."

When had the wall been built? The division was much greater than the color of their skin, Sandra thought. Their mother's hands had always touched her face out of necessity—removed the crumbs from her mouth, crust from her eyes. But she stroked Jimmy's face with such ease, not a hint of duty. And The Old, The Venomous, The Familiar opened up cat-like eyes, slithering around Sandra's spine, tempered only by the smile on her face.

Everyone around the table watched the heartwarming interaction between Jimmy and his mother. This was the lady who loved him when no one else did, when he was down and out, strung out. This was the woman who played with him, ignoring Reverend Hamilton's accusations of adultery, that Jimmy was not his, only accepting later that he was his son. Jimmy was Hyacinth's first child, and, for four years, her only child. All those years after he left, she yearned for Jimmy to return home, but he never did. Yes, he sent pictures, but it wasn't the same. Hyacinth couldn't feel his warm skin, couldn't stroke his hair. They couldn't take long walks together, and how she loved those walks with her son. She listened to Jimmy as he told her about his dreams of becoming a musician. Jimmy wanted to be everything, except a preacher.

When he was young, Jimmy wanted to take his mother away from this house, away from the reverend, wanting his mother all to himself. There were many nights when he heard his mother cry, but, in the morning, she was always cheerful. Had he been dreaming the night before? One night he awoke and climbed out of bed. He saw his mother sitting in the dark living room, the moonlight upon her. Jimmy walked to his mother and kissed her. He asked her, why she had been crying. She said he was too young to understand. She then asked, why he wasn't in bed. Jimmy sat on his mother's lap. They talked about all sorts of things before he fell asleep. As Jimmy grew older, he realized that the nights his mother cried were the nights his father was out of town. There was always a convention. His mother was left alone quite often.

Les always felt uncomfortable around Reverend Hamilton. To Reverend Hamilton, they were living in sin, no getting around it. When Reverend Hamilton looked at Les, Les felt as if he could see right through him. At times he stared at Les so hard Les couldn't look him in the eye. It was night now, and Les saw light snowflakes through the window. He thought about the drive home, wanting to leave at that moment, but he knew they were going to stay for a week. A whole week! Everyone was sitting around the fireplace. The fourth movement of Beethoven's Ninth Symphony played softly in the background. Les decided to retire early. Whenever he and Sandra came to visit, they slept in separate rooms. Reverend Hamilton wanted it that way, a message to them that he did not sanction their lifestyle.

Hyacinth was in an extremely gay mood. She sipped blackberry cordial and bounced to the Joy theme. Gee's head rested on Jimmy's shoulder. They were sitting on the couch, feeling warm and cozy by the crackling fire. Sandra was trimming Reverend Hamilton's nails while he sat in his wingback chair. When she was a little girl, she always trimmed her daddy's nails. Afterwards she'd put two coats of clear nail polish on each fingernail, making sure each coat was straight and even. It amazed Sandra that his hands were still strong and powerful.

Lilly sat quietly next to Hyacinth. They were two peas in a pod.

"Lilly," Jimmy asked, "how's Mr. Johnson?"

"Jimmy, you sure been away too long. My Raymond done met the Lord three years ago."

"I'm sorry."

"Don't be. He's happy."

"We all must meet the Lord one day," Reverend Hamilton interjected. "Some sooner than others."

Hyacinth hated when Reverend Hamilton spoke that way. It was a reminder that things would not remain the same. She looked out the window. "Oh! Look, Trevor, it's snowing. Remember that year when we first got married? Now, that was snow!"

"Yes, darling, I remember. Sometimes we'd take a walk in all that snow, ice crunching beneath our feet. Your nose always turned red. You looked like Rudolph. Seems like yesterday, doesn't it?"

"Ummm, it sure does."

Hyacinth was transported to another time, another place. She and Trevor were young again. She was thinking of the day he first kissed her. It was a beautiful spring night. They were sitting on the bench in the backyard. The moon was bright, the smell of freshly mowed grass was in the air. Hyacinth had lived with the Hamiltons since she was three years old. Trevor's parents— known as Grandma and Grandpa Hamilton to Hyacinth—had taken her in when her mother died in a car accident. So she only had a vague recollection of her mother, a Barbadian woman. She never knew her father, an Englishman who loved the sea. To Hyacinth, Grandpa and Grandma Hamilton were her parents. And, for a long time, she fought any feelings she had for Trevor. It seemed as if they were related somehow. It didn't seem, well, Godly. But Trevor was persistent. He knew what he wanted, he always had.

At five, Trevor told his parents he was going to become a preacher. He said it with so much conviction, they knew it would be true. His mind never swayed like other boys his age—those boys who wanted to be doctors in the morning and policemen in the evening. Not Trevor, he was going to be preacher. That was final.

It appeared that every step he took in life was leading to the day when he would become an ordained minister. So, of course, he needed the perfect wife. Hyacinth was it. Sure, Trevor had his fun behind a tall tree or under a bush with loose girls in the neighborhood. Sure, he would slip his fingers up their shirts and rub their breasts. Sure, he even went a step further, allowing them to hold his growing manhood. When his parents weren't home, he'd even slipped them beneath his sheets. That's what girls were for, wasn't it? But not a wife! She had to be pure, chaste. Trevor knew his parents wouldn't allow Hyacinth to go anywhere but to church and school. And Trevor liked it that way. Trevor had chosen a mate way before Hyacinth had any idea how he felt about her. She was his. That was all there was to it. Hyacinth didn't have a say in the matter.

When Trevor first kissed Hyacinth, she felt the urgency of his virility. It was a powerful sensation. She felt the warmth of his body next to hers. She looked up at him. He kissed her again, darting his tongue inside her mouth and over her perfect teeth. He sucked on her tongue. He nibbled on her neck, leaving a red mark. It thrilled him to see that red mark! Hyacinth hadn't known what was happening to her. She was only seventeen, still a child in many ways. And Trevor liked it that way. That night Hyacinth couldn't go to sleep, thinking of that kiss. She had never been kissed before, not like that. Grandpa Hamilton had only kissed her on the forehead or on the cheek, but this kiss made her feel womanly.

Trevor was clever. He knew the first kiss was the kiss most people never forget. It could be many years, with many lovers in those years, but most people will remember their first kiss. He had Hyacinth. He just knew it. But he didn't dare touch her: He had the other girls for that. He wouldn't touch her until their wedding night the following year.

Now Hyacinth touched Reverend Hamilton's hand. This was the only man she had ever known intimately. To her, he was life itself. Her life began the day he kissed her on the bench. Jimmy looked on as his mother tenderly touched his father's hand. Reverend Hamilton looked at Hyacinth with so much love it made Jimmy reconsider his idea about their marriage. No doubt, during the early years, there were problems. But now, new elements were added to the ingredients: age and the possibility of death. Looking at Jimmy's parents, Gee whispered, "I love you."

Jimmy whispered, "I love you back."

Jimmy glanced at Sandra; it was the first time he'd seen his parents displaying open affection. A week ago, Sandra asked him if he'd ever thought about his own mortality. But not until that second had Jimmy really contemplated death and the people he would leave behind. Jimmy was sure these thoughts now occupied his father's mind. He had missed many years in his father's life—birthdays, Father's Days, family reunions, Christmas. Laurence and Rita had never known their grandfather. They knew their grandmother; she flew to Santa Monica every year before being confined to a wheelchair. But their grandfather would probably remain a mystery to them, and to Jimmy. Jimmy realized he hated his father with so much intensity because he'd loved his father with equal intensity. It had taken thirty-six years for Jimmy to understand this, right there on his father's couch. Reverend Hamilton paid the price for being a father, the one person that a son will put on a pedestal. Reverend Hamilton had simply fallen from grace.

Would he ever fall from grace? Jimmy asked himself. Openly or secretly in his own children's eyes? How would he redeem himself? How could Reverend Hamilton?

Around twelve o'clock, everyone retired except Jimmy and his father. They sat watching the fire. The wood crackled in their silence.

"Why did you postpone the tests?" Jimmy asked, crossing his legs, the reflection of the fire in his caramel-colored eyes.

Reverend Hamilton looked at Jimmy, then back at the fire. He didn't respond right away. "I wanted to take care of some business first," he said nonchalantly. "In a couple of days, the doctors will be waiting for me."

"What kind of tests will they be taking?"

"A biopsy." Reverend Hamilton leaned forward to stoke the fire. "Funny, I just went for a routine check-up. Felt fine overall. Well, I had chills, fever, diarrhea, and night sweats, but I thought that it was Lilly's chili!" Reverend Hamilton roared, his mouth a large cave. He realized he was laughing alone. "It's a joke, Trevor, although dry it may be!"

"I don't think it's funny. Don't shield me from anything. I want to know."

Reverend Hamilton sat back in his chair. He told jokes when he was ill at ease; it helped him deal with difficulties. But he knew this was not the time by the look on his son's worried face.

"It's true I'd experienced chills, fever, and night sweats, though. That prompted me to get a physical," Reverend Hamilton said soberly. "The doctors detected a mass on my chest X-ray. They also found enlarged lymph nodes in my groin, armpits and throat. They suspect cancer. Don't repeat all of this to your mother, I don't want her to worry too much. I'll let everyone know the details once the test is taken and the results come back."

"I'd like to drive you to the hospital, if you don't mind."

"I'd like that. I'd like that."

"It will be all right. With the advanced medicine these days, I'm sure things will work out just fine."

"I always wondered why you hated me so." Reverend Hamilton abruptly changed topics. "I just couldn't understand why you defied me in every possible way, all of a sudden."

Jimmy shifted in his chair and rubbed his face from forehead to chin. He sat forward, exhaled. "All of it doesn't matter anymore, but I knew about you and Sister Trudy. I knew about our half-brother. I saw you and Sister Trudy in the back of the church one day. You were doing things I didn't understand, but that I knew betrayed Mama. I was just a kid."

Reverend Hamilton hung his head low. It had been many years since he had thought about Trudy. She had left Cambridge a few months after their baby was born. He would be about twenty-seven years old now. Trudy didn't leave a forwarding address or anything, just disappeared. Reverend Hamilton felt deep shame.

"I'd asked the Lord many times to forgive me. I think he has. I'd like to die with a clear conscience. I'm asking you, can you forgive me?"

Jimmy touched his father's shoulder. "I think I can. Sure, I know I can."

Hyacinth was clearly agitated in the days that followed. Lilly sensed it while she combed her hair. Hyacinth knew her husband was in the hospital. After that, God knows what? She squirmed in her wheelchair.

"Now, now, now, you just settle down. I know you want to look pretty and all. Come on now."

Hyacinth grabbed the brush from Lilly and threw it across the living room. It landed on the mantelpiece near Jimmy's bronzed baby shoes. "For Christ's sake, Lilly! I'm not a damn baby, so stop treating me like one. My husband is in the hospital, and I'm scared. Can't you understand that?" Hyacinth burst into tears.

Lilly was stunned. She'd never heard Hyacinth speak that way—nobody ever heard Hyacinth speak that way. Lilly stood there, a healthy distance from Hyacinth. Sandra rushed into the room and looked at Lilly. Lilly returned her gaze, then they both looked at Hyacinth. Sandra walked toward her mother, but Hyacinth held her hand up as if to say, "Stop!" Sandra stood still, not knowing what to do. Her mother sobbed uncontrollably. Sandra turned to Lilly, "Please excuse us." Lilly walked out, closing the door behind her.

"All my life," Hyacinth said between sobs, "all my life, people always treated me as if I were a child, as if I were a paper doll. Well, I have more sense than people give me credit for! But people always see me as helpless, someone who needs to be taken care of, or somebody they can trample on. And now I seem even more helpless with this stupid wheelchair. Well, I hate it!" Hyacinth continued to cry.

Sandra pulled a clean tissue from the pocket of her flannel robe and handed it to Hyacinth. She sat down on the couch opposite her mother.

Hyacinth blew her nose. A portion of her hair stuck up in the air. "Yes, it's true I was a naïve young lady," she said, balling the tissue in her hand, "but that's because Grandpa and Grandma Hamilton sheltered me. I never experienced lots of things like…like…like working in an office, buying myself clothes with my own money, dating other men. Your father is the only man I've ever been with! I'm not complaining. I love your father. You know that your father has always taken good care of this family, especially when you and Jimmy were children. We never went without anything, you know that."

"Yes, Mama, I know." Sandra placed both fists to her face as she leaned forward, pressing her knuckles against her lips.

Hyacinth blew her nose again. "But there were times when I wanted to break free. When I was young, I used to paint birds, you know. All kinds. Your father thought that they were beautiful, but he thought that it was a lady's pastime— just sit and paint silly little birds. But those birds were a yearning, Sandy. Yes, indeed. Sometimes I wanted to fly…fly…fly. Bluebird, bluebird, through my window. Bluebird, bluebird, through my window. Bluebird, bluebird, through my window…"

What will be waiting near the end of the road? Sandra thought. Will it be real peace and contentment, or bluebirds? Dutifully, Sandra smoothed back her mother's hair while she rocked in her wheelchair, singing her little song of longing.

A few days lapsed before the definitive diagnosis was given. Reverend Hamilton had B-cell non-Hodgkin's lymphoma; it was stage III, intermediate grade, since the cancer had spread to his lungs. A bone marrow biopsy was taken thereafter to see if the cancer had spread to his bones. Reverend Hamilton was lucky; it had not. Sandra and Jimmy sat beside Reverend Hamilton as the doctors explained the various stages of non-Hodgkin's lymphoma. As they understood it, there were stages I, II, III, and IV, and each stage had grades, low, intermediate and high. Sandra wrote every bit of information down.

The doctors wanted to begin with the oral chemotherapy, Busulfan. Busulfan came in two-milligram pills; the number of pills varied by the weight of the patient. Their father needed to take eighty-eight milligrams, amounting to forty-four pills per dose. Reverend Hamilton would receive a total of fourteen doses over four days. The pills would be put into large capsules so that Reverend Hamilton would not have to swallow each pill. He would take Zofran and Phenagran for nausea, and Dilantin to prevent seizures, a common side effect of this kind of chemotherapy. After the Busulfan, Reverend Hamilton would undergo intravenous chemotherapy, VP-16 and Cytoxan. The VP-16 would be a thirty-eight-hour dosage, followed by two doses of Cytoxan, 5200 milligrams each. The doctors would wait and see how Reverend Hamilton responded to treatment. They would check his blood count regularly, and test his spinal fluid for lymphoma.

Once the oncologists left, Reverend Hamilton stood in front of the window for a very long time. What could anyone say? They knew there was a long road ahead. Hyacinth wanted to see her husband, but most thought it inadvisable. Sandra hugged her father, but he didn't hug her back, just stood there looking outside the window in a stupor. Jimmy decided he would stay in Cambridge during his father's chemotherapy. He thought it would be best for Gee to go back to Santa Monica to be with the kids. Sandra thought it would be best for Les to go home, too. Sandra and Jimmy hugged each other in the corridor of the hospital. It was all a bad dream. Reverend Hamilton had always been invincible. They hoped that he would beat this awful thing, this menace that took away fathers, mothers, and children. The word cancer was now real to Sandra and Jimmy. It was not someone else's plight—it was theirs.

On their way to their father's church, they looked at little children romping in a nearby playground in the cold January sun. People hustled to buy groceries, a man walked into a barbershop, and a dog chained to a pole anxiously waited outside the bakery for its master. Life went on pretty much as usual. Other than family members and doctors, no one else knew of Reverend Hamilton's upcoming fight. He had always been the person other families called on in time of need. He was their minister, their comfort. Who would comfort Reverend Hamilton while he was being prepared for treatment?

Sandra and Jimmy knew there would be many prayers from members of his congregation and the elders of the church. Jimmy thought he and Sandra needed to restore their faith in the power of prayer. It had been so long since either one genuflected in the traditional way they knew as children. Both had forgotten how to call on God. They entered their father's empty church. Jimmy bowed his head, reaching for his sister's hand. Sandra held Jimmy's hand tightly. Jimmy prayed until tears rolled down his face. He was surprised how much he remembered how to pray, like riding a bicycle. Sandra, on the other hand, had never learned how to ride.

Chapter 3
MAMA

"Bluebird, bluebird, through my window. Bluebird, bluebird, through my window. Bluebird, bluebird, through my window."

Jimmy was worried about his mother. Reverend Hamilton had been in the hospital for one week. No one could convince Hyacinth to eat, not even Lilly. Hyacinth sat in her wheelchair and rocked all day long, singing her little song of longing.

"Mama! Mama! You got to eat something. Mama, can you hear me?"

Hyacinth stopped and looked at Jimmy. "Sure, I hear you, Freckles. Bluebird, bluebird, through my window. Bluebird, bluebird, through my window."

Jimmy was frightened. His mother had not called him Freckles since he was seven years old.

"And you better eat your string beans, Freckles, or you won't get any cake. You know how much you love Mama's banana cake. Bluebird, bluebird, through my window. Bluebird, bluebird, through my window. Bluebird, bluebird, through my window." Hyacinth had slipped into the safety net of the past. There was too much uncertainty in the present.

"If you'll eat something, Mama," Sandra said, "we can go see Daddy. Wouldn't you like that?"

"We'll go see Grandpa Hamilton?"

Sandra sucked her teeth. "No, Mama! Your husband, our father, Trevor! After you eat, we'll go see your husband, Trevor."

"Trevor? My husband?"

"Yes, Trevor, your husband."

"Trevor is dead! Bluebird, bluebird, through my window. Bluebird, bluebird, through my window. Bluebird, bluebird, through my window…"

At the hospital, Jimmy couldn't understand why only two visitors were allowed to see Reverend Hamilton at a time. It was such a stupid policy. The rule prevented a circle of family members and friends to gather around his bedside to say a little prayer. But what really annoyed Jimmy was that he had to wait in the hospital lounge with Aunt Enid while Uncle Rufus and Lilly were visiting his father. Jimmy hated Aunt Enid. Long ago, Hyacinth told Jimmy that Aunt Enid despised any woman better looking than she was, and that would account for the entire female population in Cambridge—plus a few men, too. To make matters worse, Aunt Enid disguised her inferiority complex with loads of pompousness; she talked to people with her nose turned up in the air as if she smelled something bad. Aunt Enid made it her business to read all the modern-day bestsellers as well as the classics. It was mandatory for her to keep abreast of current events—weapons to compensate for the no-getting-around-it homeliness. And God forbid if you ever made a mistake in life; Aunt Enid never ever let you forget it. To Aunt Enid, Jimmy was a junkie. Always was, always would be.

Hyacinth paid dearly for her beauty when it came to Enid, since Grandpa Hamilton had paid more attention to her than he had his own daughter. Enid made it clear to Hyacinth she was just a visitor, an orphan who was taken in because of pity—and pity alone.

But it didn't stop there: In the Hamilton's household cleanliness was close to Godliness. So Enid put her soiled Kotex pads under Hyacinth's bed, assured that Grandma Hamilton would find them and give Hyacinth the whipping of her life. Every other month, the whole neighborhood heard Hyacinth's sorrowful wailing. Oh God, how Hyacinth's life turned to hell when Enid attended college. Each book that Enid read, everything she learned, became ammunition to cut Hyacinth's throat. Enid was as skilled as a surgeon at making Hyacinth feel worthless. Late at night, Hyacinth would sneak outside the house. She'd cry until there were no more tears to cry. Hyacinth had told Jimmy all these things long ago, so Jimmy hated Aunt Enid like he hated rats, cockroaches, and other vermin.

Uncle Rufus greeted Jimmy in the hospital lounge. The smell of liquor seeped from his pores. After Uncle Rufus lost his right leg to diabetes, liquor was his answer. It helped him deal with unpleasant situations. Jimmy knew Rufus took a shot of bourbon before leaving home. If he hadn't, Rufus wouldn't have been there. It must be difficult for Rufus to see his big-time brother fatigued and nauseated from chemo, Jimmy thought. Rufus always lived in Trevor's shadow, and years ago he'd wished bad things upon him. But then they were teenagers, kids. Everyone predicted Trevor would be the one who'd become somebody. Trevor was smart, tall, slim, good-looking, and a great talker. Rufus was not so smart, short, stocky, not so good-looking, and he stammered. No way could Rufus compete. So it wasn't surprising to Rufus that Trevor had won Hyacinth's hand in marriage. Rufus had loved Hyacinth, truly loved her, long before Trevor. Rufus had watched Hyacinth turn into a shapely young woman. It made something stir within him—she had entered his dreams, had crowded his thoughts every waking moment.

Seeing Rufus made Jimmy think about the good old days, when they had shared bottles of Johnny Walker Red. He remembered knocking on Uncle Rufy's door many years ago, on that Sunday morning when he'd left home with nothing but pocket change, his electric guitar, the clothes on his back, stoned. Rufus greeted Jimmy with open arms and a stiff shot of bourbon.

"How is he today?" Jimmy asked.

Uncle Rufus looked to the floor, leaning heavily on his left crutch, his stomach spilling over his pants. "He...he...see...seeems o-kay, but ver-ver-ver-y tired." Uncle Rufus seemed tired himself. "He's go-go-go-ing to be-be-beat this thing, right?"

"Sure he is. He'll pull through, he always does!"

Rufus grinned, his fleshy face like a bulldog's.

"Tha-that's for sure. So, how's your moth-er?"

"She seen better days. I guess things will get better once Dad is released from the hospital. For Mama's sake, I hope his release is soon, very soon."

Reverend Hamilton pondered Revelations 21:3. It had new meaning for him, his family: "And God himself will be with them. And he will wipe out every tear from their eyes, and death will be no more, neither will mourning nor outcry nor pain be anymore." Tears stung his eyes. He yearned for the day when death, mourning, and pain would be no more. But, in his life, at least, there were pleasant moments sandwiched between the painful ones. Reverend Hamilton received many get-well cards from members of his congregation, and Reverend Dexter, the new assistant pastor, visited him frequently. The young pastor's enthusiasm made him smile.

It was the last day of the Bulsufan chemotherapy. His stomach was terribly upset, but the quick-acting Phenegran helped to stop the nausea. In spite of what Jimmy had told him, Reverend Hamilton felt it was best not to see his wife, believing Hyacinth was not strong enough to see him in his weakened state. But he spoke to Hyacinth over the phone, convincing her he was alive. It pleased him to know that she had then eaten a full meal, although she still rocked in her wheelchair, singing her bluebird song. Hyacinth had forgotten how to be away from him for extended periods of time, he thought. Many years ago, while still a young woman, she'd grown accustomed to being alone. There were many nights of tears, no doubt, but little Jimmy was by her side. Now, at the age of sixty, still recovering from a stroke, Hyacinth was as dependent as a baby. Without her husband in sight, it was as if he'd disappeared, never to return. So Hyacinth walked down a familiar pathway, the pathway to the past where there was no uncertainty. She had already lived it, knew what would occur. The fear of the unknown was the enemy Hyacinth couldn't conquer. Each day she regressed deeper into the past.

For the first time, Reverend Hamilton wondered if Hyacinth had ever had any life aspirations. If she did, she never expressed them, or worse, he'd never asked. Hyacinth's role in life was the dutiful wife of a prominent minister. Until now, he never thought of Hyacinth as being anything else, but who was the person behind the role of the dutiful minister's wife? Many years ago, Reverend Hamilton envisioned that, at the brink of his death, he'd have the opportunity to peer down the long corridor of his life and be satisfied with what he saw. He had fulfilled all of his aspirations, all of his dreams. As a young man, he'd walked into the world with chisel in hand, carved out a chunk for himself and his family. He had successfully done what all men are expected to do—but was this at Hyacinth's expense?

Mrs. Kipins was different from all the other high school teachers, Hyacinth thought. She always gave a word of encouragement. "Listen, Hyacinth. Listen to the inner voice of your heart and let that inner voice transfer itself to your pen."

Hyacinth never knew she had a voice, but Mrs. Kipins said every person had a voice, so that included her. Once Hyacinth knew that she had a voice, she wondered who would care to listen to it? In the beginning, Hyacinth's inner voice lacked direction and focus—much like her voice in the world. But her voice in the world was not her own choosing. Hyacinth was not born a Hamilton. She was born a Brathwaite. Hyacinth Jeanesta Brathwaite. Enid was right all along: Hyacinth was just a visitor, an orphan with no real say in the

Hamilton family. But the more Mrs. Kipins encouraged Hyacinth, the more her inner voice began to take form. Hyacinth kept her inner voice a secret for fear Enid or somebody else would try to destroy it, diminish it somehow. She kept her secret well into womanhood.

There wasn't much comfort to Hyacinth during those nights when Trevor was out of town for one Baptist convention or another—not that he hadn't taken her to any of these conventions. Trevor took Hyacinth when it suited his purpose, like when he had to meet another minister for the first time. Appearances were everything. The presence of his wife would show Trevor was indeed a devoted family man.

But there were many lonely nights, so lonely they were palpable. Hyacinth had translated the pain, the hurt, using her inner voice:

> *Inside, you're cold and dark.*
> *And even though sunshine is in your glowing smile,*
> *your eyes do not lie when I ask, "Where have you been?"*
> *Your corrupt breath is cold cool wind ruffling lakes of hidden tears.*
> *I know as well as you, but try to forget, and make conversation of simple grain.*
> *And all the while listening to myself not really speaking at all.*

Over the years, Hyacinth went through the dusty boxes in the attic containing her inner voice, her pain, her hurt. Hyacinth recorded her inner voice loudly, clearly, with focus and direction. They were reminders that she'd forgiven Trevor for everything he'd done, but she could never ever forget. How could she? They could be read at any time, at any moment—and the hurt relived. Drifting out of her daydream, Hyacinth's eyes focused on Sandra diligently hanging freshly ironed shirts and blouses in the bedroom closet. Hyacinth felt drowsy from the sedative her doctor had given her earlier. Her voice was low, raspy, practically inaudible when she called her daughter's name.

Sandra stopped and turned toward her mother. "Mama? Did you call me?"

Hyacinth shifted her body so that she lay sideways in bed, patting its edge.

"Are you okay, Mama?" Sandra sat down.

Hyacinth nodded and cleared her throat. "Do you have a voice, Sandy?"

Sandra looked at her mother in annoyance, fearing she was now bordering on a new absurdity. "Of course I have a voice, Mama! I'm talking to you, aren't I?"

Hyacinth shook her head. "No, not that voice. Here." She pointed to Sandra's heart. "Do you ever write what you feel?"

Sandra's eyes softened. "No, Mama, I don't. Sometimes I should. Maybe it would give clarity to what I'm feeling. Sometimes I feel too much. These different feelings crowd one another, bump up against each other, cause confusion...you know."

"You mean those feelings you have for Les?"

Sandra looked at her mother in surprise. She didn't understand her. One day her head was in a fog, talking complete gibberish. Another day she appeared to have all her senses. "That and other things, Mama. But I do love Les, although our relationship is near its end."

"Sometimes endings are beginnings, Sandy. It's just that we hold on to the ending, because sometimes we're afraid of the beginning. The newness of it all doesn't seem to fit right. You know what I mean?"

"I do, Mama, I know exactly what you mean. You know," Sandra shook her index finger in the air, "I just thought of something."

"What?"

"I don't have a voice, Mama, but I have an eye. When I take photographs, sometimes they convey what I'm feeling. When I'm lonely, I may take a picture of a still pond with no visible sign of life, just a lonely, smooth, glassy surface. But when I'm angry, I seek out approaching storms, dark clouds."

"A voice, an eye. Same thing, Sandy, same thing. It's all part of the human experience to record, to document what we feel. It helps us focus on what we're feeling, I suppose. But in order to document what you feel, you must live inside." Her mother pressed a finger to Sandra's chest. "Your soul must be facing you."

"That's beautiful, Mama. When did you get so wise?"

"I've always been, just tucked away like hidden treasure. When you get a chance, Sandy, go into the attic and look for green cardboard boxes. I have a voice of a lifetime in those boxes." Hyacinth yawned and closed her eyes.

Sandra looked at her mother, noting how peaceful she looked. Wow. Never in a million years would she have thought her mother had a penchant for writing. She wondered if Jimmy knew about this. Sandra dutifully pulled the comforter under her mother's chin. The house was still, quiet. Sandra walked into the hallway and pulled down the stairs leading to the attic. The attic contained many mementos of their lives: her old roller skates, Jimmy's bicycle, Daddy's golf clubs, Mama's first sewing machine. Sandra rummaged through a lot of rubble before she spotted three boxes. Each box had the inscription H.J.H.

CHAPTER 4
SANDRA

Who will tell our story once we're gone, of the day we were born, how we laughed, when we cried? Who will be worthy to give an accurate account, to assure us that the mountains of pain we endured are not leveled upon the lips of those who tell it? Who will be the keeper of our history? Our sons? Our daughters? But the one who documents her own life ultimately becomes the teller of her own tale.

Sandra read in disbelief. Just who was H.J.H.? Why hadn't she been introduced to Sandra long ago? This was a woman who had feelings, wisdom. She could have given Sandra sound counsel during the bad times when she clung to a pillow where Les just lay, trying to capture his fading body heat right before she heard the jingling of his belt buckle and footsteps. Sandra sat in the attic and read and read and read. She felt her mother's pain in every paragraph, sentence, word, syllable, and punctuation. The pain was hers, too.

Her mother had written, "The only woman truly protected from life is a woman who hasn't lived, a woman who hasn't loved, because life, like love, is a journey unknown. We only know that we want to live, we want to love, but who really knows what life and love may offer? Both may hurt or heal."

So later that evening, it wasn't too surprising to Sandra when the woman on the other end picked up the telephone. Sandra hung up. She dialed her home number again. Slowly this time: 7-1-8-3-6-0-0-0-7-9. The telephone rang once, twice.

"Hello."

It was the same woman.

"Who's this?" asked Sandra.

"Who's this?" The woman replied.

It sounded like…like…Jade?

"Is Les there?"

"He's taking a shower. You can leave a message."

"Tell him Sandra said, 'It's over!'"

Click.

There are moments in life when sometimes a woman would rather not live, because of the illusion of love. It's over. Sandra's words resounded in her head, bouncing off the walls of her skull. It's over. It's over. It's over. Now where do I go from here?

The following weeks were like all the other weeks in Sandra's life: moments of joy and sorrow. Reverend Hamilton was released from the hospital as an outpatient. His doctor's visits consisted of countless blood work, X-rays, and CT scans. He was given antibiotics and antiviral medications. The mass in Reverend Hamilton's chest was shrinking. His lymph nodes were stabilized. Now he was sporting a stylishly bald head.

Reverend Hamilton was in good spirits, but people noticed he'd developed an occupation of staring outside windows for long periods of time. His eyes did not focus on anything in particular. Two weeks after being released from the hospital, Reverend Hamilton said it was time for Jimmy to go home. Jimmy did go home, but called his father at least three times a week, every week.

Sandra told her father she was going to stay indefinitely to make sure everything would be all right, but her mother knew the truth. Truth was, Sandra didn't want to face Les. Standing naked in front of a full-length mirror, Sandra thought of the hassle in starting over. She turned sideways, pressing the slight curve of her pelvis. She believed she still had a good body. She moved closer. There weren't any wrinkles yet, just a faint line across her forehead. She grinned, tonguing the gap between her front teeth before raking her fingers through her kinky curls. She turned off the running water in the bathtub. The suds were lofty and high. She dunked her big toe into the water, then slipped into the bathtub. Sandra grabbed the nearby wine bottle and poured abundantly.

She gulped down the first glass of red wine, hoping that the alcohol would numb the pain and fear. She felt the wine go to her head immediately. For weeks, Sandra's diet consisted of a nibble of bread, maybe a slice of cheese, a sip of water, nothing more. The lump of grief wouldn't allow anything else to pass her throat. The empty nights brought fitful sleep, crying spells, dreams of Lester

Ricks. Sandra placed one hand over her face, squeezing her eyes, hoping she'd disappear. She'd always done this as a little girl. She'd squeeze her eyes, hoping to escape from her father's disapproval. Her father's disapproval could have come in the form of an angry look, or worse, not look at all. Being invisible was far worse to an eight-year-old.

Sandra never remembered what bad thing she'd done. Maybe she kept squirming in the pew, or yelling and playing with other children in Sunday school. Who knows? But what Sandra did know was that she would throw her arms around her father's neck, look into his eyes. "See me, Daddy!" He could have been sitting in his study poring over an article or preparing for the next Sunday's sermon. "Daddy, Daddy, I love you," the little girl with wooly hair and missing front teeth would say. But when she looked into her father's eyes, his head would turn right. If Sandra's turned right, his would turn left. If Sandra's turned left, his would turn right. It went on like that—Sandra didn't exist. She yearned for a beating. Didn't the Bible say he who spares his rod hates his son, but he who loves him disciplines him promptly? "Where's the rod, Daddy? Jamie gets a beating from his daddy, then his daddy hugs him. I want a beating, Daddy, please!" Later, Sandra would exhaust herself from crying, then become angry with herself for being a bad girl, and squeeze her eyes to disappear. Like her daddy made her disappear.

Sandra poured another glass of wine, gulping that one down, too. She felt lightheaded, but the pain was still there. Fear still lay hard against the soft lining of her throat—thick like phlegm. Her tears merged with the bath water. Her mind rested on Les. She once thought that Les was different from her father, realizing later that they were different only in lifestyle and appearance, but were the same men, with different methods. Sandra grew up. Like any young girl, her father was the world to her—God, even. If she were good, he'd raise her to the sky. If she were bad, he'd drop her to the ground. With the onset of young adulthood comes assertiveness. Her father's translation: aggression, disobedience. In Sandra's mind, she was still Daddy's little girl, but with a mind of her own. Yet from the time she had taken her first step during her formative years, her father had formed her mind. And Trevor wanted to keep it that way. She was his baby girl.

Whenever Sandra would forget that, he'd stop loving her, deliberately ignore her, make her disappear—again. Sandra still loved him, but also hated him. He'd never see she was just his daughter who cried, had feelings, who thought— thought it wrong for him to touch her that way. It was always around midnight. Mama asleep. Jimmy gone. The creaking sound at her bedroom door made her heart pound, and at twelve years old, she knew it wasn't the Boogieman. She'd pull the Cinderella sheets over her head, pretending to be asleep, squeezing her eyes, hoping to disappear.

When Les walked into Sandra's life, he brought a bucketful of promises she thought would fill her emptiness. Marriage was never an option for Les. He was free-spirited. He explained this to Sandra right from the start. He thought Sandra understood. Sandra thought she understood. At that time, she did. But Les promised he would never hurt her, would always be there for her, that she could be herself, that she could tell him everything. Sandra told him everything. Sometimes they'd lie in bed, Sandra on top blowing soft air on Les's hairless chest. Les would turn over, placing Sandra beneath him. He'd look into her eyes with all the sincerity in the world, and Sandra knew she was home, that she'd never disappear. Sandra trusted Les, revealed to him all the penned-up anger inside. She'd taken Les down every frustrating lane of her childhood. Les listened to every word, tallied every event.

Sandra wanted to start a family after turning thirty, and felt the weight of turning thirty with no wedding ring. So she nudged at the idea—again. She remembered that she had curled up against Les's warm body while he was sitting on the sofa. She placed her head on his chest. Her head rose and fell with each breath. Les ran his fingertips through her hair, massaging her scalp. She had made her move.

"Les, do you ever think about getting married? About having children?"

"Never."

"Why?"

"Because."

"Because why?"

"Because we've been through this before, Sandra."

Sandra detected the irritation in his voice, but continued the inquiry. "Listen, I'm thirty and you're thirty-six and—"

"I know how old I am!"

"Good! So we both know we aren't getting any younger. Don't you want a daughter or son to continue in your footsteps after you're gone?"

"Well," Les paused, looking to the ceiling, "maybe a son. Yeah, a son." Les shifted in his seat, causing Sandra to remove her head from his chest. He looked directly into her eyes with all the sincerity in the world. "Yeah. Yeah. Maybe I would like to have a son if my father had messed up my mind and shitted on me and made me feel like I was invisible and I was trying to recapture the things in childhood that I, myself, didn't have. And when the kid is born, I'd probably look at him and say, 'I brought you into this world because of me—this had nothing to do with you, you see.' Now pass me the remote. This basketball game, like your game, is boring the hell out of me!"

Who let the air out of the room? Les had the power to not only diminish her, but demolish her. Like her father, Les enjoyed it, and he had gotten his wish: Sandra hadn't mentioned anything about a child or marriage for a while, not until the following year on her thirty-first birthday. But even then she'd asked herself, "Why would I want to marry Les, anyway?" The answer to this question had never arrived at Sandra's doorstep, and her longing for Les was just as mysterious to her as it was to grasp the understanding of how she could love and hate her father at the same time. Sandra drained the last drop of wine from the bottle. The combination of alcohol and maddening thoughts made her contemplate death, her death. Kill yourself. Sandra rubbed her forehead.

The water dripped into her eyes as she pondered various methods: sleeping pills, gun, poison. But what about the ramifications of her death, the people she would leave behind? How would her suicide affect them, their lasting memories of her? Sandra quickly resolved that death, like life, had many, many complications.

When Sandra emerged from the bathroom, she tried her best to appear sober. Hyacinth did not say a word, but she still smelled the alcohol beneath the thick veil of Scope.

"Where's Daddy?"

"He's in his study. He's working on a sermon for this coming Sunday. I still think it's too early for him to go back to ministering, but the doctors say your father is doing well, and that he could go back to work on a limited basis. His last CT-scan showed that the mass on his chest is practically disappeared. So that's good news. I'm so happy!"

"I know, Mama, it shows. I see you're even using the walker now. You are taking small steps on your own. That's great, Mama."

Hyacinth beamed with pride.

"Look at you! You are so proud of yourself, aren't you?"

Hyacinth blushed. "Well, the Lord doesn't like it when one is puffed up with pride, but—"

"Oh! Mama! This is progress. You should be proud!"

"Come here! Come here!" Hyacinth whispered. "I want to tell you a secret. I was going to wait until your father's next visit to the doctor, but I'm going to tell you now." Sandra sat beside her mother on the couch. Hyacinth looked like a mischievous schoolgirl. "Well! You know that our forty-second wedding anniversary is coming up."

"Yes, Mama. I know."

"Well! Depending on what the doctors say, your father and I are planning to take a cruise to Bermuda! What do you think?"

"Oh Mama! That's great! Les and I were planning—" Sandra stopped. She looked baffled, rubbing an invisible spot on her hand.

Hyacinth moved closer: "I'm sorry about Les." She then caressed her daughter's cheek.

Sandra jumped, placing a hand over her mouth. Tears filled her eyes, but would not fall pass the rim. I hurt, Mama. I hurt so bad, her eyes said.

I know, baby. I know. I'm here for you now, Hyacinth's eyes replied. If I could, I would kiss the pain away. Lord knows I would.

CHAPTER 5
REGIONS

The region of rock bottom—Sandra drew closer to it each day. A sea of empty wine bottles collected beneath her bed, some standing upright like bowling pins. Every evening, Sandra pushed her chair away from the dinner table, food untouched, with three pairs of eyes staring at her plate, then back at her. Her mother, father, and Lilly never said a word as she slipped upstairs with a bottle of wine in hand, the soft click of the bedroom door her refuge. A bottle of wine had more to offer Sandra than life: Chardonnay was her backbone to rustle up the nerve to call Les, the fifth time. He was not home again, forcing her to leave another message. A swig of Merlot was the jolt to restart Sandra's heart each time the phone would ring, but never for her, never Les. Sandra would sit in the middle of her bed, hugging her knees to her chest, her eyes focused on the phone as if her pupils alone would will it to ring.

Two bottles of Zinfandel comforted Sandra after she'd backed up against a wall, sliding to the floor in a crouch. Her faced crumbled and she opened her mouth in a long wail. Just minutes before, she'd spoken to Les, finally reaching him at home. His words were pointed, hard-edged, the voice he used when he was bored, "You said it was over. We both know it's been over a long time now. Let's leave it as that." Sandra wanted to say all the things she'd rehearsed: "It's better the second time around. We could make it work if we tried." She began, then stopped, choking on her words. The words weren't coming out right, not the way they were supposed to. "What are you trying to say, Sandra?" Les's voice traveled over the phone line, sounding irritated, carrying more distance than their separate locations. He sounded like a stranger to her, like they hadn't spent ten years of their lives together. Ten years! That's when she realized she had lost him. She opened her mouth anyway, searching for salvageable words, but all that came out was a whimper.

Sandra remained crouched in the corner for a while, hands over her face. She then reached for the first bottle of wine. Wine always made things better, yes. Sandra recalled sneaking into her father's wine cabinet, taking great gulps of sherry, then wiping her mouth with the back of her hand before replacing what she had drank with water. At twelve years old, Sandra knew that Daddy was a Scotch man. He'd never miss the sherry, never know about its substitute. Harvey's Bristol Cream had always lightened the filth that lay heavily inside her as well as the burden of her secret, and Sandra hadn't jumped as much when his hands fumbled with the knob of her bedroom door. Later, wine loosened her up with Les. She tried pot once, but that only left her paranoid, and made Les mad, for she was too freaked out to give him any. But with wine, everything was all right, sweet. Les was always satisfied. Sandra was always satisfied. Yes, looking deeply now, wine was always there comforting her, calling her, lurking.

After realization had set Sandra's mind in a cast, separation from Les was the physical ache that lay in her chest and stomach. Everything was an effort, even to speak. She opted for silence. Days drifted in silence, silence of not wanting, of not hoping.

Fingers brushed through Sandra's hair daily, sometimes mingling with the comfort of wine. They could have been her mother's, could have been Lilly's, two women from another generation who comforted. Hyacinth's hands moved with newfound purpose: washing Sandra's armpits, feeding her opened mouth. Her hands no longer touched Sandra out of necessity, but of love, of remembrance. She'd been to this place before, a place no mother wanted for her daughter. As Hyacinth's purpose increased, Sandra's decreased. Her life with Les was gone, gone. But there was the silence. She surrendered to the silence. It was easy, surrendering—the closest she compared to dying.

Only Sandra's eyes moved when Lilly propped her head on plumped pillows; they shifted from curtains to closet, from closet to nightstand, from nightstand to dresser, always following Hyacinth. Keep your eyes on Mama, she kept thinking. Watch Mama. Hyacinth's presence was Sandra's anchor after the world around her floated away. She'd awoken one morning, and thought that she was still dreaming. Everything appeared small and far away, like viewing the world through the lens of her camera. And the world was black and white like her pictures she framed and hung on her living room wall. She hadn't broken her silence to tell anyone, just kept her eyes on Mama, her only sense of reality. Yet in this prison of depression, Sandra's world was clear without the nuances of color. The good times she shared with Les weren't really good times at all. From the view of the new lens, Les had never loved her.

She wanted him to love her, tried her best for him to love her. But never had he said he loved her. Always said he loved her big butt when he grabbed it from behind, pressing his manhood against her. Had always said he loved her tight thighs, full chest—always a part of her, but never her. There was clarity to this world that Sandra had never seen before. Les never loved her. Period. The thought brought tears to her eyes, but everything was crystal clear now—everything, like black and white.

Lilly's hum soothed the invisible lacerations that crisscrossed Sandra's body. She sat in a chair near Sandra's bedside and hummed. It was something slow and mournful. Could have been an old Negro spiritual, like Lilly's eyes had seen the tilt of many slave cabins. Lilly talked between her humming, not expecting Sandra to reply or comment. She just talked, knowing that words had medicinal properties at times. "You got to break out of this, Sandy. You hear me? The Lord is not ready for you yet. Um Ummm. Just call on him, baby. Call on him. Um Ummm. Say it, baby. Say Jesus. Um Ummm. He's a friend to the friendless. Yes he is."

This would have been enough to lift anybody up, but Sandra's spine willfully pressed itself against the mattress, preparing for the long haul. She would have to ride this one out! This grip on her person was stubborn, had fighting spirit. It wanted to live. Sandra didn't have the strength to fight. Her muscles had grown weak from lack of exercise and little food. She didn't even have enough strength to stand. Whenever she attempted to step out of bed, her legs were logs resistant to being led. She held onto pieces of furniture, her back hunched like an old woman, taking baby steps toward the bathroom. Usually Mama or Lilly trailed behind her. Sandra's body was a shell, and every part of it hurt, even the slightest brush of linen made her skin ache. So she didn't move much. She just lay in bed, surrendering.

Hyacinth sat on the edge of the bed one evening, telling Sandra about the world outside. Jimmy was planning to open another health food store. Gee asked for her incessantly. Laurence and Rita maintained good marks in school, and as a reward, they were going on a family vacation to Hawaii.

Vacation? asked Sandra's eyes. Her brows bunched.

"Sure, baby." Hyacinth rubbed lotion on Sandra's fragile hands. "School is almost out. We're in May now."

May?

"Yes, May." Her mother smiled. "The world is waiting for you to become part of it again, baby."

Sandra lowered her eyes. Seemed like the world was doing just fine without her. May, already?

Hyacinth placed the bottle of lotion on the night table, snapping the cap in place. She massaged Sandra's fingers gently.

May, already? Sandra looked around the room, like looking down a long tunnel. The curtains appeared to be made from lighter material. The bedspread was no longer the heavy quilt. Her gown was no longer heavy flannel. She hadn't noticed all of this before. She'd only noticed Mama's face. Sandra squeezed her eyes, terrified! For the first time, she was afraid of what was happening to her. This wasn't something she could just snap out of! She wanted to scream, but she was afraid of that too, afraid of what might gush out. Her throat was dry. She wanted wine, but she recalled the clamor of empty wine bottles when Lilly had removed them from beneath the bed. All she needed was a drop, just a drop.

A spurt of air escaped Hyacinth's nose.

Sandra looked up, realizing that her mother wasn't massaging her fingers anymore. Hyacinth was lost in thought, her hands on her lap.

Sandra sensed something was wrong. She shook her mother's hand. What is it, Mama?

Hyacinth leaned forward and cupped Sandra's face with her hands. She looked into Sandra's eyes for a good while. Finally, she said, "It's Les."

Sandra's eyes widened. Les?

"He called tonight, baby," she said cautiously. "Well, he called several times before, but we told him that you weren't feeling well." Her mother sighed.

Sandra tucked her lips inside her mouth, waiting.

"Baby...he...he wants to work out an agreement about the house and business. He says that you both should arrange a meeting to iron things out. You have to talk to him, baby. Put closure to this."

Sandra quickly turned her face away from her mother, tears streaming down her cheeks. She turned on her side, facing the wall. She pulled the covers over her shoulders, forming her body into a ball. And the ache in her chest turned into a fist.

The fist grew. Sandra shot up in bed that night, holding her chest. The fist seemed to be pumping rather than her heart. All the bad things that people had ever done to her flooded her mind, going back to grade school. She always took it, didn't protest much—not that she couldn't, wouldn't! Her need for acceptance was far greater than the need to defend herself. She wanted to be everyone's darling. Now sitting in darkness, Sandra realized that the cost was too great. Where did it get her?

Her fingers fumbled for the brass base of the lamp, pulling the slender chain to turn on the light. She felt like smashing something, felt like smashing the whole world. She changed her mind, grabbing a handful of tulips in a vase on the night table instead. She crushed them between her palms and cried. How dare they bloom.

The footsteps approaching her bedroom this morning were much heavier than Lilly's or Mama's. The sound of the gait had manly confidence. Each step was solid, certain of where it was going, where it had been. Sandra knew that the footsteps were her father's. Don't enter this room, she thought. The footsteps were getting closer. Don't enter this room. Keep your ass out of this room! The fist in her chest pounded. The footsteps stopped in front of the doorway. Sandra grabbed a handful of sheets. Keep moving! This world of clarity, Sandra later realized, had two compartments: one of inexpressible sadness, the other of hate. Both were crystal clear. The emotions that Sandra had tucked away from the outside world now stood naked. Bastard! The footsteps moved forward. Get out of here! Tears slid down the side of Sandra's face, settling in a small puddle on the sheets. Her body was facing the wall. She felt the depression on the bed from her father's weight. Did you come to get some, Daddy? Is that what you want? Is that all you men want? She buried her face in the pillow. A tremor moved in her right foot.

"You can't go on like this, Sandy." Her father's voice was tinged with sorrow. "It's not healthy. Do you hear me?"

Shut up!

"Sometimes things seem so hard to bear. But God pulls us through. I can't begin to tell you how I felt when I found out I had cancer."

Drop dead!

"Now I don't know how you feel…" He paused.

Got that right! You son of a bitch!

"But you can get through this. I know you can."

Sandra felt the shift of his weight, his hand on her calf through the sheets. Get off me!

"Now I know at times I haven't been the best father, but you and Trevor Jr. mean the world to me. I can't lose you, Sandy. Say something, please."

Silence.

He sighed. "I remember the day when you were born. You were such a cute little thing. A daughter, I kept saying over and over, a daughter. It was an experience, different from the birth of a son. I felt like a warrior, like I had to automatically protect and defend. It may sound silly to you, but that's how fathers feel toward a girl, more so than boys." He paused again. "But then, sometimes fathers get confused about their daughters." He removed his hand. "They…well…they…Oh, I don't know." He rested his hand on her calf again. "What I'd done I confessed to the Lord, Sandy. He truly forgives. And no matter how strange this may sound to you, I've always loved you. Always."

Something in Sandra snapped. She suddenly sprang up on all fours, wild-eyed. "Liar!" She barked. "Liar! Liar! Liar!" Her throat felt raw and cracked. "Liar!" She looked at her father's frightened face, his hand over his mouth. He looked so far away as he slowly backed out of the room. Then moments later, Lilly and Mama rushed inside, practically knocking down furniture, and him. Their eyes were wide open and mouths agape. They were stunned that Sandra had broken her silence.

Sandra jumped to her feet and grabbed the brass base of the lamp, knocking off its shade. She advanced toward her father. "Liar!" But Lilly and Mama grabbed her wrists, stopping Sandra cold. She dropped the lamp and crumbled to the floor. "Liar, liar, liar," she said, rocking back and forth on her knees, hands plastered to her ears. "You liar."

CHAPTER 6
PRAYERS AND
SUPPLICATIONS

"Well, at least you're talking again," Jimmy said over the phone. "I was really worried." He breathed into the receiver. "Remember what I said awhile ago, that whatever happens between you and Les, don't lose yourself in the process. He's not worth it, Sandy. Nobody is."

"Did I tell you Les never loved me?"

"What?"

"He never loved me. Les."

"Sandy, please! Listen, when you hit rock bottom, there isn't any place to go but up. Gee used to tell me this when I was strung out. I didn't believe her at first, but it's true. Now with everybody's prayers, you're going to pull through this. I guarantee you. Okay?"

"'Kay."

Although Sandra did not feel like it, she managed to get up to wash herself. Her world was still mainly black and white, but some days there were traces of color. Clarity was still there with a vengeance—luckily, her father stayed out of her way. One thing about vengeance, Sandra concluded, it added strength to limbs. Her gait was progressively steadier each day.

Her mind rested on Les. In such a rush to finalize things! Yeah, well, let him wait! Tired of him trying to light a match to my butt! Sandra thought, as her feet fumbled for her slippers. She stood up and stretched, catching sight of herself in the full-length mirror. Sandra smoothed the gown close to her body. She must have lost as least twenty pounds! All the more reason for making Les wait. She certainly didn't need any of her clothing from home. They wouldn't fit her anyway. All she needed were the gowns and robes Mama bought her, perfect clothing for the house. Sandra didn't need any clothing for outside, for she was not planning to go outside. What did the world have to offer? No, she would stay inside her bedroom, sharpening knives, and when the time was right, she would arrange to meet Les on her own terms.

Everyone else in the world was active, though. Lilly and her church friends were planning bus trips here and there. Jimmy, Gee, and the kids had returned from their trip to Hawaii, had sent some beautiful pictures, too, of Diamond Head, Haleakula. And Mama and Daddy were preparing for their cruise to Bermuda. Sandra dropped her hands heavily to her sides. A cruise to Bermuda, a trip to Hawaii, she thought, recalling some of the few pleasures the world offered. Sandra peeked through the slats of the blinds, watching the children head back to school. September must be the worst month in the year for kids, she thought, having to go back to school after the long, hot summer, after all that fun. Two little girls with spindly legs were walking down the sidewalk, arm in arm. They were dressed in plaid pleated skirts and white blouses. Sandra thought of Janet, her best friend in grade school and through college. She and Janet walked arm in arm like those two little girls, dressed like those two little girls, heading toward school. Now Janet was a married woman. "Happily married to Carl," Mama had said. "You remember Carl, don't you?" One of the little girls giggled, quickly covering her buckteeth. So innocent, Sandra thought, shaking her head. Who knows how their lives would eventually turn out? How life would eventually turn out?

Sandra put on her robe and gathered her toiletries, heading toward the bathroom. She noticed her parents' bedroom door was cracked. Sandra stopped, listening to the hushed tone of her father's voice. She moved closer, gazing through the crevice.

"What am I to do?"

"Nothing," her mother said. She was dressed in a flowered house dress, looking as if she had just gotten back from Bermuda. "Do you want me to pack this shirt?"

Her father turned to face her mother, as he sat on the bed, placing a hand on one of the tall mahogany bedposts. On the end of each bedpost was a beautifully carved pinecone. "Pack anything you like. I trust your judgement." Her father then turned around and placed an elbow on his lap, resting a cheek in his palm. He looked to the floor, dejected. "I don't know. I don't know."

Her mother neatly folded the shirt into the suitcase on the bed, then sat next to him. She absentmindedly pulled a thread from the sleeve of his terrycloth robe.

"If looks could kill, I would be dead already," he said.

She sighed. "Listen to me. Our Sandy is going through a bad time right now. Sometimes a man can turn a woman's mind inside out, and he thinks nothing of it! The only thing we can do is to be there for her. Once Sandy gets over this, whatever she feels toward you will subside. You're a man, too. So she's resentful. It'll pass." She placed her hand on top his.

Her father was quiet for a while. He then sat up and looked into her mother's eyes. "I haven't always been a good husband to you. I know."

Her mother stood up and rubbed his shoulder. "You've done the best you can."

"Have I?"

Her mother walked around the bed and continued to pack without saying a word. She had a pained look on her face.

It must have been hard on Mama, Sandra thought. Sympathizing with her daughter, yet paying allegiance to her husband whom her daughter hated. Mama was like the meat between the sandwich, caught between the middle—a very bad place to be.

Her father stood up and adjusted the belt of his robe. He walked toward her mother, turning her around to face him.

Her mother had a pair of socks in her hand, pressing them against his chest.

He held her, kissing her gently on the lips. Afterwards, he said, "As God is my witness, I'm going to make up for all the things I haven't done."

Her mother threw the socks on the bed and held his face. "Oh, Trevor. For now on, I think things are going to get better. I have a feeling. I think the worst is behind us. We'll be a family again."

Her father grabbed her hands and kissed them. "I hope so." She turned around and continued to pack, as he cuddled up against her. "Make sure you pack the sun screen. You know how you burn."

Her mother laughed a school-girlish laugh.

That afternoon, Sandra and Mama sat down in the den for tea. They'd done this a number of times; it was an event Sandra enjoyed. She looked forward to the little things in life, not asking for much. Tea with Mama was the world, and only the two of them occupied it. Sandra didn't know what she was going to do with Mama in Bermuda for two weeks. But she quickly shook off the thought, not wanting to dwell on that now. Mama's eyes were enveloping her, and she enjoyed the attention. Mama's face, from Sandra's view, was like a black-and-white picture, with just a hint of pink at her cheeks. Sandra still hadn't said anything about her sight, afraid that Mama would panic. Maybe Sandra should've been in a panic. Yet for some reason, she was certain that her sight was related to her depression, psychosomatic or something. Anyway, it was getting better already. Objects no longer appeared far away, and now there were even slight nuances of color.

The lemon cookie melted in Sandra's mouth. "Um, good."

Her mother smiled. "Like them, huh?"

Sandra nodded her head gingerly.

Her mother put her cup of tea on a tray, then sat back in a plaid reclining chair. "That's an old recipe. Grandma Hamilton gave it to me years ago. I used to make them for you when you were little. You ate them by the handful."

Sandra stopped chewing. "I don't remember that." She frowned. "I thought you only made cookies for Jimmy." Her words cut Mama's heart. She suddenly realized it. She saw it in Mama's eyes. "What I meant was…well…I…"

"No need to explain." Her mother sighed. "Events always look different from a child's point of view. I understand." Her mother fingered her wedding ring. "A good mother loves her children, but sometimes things occupy her mind, and she doesn't realize at the time how it affects them. You'll understand when you have yours." She cracked a sad smile.

Sandra placed the cookie on the plate and rearranged the knitted blanket on her lap. "I'm not going to have children."

"What makes you say that, Sandy?" Her mother looked concerned.

"Who's going to love me, Mama?"

"A sensible man! That's who." Her mother got up from the chair and sat next to Sandra on the love-seat. She placed her arms around Sandra's shoulders. "And right now you are loved by your Mama, Daddy, Lilly, Jimmy, Gee, Rita, and Laurence." Her mother took a deep breath. "There!"

Sandra laughed. She hadn't laughed in months. Maybe Mama was right. The worst was behind them.

"I'd prayed long and hard to hear your laughter. Do it again."

Sandra laughed harder. "Oh Mama," she said, covering her smile.

Her mother gently removed Sandra's hand from her mouth. "Don't, don't ever cover that smile." She hugged Sandra tightly.

All Sandra ever wanted was to be hugged by Mama, to have Mama all to herself. Better late than never, she thought.

Bermuda was a beautiful place, according to Mama's letter. So far they'd visited the parishes of St. George's, Hamilton, and Devonshire. "It's like a sunlit fairy tale," Mama wrote. "And your father can't get enough of the Bermuda fish chowder served with black rum and sherry peppers. He's pretty heavy on the black rum." Mama drew a smiling face. "Tom Moore's Tavern is a must. The food is heavenly. I must have gained ten pounds…Bermuda is a great place to plan a wedding, Sandy. I can see you in your long wedding gown. It can happen, you know. I'm praying on it. I know that you're probably shaking your head right now." Sandra laughed, because she was shaking her head. "I guess I'm just an old romantic at heart," Mama continued. "Your father and I have just renewed our wedding vows."

Upon reading the last sentence, Sandra placed the letter on the bed and clasped her hands on her lap. "Mama and Daddy renewed their wedding vows." The words pinched Sandra's throat like a fishbone. And he just gets away with it, she thought. Maybe it was time for her to renew her life. Start all over again. She couldn't live in this house forever.

Sandra turned the bottle upward and guzzled, recalling how she'd stumbled over the bottle of Merlot when she was rummaging through her closet. She was rummaging through her closet after she'd seriously thought about Jimmy's proposal. If she accepted, she would need clothes. The jeans she'd packed back in January were now two sizes big. All the other clothes were too warm for Santa Monica. The place sounded happy, Santa Monica. Had a nice ring to it. Jimmy said she should spend time with them, breathe fresh air, get some sun and sand.

"Come on! You haven't seen the new house yet, Sandy. We live on Stanford Street now. It's north of Wilshire Boulevard in the College Streets section. We have three bedrooms, two bathrooms, a family room, den, dining room, a fabulous kitchen, a pool, and lots of surrounding property—a far cry from Brooklyn."

"What's wrong with Brooklyn?"

"Nothing, if you don't mind living like an animal in a zoo! Face it, Sandy, the place is overcrowded. Oh, yeah, we have a huge backyard, and we're only a short distance away from the restaurants and shops on Montana Avenue. You'll love it!"

"That all sounds good, Jimmy, but what will I do? I'll probably get in the way."

"Don't be silly! What will you do? Live! And manage the new store for me.

I'll pay you."

"Serious?"

"Yeah."

What other options did she have? Lately, she'd been looking at slim pickings. Well, no pickings, really. No man. No home. She would still see Mama if she moved to California. Mama had said she was going to resume her yearly visits to Santa Monica now that she was through with that wheelchair. What did Cambridge have to offer? Nothing but the same old people she grew up with, most of them happily married, which was like rubbing salt in the wounds. "Did you know that Sandra was back home?" they'd say. She could hear them now.

Maybe she would change her name when she moved to California. People couldn't call her if they didn't know her name, couldn't call her a failure. Maybe she would assume a whole new identity when she arrived in California. She was good at creating identities. Hadn't she pretended to be a loving daughter to her father for how many years now?

Sandra sat forward on the edge of the bed, bottle of wine dangling in front of her legs, thinking. With her free hand, she twisted a portion of her hair. She then took a healthy swig. "Well," she said, "people say California is wine country."

The pure light of the sun was blinding this morning. Once Sandra believed that the sun was God greeting the world, and the wheels of His golden chariot created the colors at sunrise as He rode across the sky. That was in her days of innocence, so long ago. The sun and God had walked out of Sandra's life when her father had walked into her bedroom at midnight.

Sandra moved away from the bedroom window and sat down in a chair, placing a hand on her stomach. It still felt queasy, sour. Wee hours in the morning, a real scrimmage ensued, causing her to race to the toilet to vomit. A grand upchuck. Sandra remained squatted on the black-and-white tile floor, hanging onto the bare rim of the toilet, its cushioned seat above her head. Damn Scotch! She was never able to handle liquor. That's why she stuck with wine. But she was out of wine, and she was nervous about her trip tomorrow. She needed something! Each time Sandra thought about the trip to California—her new life, new self—she'd get nervous. She was like Mama: She hated change, too. It frightened her. So last night she slipped into her father's study and drank Scotch.

He very rarely touched it now. Dead sure he wouldn't miss it.

"You're up early this morning," her mother said, standing in the doorway. "You must be excited about your trip."

Sandra smiled, quickly sitting upright. "Sure am!"

Her mother walked into the room and sat on the bed, dressed in her Sunday best. She wore a tailored suit—it could have been brown or maroon or a maroonish brown, Sandra couldn't quite determine—and a lady's hat that looked like a fedora, with a feather in its band. Her pumps were highly polished, her stockings straight, and her cape-like coat draped over her shoulders. She held supple leather gloves in one hand, a clutch bag in the other.

"You look nice, Mama."

"Thanks. I can't stay too long. Your father is going to minister a special service this morning, so we have to get to church earlier than usual." Her mother fingered the brass headboard as she said this, then looked at Sandra. "Are you sure about this, Sandy?"

"Course I am, Mama!"

"You can always stay here until you decide what you really want to do."

"I've already decided, Mama. Don't worry. The change will do me good."

Her mother attempted to look into Sandra's eyes, but Sandra kept her eyes lowered. She knew that Mama could read eyes, could read the truth.

"Are you happy, Sandy? Happy about what you're doing?"

Sandra looked toward the shag carpet. She didn't want to downright lie. "For the most part, yes. I'm not as depressed as I was months ago about my future. I have something to look forward to, a new life, a new me."

"Well, as long as you're happy." Her mother stood up and kissed Sandra on the cheek. "I have to go now. I'll see you later. And don't forget—Lilly and I made dinner reservations for tonight, so get dressed." She headed toward the door.

"Mama?"

Her mother turned around.

"Thanks for the money. Once I finalize things with Les, I'll pay you back. I swear."

"I'll hear nothing of it. It's a gift from your father and me."

"Thanks a lot."

"Just one question."

"Yes?"

"Did you pack the outfits I bought for you in Bermuda?"

"The first things I'd packed."

Her mother smiled and walked out the door, her coat swaying behind her.

Sandra listened carefully to Mama's footsteps as she descended the stairs, listened for the slam of the front door. She collapsed on her bed, holding her stomach. Damn! That's it! No more Scotch. She lay flat on her back, looking toward the ceiling. She thought about her new life, her new self, and she bit the side of her lip. I sure hope Mama's right, that the worst was behind them, behind her, she thought.

CHAPTER 7
HOPES

The weeping willow tree in the middle of Jimmy's front yard impressed Sandra. His home impressed her, too. It was a traditional-style family house: wide, spacious, white, with a gray, sloped roof. A well-kept lawn abutted both sides of the stone gray pathway leading to three brick steps and a red front door. Alongside the house were flowers—French marigolds, dwarf sunflowers, petunias—surrounded by carefully arranged white rocks. The pungent bushes were well manicured, and in the middle of the lawn stood that massive weeping willow tree, roots clinging to the earth.

The back yard was huge, containing a good-sized pool, a deck, a stone paved patio, and a greenhouse. Sandra loved the patio with its white wicker furniture, the white tables with ample umbrellas for shade. "Yes, I can get used to this," she said to Jimmy.

"I told you it's a far cry from Brooklyn," he said, smiling.

The sun was roasting. Sandra's white gauze halter-top and matching wide-legged pants that Mama had bought in Bermuda were perfect for the weather. Sandra was thankful she had changed her clothes at LAX airport. "Come, let me show you Gee's greenhouse." Sandra followed Jimmy to the grassy far end of the yard.

The air was hard to breathe inside the greenhouse, like the heavy air in a rainforest. Flowers were everywhere: tropical hibiscus, African violets, and exotic orchids. Some flowers were hanging in baskets, but most were in terra cotta pots placed on long metal tables alongside garden tools. Sandra sat down on a metal bench, looking at a big ceramic frog with a gurgling stream of water spurting from its open mouth.

"This is where Gee unwinds," Jimmy said. "Her sanctuary." He lightly touched the hanging flowers with his fingertips.

Sandra looked around. "You and Gee must be doing all right. Greenhouse, pool, patio, big house."

Jimmy laughed. "I guess you can say that we've been blessed. We saved for this. We were surprised along the way, too."

"What do you mean?"

"Well, Gee's Uncle Fritz died. He'd left her a good sum of money."

"That always helps." Sandra chuckled.

Jimmy stared at her. "You look good. Lost some weight, but you look good. Let's hope that the worst is over, eh?" He winked. "Come, let me show you inside."

Inside was fabulous, from bedrooms to bathrooms, but Sandra liked the living room most. It had high beamed ceilings, polished oak floors, a stone-face fireplace, and six adjoining floor-to-ceiling windows.

"I like this room," Sandra said. "This is nice." She sat on a cowhide sectional large enough for ten people.

"I'm glad that you like it," said Jimmy. "This is your home now."

And it felt like home to Sandra, until later in the evening when Gee served dinner out on the patio.

Lit candles illuminated the darkness. Gee placed a white linen cloth over a table, achieving an elegant restaurant effect. She then placed breadbaskets and bowls of fruit in the middle of the table as centerpieces. For starters, consommé. The main course: an assortment of grilled seafood, mixed green salad, and roasted red potatoes. Dessert was raspberry basil shortcake with whipped cream. Looking at the seafood, Sandra knew Gee had prepared dinner especially for her, since everyone else at the table was a vegetarian. Sandra yearned for the filling of the wineglasses. At last, Gee uncorked a chilled bottle of sparkling white wine, nonalcoholic. Sandra's face dropped. She was not at home. She soon realized that this Hamilton family did not keep a drop of alcohol in the house. Damn!

"So, Aunt Sandra, how do you like this part of Santa Monica?" Laurence asked, taking a sip of his mock wine.

"She just got here, Laurence," Rita said. "She hasn't seen much yet!"

Laurence's head swiveled toward Rita. "Am I talking to you?"

"No, but I'm talking to you!"

"You're not talking to me!"

"All right now," Gee said, clapping her hands.

Rita looked at Laurence, rolling her eyes and scrunching her face.

"I saw that, Rita," Jimmy said.

Sandra cleared her throat. "Well, even though I haven't seen much, I like what little I've seen."

"That's cool," said Laurence, nodding his head. "I love it, the people, my school."

"What school is that?"

Laurence placed his fork on the side of his plate. He rubbed his palms on the front of his red tank top, glad to be conversing. "Santa Monica High School. It's great. Lots of famous people graduated from there: Sean Penn, Charlie Sheen. Who else? Let me see."

"Is that the reason why you're going?" Jimmy asked, looking up from his plate.

"No, Dad." Laurence slumped in his chair, lowering his eyes. He immediately shot up in his seat, looking at Sandra. "I'm going to Santa Monica High School because over ninety percent of its graduates go on to post-secondary educational institutions, including some of the nation's finest four-year colleges." He turned to his father. "Well, did I get it right, Dad?"

Jimmy and Gee burst into laughter.

"Boy, you are too much," Jimmy said, grinning.

Laurence turned to Sandra again. "Math is my favorite subject. I swim, play basketball, and I'm also on the debating team."

"Wow!"

"Yes, our Laurence is a busy bee," said Gee. She rubbed his dreadlocks as Laurence grinned ear to ear.

"What about you, Rita?" asked Sandra. "Are you as active as Laurence?"

Rita nibbled on a roasted potato positioned on the tine of her fork. "Not really. I like to write. English is my favorite subject."

"She writes wonderful poetry," Jimmy added.

Sandra looked at Rita. "Did you know that Grandma wrote poetry?"

Rita looked at Sandra seriously, her wide hazel eyes blinking. "No, I didn't." She quickly turned to her mother. "Could be hereditary, Mom."

"Could be," Gee replied, rubbing her palms. She folded her forearms at the edge of the table. "I'm done."

Sandra looked at Gee's long flowing hair. Her bell-sleeve dress with embroidery in front made her look like somebody's love child. Rita looked like Gee, Sandra thought, except that Rita had dreadlocks. Her dreadlocks, the color of wet sand, were gathered in a bunch on top her head.

Jimmy leaned forward, looking at Sandra. "I didn't know that Mama wrote poetry."

"There are boxes of poetry in the attic, dating way back."

"Really?"

"Really." Sandra bit into a jumbo shrimp.

"What did she write about?"

"The Reverend."

"You mean Dad."

"Yeah, him."

Upon saying this, Sandra felt four pairs of eyes staring at her, questioning. Jimmy sat back in his chair. "You've changed."

"No. I haven't," Sandra said, her words clipped. "The world has."

Since that evening of mock wine, Sandra brought her own—the real McCoy—stashing the bottles underneath the sofa bed in the den and behind the counter in the health food store she managed for Jimmy. The job was boring, but her training was worse. What did she care about the benefits of valerian root tea? She listened to Jimmy as he rattled on about the uses of alfalfa.

"Alfalfa?"

"Yeah, alfalfa. It alkalizes and detoxifies the body, acts as a diuretic, eases inflammation, lowers cholesterol, balances hormones, and promotes pituitary gland function. Are you writing this down?"

Sandra grunted, scribbling words that seemed like nonsense to her.

"Good. Now alfalfa also contains an antifungal agent, which is good for anemia, bleeding-related disorders, bone and joint disorders, colon and digestive problems, skin problems, and ulcers. Alfalfa must be in fresh raw form to provide vitamins. Sprouts are especially effective..."

Did Jimmy really expect for her to remember all of this? Sandra thought. She dropped her hands to her sides. "Does this really matter? I mean, we all are going to die anyway."

Jimmy stared at Sandra as if she had two heads. "It matters to our clients." Then he moved to cat's claw, milk thistle, aloe vera, dong quai, and yarrow, without skipping a beat.

This was Jimmy's world, not hers, Sandra thought. Her mind drifted, going back to her days at Nubia, her African clothes boutique. Sandra remembered going through the racks of clothing with a customer, rattling off the diatribe she'd heard Les say time and time again: "Yeah, Kemet was the beginning of

Egyptian civilization, but Western cultural imperialism has tried to rob Africa of her history! Those intellectuals fail to recognize Kemet as a culture of Africans that existed way before the Assyrians arrived in Egypt. And the name Kemet simply means 'home of the blacks.' Huh. Thousands of years ago, Herodotus called all Africa Ethiopia. 'Cause an Ethiopian to the ancient Greek was any man with a black face!"

"I hear you, sister! Speak on," the customer had said.

Now this is what their clients wanted to hear. At least according to Les. They wanted to hear about things that really mattered to them, a piece of their missing history. They also wanted clothing from an African country, the closest to Africa some of them would ever get.

Sandra looked through the plated-glass window. On the boardwalk of Venice Beach were blonde, tanned, buxom women wearing bikini tops and cutoff jeans, Walkman headphones to their ears, on roller blades. Everything was different to Sandra.

Jimmy slapped his thighs as he stood up from his chair. "Well, that's enough training for today. Our customers will be strolling in soon."

Thank God, Sandra thought, secretly rolling her eyes.

The tinkle of the bell above the door caused Jimmy and Sandra to turn their heads. It was Laurence, his face bright and cheery. "Hey! Hey! Hey! Hey!"

Sandra smiled. Laurence was her man. She had fallen in love with him from day one. Rita was aloof, she stuck to her mother, and didn't say much. But Laurence was free-spirited. During the first month, he had shown Sandra all around Santa Monica: Pacific Park, Palisades Park, Muscle Beach, Looff Hippodrome Building, and the happening eateries downtown. Sandra drove. Laurence directed. Many times he had tried to persuade Sandra to let him get behind the wheel.

"No! You're only fifteen," Sandra found herself repeating.

"Ah, man!"

"Ah, man! Nothing."

"I'll give you money. Come on! Name your price."

"Boy! You think I'm poor and stupid? Put your money away!"

"You drive a hard bargain, Sandra."

"That's Aunt Sandra to you!"

Then they both laughed until they cried.

Laurence made Sandra forget herself, forget who she was. In this way, she was almost a new person. She laughed more.

"Hey! Brother man," Sandra yelled, "What's happening?"

"You for the moment, my sister," Laurence chimed. He turned toward his father. "Hey! Dad."

Jimmy smiled. "Listen, I'm heading towards the other store. You want to come, Laurence?"

"I want to stay with Sandra. Okay, Dad?"

Jimmy shook his head, laughing. "It figures. Two peas in a pod." He touched his son's shoulder as he walked toward the door. "See you two later," he said.

Later that afternoon, Sandra and Laurence walked along the boardwalk of Venice Beach. Sandra teased Laurence as he scoped out women.

"Here we go again. Another brother into white chicks," Sandra said, throwing her hands in the air. "What are sisters gonna do?"

Laurence waved his hand at Sandra, sucking his teeth. "Please!"

"So you're a boob man, huh?"

"I am not a boob man! Your mind is always in the gutter."

Sandra pinched him.

"Ow!" Laurence rubbed his arm.

There was a moment of silence.

"Well, if you must know, I'm a breast man, stated correctly."

Sandra stopped in her tracks and burst into laughter, holding onto his shoulder. "I'm telling your father!"

"He already knows!" Laurence shoved his face in Sandra's face.

They both laughed this time, Sandra doubling over.

Afterward, they drove along the palm tree-lined streets to the trendy shops and boutiques. Sandra bought a straw hat and a couple of dresses. Laurence bought jeans and t-shirts. They had lunch at a sidewalk café, watching the street performers and musicians, the herd of tourists, and the plastic wannabe movie stars and the real ones, too.

Sandra stole a French fry from Laurence's plate.

"That's going to cost you," he said, before taking a huge bite from his veggie burger. He pushed a stray dreadlock from his face. The rest of his auburn dreadlocks fell to his shoulders, like a lion's mane. He chewed heartily.

Sandra looked at Laurence's bare arms, his forming muscles.

"What are you looking at?" He threw a French fry in the air, catching it in his mouth.

"Your muscles."

"Yeah, I've been working out." He flexed his biceps, smiling.

"I see. I guess the girls are all over you, huh?"

Lawrence shrugged. "I got a few babes."

They laughed.

Sandra wiped the beads of sweat forming on her nose. She then picked at her pasta salad, scattering it around her plate.

Laurence looked at Sandra. "Not too hungry, are you?"

"Nope."

"Do you want it?" He quickly reached for her plate.

"Take it, greedy boy, here."

"I'm not greedy. Just growing." He winked.

Sandra motioned the waitress for another glass of wine.

Laurence frowned. "You drink a lot. You already had four. Why do you drink so much? Every time we go out, you have to drink."

Sandra stared at Laurence. His face no longer looked like a pleasant fifteen-year-old, but a younger version of Jimmy looking back at her disapprovingly, his caramel-colored eyes unblinking. "So you're my daddy now?"

"No." He shrugged. "Just your nephew who thinks that you drink too much. Mom says when people drink like you, they have problems—deep-seated ones."

The waitress placed the glass of wine in front of Sandra.

"Thank you." She paused as the waitress walked away. "Well, you know what, Laurence?" Sandra said, taking a sip of wine. "Mothers are not always right. I just like the taste of it. That's all. No biggy."

He stared at his plate. "Well, I still think that you drink too much."

"Laurence, have you told anyone about my drinking?"

"No." He looked at her.

"Are you sure?"

"Yes! I swear!"

"Good. Let's keep it that way."

Sandra was used to the flow of this Hamilton family after four months. There was always a hustle and bustle in the morning, everyone scurrying to work or school, but the evenings were relaxed, and it was mandatory for everyone to be present at the dinner table. Gee wouldn't have it any other way. Sometimes Sandra helped Gee in the kitchen. They'd laugh and sing songs as they prepared vegetarian meals. Jimmy joined in from time to time, showing off his rendition of Marvin Gaye's "Let's Get It On" while he sidled up to Gee. Gee's face would turn beet red, laughing hysterically. It was fun to Sandra, a sure way to forget her woes.

But by nightfall, the house was quiet, with everyone tucked in bed. The stillness provoked Sandra's thoughts, thoughts about what she would eventually do with her life, believing she remained at a standstill. Nothing had changed really, except for the fact that she no longer lived in her father's house, and that Les was almost a figure in a far corner of her mind. They had long since finalized business, and when he popped into her head from time to time, she still thought of knives.

A few men had asked Sandra for a date since she moved to Santa Monica, all patrons of the health food store, but Sandra politely declined. There was Glen, a recent divorcee who couldn't get over his ex-wife in spite of his efforts. James was a fine brother, but needed to decide whether he was gay or straight. Clarence, a hunk of a man, was more interested in her chest than anything else. She recalled their first conversation, how they were discussing the benefits of Japanese green tea, and out of the blue he said, "Umph! Your chest looks good. What size are you, a 36C?" That was it for Sandra.

No matter how hard Sandra tried to win Rita's favor, it was to no avail. She had tried everything: taking interest in her poetry, trying to find some common ground. Yet Rita remained distant, huddling under her mother's wings. Not only had Rita maintained a mental distance, but also a physical one. Sandra tried to brush it off. "Huh. She's just a teenager. You know how troubling teenagers can be, especially the girls," she said to herself. But Sandra was bothered by it nonetheless.

Every Saturday afternoon, Gee and Rita spent quality girl time. This Saturday they were out on the patio, painting each other's toenails. Each of their toes fanned out like webbed feet, cotton balls between them. Gee had chosen a nice nude beige, but Rita picked a horrid sky blue.

"Good afternoon," Sandra said, plopping down on a wicker chair.

"Good afternoon to you, too." Gee said. "For a moment, I thought to check on you to see if you were still breathing." She smiled, twisting her long hair into a knot on top her head.

"I'm still alive and kicking. And good afternoon to you, too, Rita."

Rita applied a second coat of polish on her mother's toenail. "Good afternoon," she said in a dull tone, without looking up.

"Had a restful sleep?" Gee asked cheerfully.

"Mom, keep still."

"Okay. Okay."

"Sure," Sandra replied. She lied. Her head was pounding from too much wine the night before. She could barely lift up her head, never mind her body. Her stomach still felt uneasy. Sandra stared at Rita sitting on a stool before her mother, bending forward. Rita wore a white tank top cut low in the back. To Sandra, Rita's vertebrae beneath her tight skin looked liked smooth stepping stones. "Will you do mine next, Rita?"

She did not reply.

Gee frowned. "Rita, your Aunt Sandra is talking to you. Answer her."

"Mom and I are going shopping after this."

"So I take that as a no, then." Sandra plastered a false smile on her face. She got up to stretch. "Seems like it's going to be another nice day."

"It's always a nice day in Santa Monica," Gee said, looking at Rita. "Sweetheart, we can go shopping later. Why don't you polish Sandra's toenails?"

"You promised, Mom!"

"Sweetheart, I'm not saying that we can't go. I'm just saying that we can go a little later. That's—"

"Mom!" Rita stood up.

"Forget it, Gee," said Sandra. "It's apparent she doesn't want to polish my nails." Sandra reached over to hug her. "Don't worry, Rita. I won't hold it against—"

Rita pushed Sandra away.

Sandra backed off.

"Rita!" Gee exclaimed, sitting forward in her seat. "Apologize!"

"But Mom!"

"But nothing! Apologize this instant!"

"But Mom, her breath always smells like liq—"

"Stop it!" Gee stood up, furious. "Go upstairs! Now!"

Rita threw the bottle of nail polish on the ground and stormed past Sandra.

Gee smoothed back the strands of her blonde hair. "I'm sorry, Sandra. I'm not sure what's gotten into her. But you will get your apology. I'll see to that!

After that day, Sandra made it her business to carry mints at all times.

"Hey, brother man, want to go to Palisades Park with me?" Sandra asked Laurence as he sat at the edge of the pool one morning. Laurence swirled his feet in the water, his chin to his bare chest. "I don't know. Maybe if you let me drive."

"Maybe I will."

Laurence swiftly looked up at Sandra, shading his eyes from the sun. "Really?"

"Well, I'll think about it."

"Okay!" Laurence heaved himself up with his palms and stood before Sandra, towering over her. "When do you want to go the park?" He brushed his hands against the seat of his swimming trunks.

"As soon as you get dressed."

"Sure!" Laurence said, running into the house.

Sandra smiled as she watched his long, lanky limbs pump into high gear. She lay on the chaise lounge, removing the sunglasses from the crown of her head onto her face. She pulled out the letter from the pocket of her shorts. It was from Mama. Sandra smiled, placing the letter to her nose. She could almost smell Mama, like scented soap.

March 2, 1991

Dear Sandy,

I'm happy that you are well in Santa Monica. I prayed that you would get acquainted with the world again, and now my prayers have been answered. I can rest easy.

Your father, Lilly, and I have missed you greatly. If the Lord is willing, I plan to make it to Santa Monica this Christmas. For the first time, your father is planning to come too! I think that it would be wonderful to have an old-fashioned family Christmas again. So I will count the months until I'll see you. Then, we will take time out for a cup of tea...

Have you met anyone yet? I've been praying for a special someone to come into your life. We both know that relationships are hard to maintain, and downright frustrating at times, but we all need someone to love and someone to love us. I find this especially true since I've grown older. My companionship with your father is much more important to me...

Sandra placed the letter on her lap and closed her eyes for a while. "Oh Mama, if you only knew," she whispered.

"I'm ready!" said Laurence, popping in front of the chaise lounge, arms wide open.

Sandra jumped, grabbing her chest. "Boy! What are trying to do? Give me a heart attack!"

Laurence laughed, pulling Sandra by the arm. "Palisades Park, here we come!"

Later that day, the fun and games at Palisades Park had worked up Sandra's thirst—for wine. She'd suggested going to a restaurant for an early dinner, which was fine with Laurence, since he was always ready for a meal. He'd ordered spaghetti with soy meatballs. Sandra bypassed the main course and ordered her first drink. Laurence frowned, shaking his head.

"What? Come on! Spit it out, Laurence. It's written all over your face."

Laurence twirled the spaghetti around the tine of his fork, without looking or responding to Sandra. She gulped down the first glass of wine, then ordered a bottle. Laurence's eyes bulged. Neither one spoke for a while. Laurence finished his entrée, moving on to ice cream and chocolate cake for dessert, his eyes cast toward his plate. He chewed slowly, glancing now and then at the R&B band setting up for the evening.

"Why you so quiet," Sandra said loudly, "don't like the comfany?"

Laurence placed his spoon next to his plate and leaned forward, whispering, "It's company. I want to go home. You're drunk."

"Am not!"

"Are too."

"I am not!" Sandra yelled.

Laurence glanced around the room. A few people looked toward their table. "I want to go home—now," he whispered.

Sandra cut her eyes and paid the check. She hadn't realized how much she'd drank, until she tried to get up. Maybe it was Mama's letter she'd read earlier that disturbed her, the mention of her father. Whatever the case, Sandra couldn't walk, and reluctantly handed over the keys to Laurence.

When Laurence parked into the garage, Gee ran outside the house, hair flying behind her like a cape.

"Sandra! Are you out of your...?" Gee stopped, assessing Sandra's state. She looked at Laurence, blinked, then looked at Sandra again.

Laurence shrugged, shaking his head as he got out of the black Lexus.

Gee's face turned red. "Go get your father!"

Sandra was fumbling with the door on the passenger's side when Jimmy walked up, Laurence trailing behind him. She stepped outside the car, then fell to the ground on her knees.

Jimmy rushed toward Sandra, yanking her arm, trying to pull her up. "What…?" He looked perplexed, staring at Gee, then Laurence.

Gee was tight-lipped, arms crossed against her chest.

Sandra mumbled something undecipherable. Her legs were folded beneath her body, limp as a rag doll.

"Come on, Sandra. Get up!" Jimmy said. "Laurence, help me."

Each took an arm and dragged Sandra to her feet, her head wobbling from shoulder to shoulder.

Gee screamed, "I won't have this in our house, Jimmy! Did Laurence tell you that he drove home? We could have gotten in trouble with the law!"

Jimmy quickly turned toward Laurence. "Why didn't you call me?"

Laurence shrugged, searching for words, "I…I…"

"Never mind! I'll deal with you later. Let's get her inside."

After much effort, they placed Sandra on the couch in the den, but she fell off, sitting on the floor with her back against the coffee table, legs splayed. She drowsily nodded, her chin resting on her chest.

"Sandra!"

"*What?*" Her eyes suddenly opened.

"Are you going to stand up or do you want me to pull you up?" Jimmy asked.

"I'll get up myself!"

Jimmy watched as Sandra struggled to her feet. "Jesus," he said. He slapped his forehead and looked to the ceiling, avoiding Gee's eyes.

Finally, Sandra sat on the edge of the couch. "I'm up, see. I'm up." She then emitted a long resounding belch. "Oh God! I'm gonna be sick."

Hours later, after Sandra had tucked herself beneath the clean sheets, after the taste of vomit had disappeared from her mouth, and the effects of the wine had waned, a sobering thought occurred to her: she was going to pay dearly for this.

The next morning Gee walked into the den.

Sandra, embarrassed, covered her face with a pillow. "I'm sorry, Gee."

Gee was back to her calm self. "So am I." She sighed and sat in a nearby chair. "Sandra, I will put it to you bluntly. You have a problem. We've seen the empty wine bottles in the bin for a while. Maybe I should have said something sooner. But it has to stop here. I can help. Do you want my help?"

Sandra didn't know what to say. No one had ever confronted her. She removed the pillow from her face. "How?" she asked meekly.

"Well, there are various ways." Gee rubbed her lap. "Self-hypnosis is one. Many of my clients have quit addictions through hypnosis. Then there's AA, a twelve-step program based on the view that alcohol is the product of disease. So with the support of a self-help group, treatment emphasizes the powerlessness over alcohol resulting in total abstinence." Gee looked at Sandra. "Are you following me?"

Sandra nodded.

"Okay. Then there's a program based on the view that alcohol abuse is the product of biological, psychological, and social factors. It also focuses on AA's twelve-step program to recovery, but in contrast to AA, the person in this program accepts responsibility for changing behavior that is excessively costly to him or herself and others. In my opinion, Sandy," Gee slapped the back of her hand onto the palm of the other, "this may be the best approach for you."

"Okay," Sandra said, in a little girl's voice. She covered her face with her hands and wept.

Gee walked over and sat next to her, rubbing her back. "Once you get help, it'll be all right. You'll see."

"I want help. I need help." Sandra grabbed a pillow and pressed it against her chest, rocking back and forth, her face an amalgam of tears and mucus.

"How long have you been drinking, Sandy?" Gee wiped Sandra's face with a corner of the sheets.

"Since I was twelve," she said between sobs.

"My goodness," Gee said sympathetically. "Why?"

Sandra stopped rocking. She couldn't tell Gee why! Then she would ask more questions: How old were you when he first touched you? Why didn't you tell someone? What did you say, Sandra? Did you say that you allowed it to go on until you were fourteen? Fourteen! How did you stop it?

Then she would say, I threatened to tell Mama.

Why didn't you threaten to tell Mama sooner?

I don't know.

You don't know?

It's not like he was hurting me.

He wasn't hurting you? So you liked it?

Then she would remain silent for a while, confused.

Two days later, Sandra was sitting in the backseat of Jimmy's car, clutching a suitcase to her chest, with her quavering chin resting on its edge, on her way to a residential treatment center called The Haven. Gee arranged everything. President of Haven Lindsay Miller was one of Gee's patients years ago, a recovered alcoholic herself, and now a close friend, and she was more than willing to accommodate Sandra for a thirty-day detoxification program. Gee made it seem as if the decision was left up to Sandra. But Sandra knew better: If she declined, she'd be headed back to Cambridge, and she didn't want that. Then Mama would find out that not only had she jeopardized her own life but her fifteen-year-old nephew's. No. She wanted Mama to believe that she was doing fine. Sandra lifted her downcast eyes toward the rearview mirror. Jimmy hadn't acknowledged her stare. She wanted to read his eyes, but he kept his face forward, eyes glued to oncoming traffic. Sandra caught a glimpse. Jimmy's eyes spoke briefly: It's a disease. I have it. You have it. Uncle Rufus has it. There's no defense.

Except for occasional pauses, Gee's conversation sounded normal to Sandra. "Sandy…are…are you okay?"

Of course I'm not okay! she thought. Then, "I'm fine."

Had Sandra been fair-skinned, the flush of her cheeks probably would've revealed the indignation or resentment or fear, even rage, but she hadn't known what she was feeling, so the emotion lay hidden beneath darkness, unidentified.

"If you're willing…truly willing…this could be a turning point in your life," Gee said.

Silence.

Gee, who was sitting in the passenger's seat, turned to face Sandra, her forehead lined with worry, but her eyes twinkled with hope. "Did you hear me?" She smiled, adjusting the strap of her white sundress.

Sandra nodded, confused, wondering how she'd arrived at this place in her life, all of a sudden it seemed. She released her grip on the blue suitcase, and a rush of blood returned to her knuckles. She looked outside the window, and saw a man bent forward at the waist, polishing a vintage, bright red car in his driveway. The sun's reflection bounced off its chrome bumper, causing Sandra to squint. It was such a beautiful day. How could anything be wrong on a day like this? she thought. It was Sunday, a lazy day; its rhythm reminded Sandra of the ocean lapping at the shore.

"You know, Lindsay's alcoholism proved to be her turning point," Gee continued, nestling in her seat, looking forward. "Opportunity presents itself in the most oddest ways. Lindsay was a mess when I first met her—an alcoholic for fifteen years—but now she's a natural born leader, teaching people how to live productively."

Why was I ever born? Sandra thought, placing the suitcase beside her.

"Sandy!" Gee's voice now sounded high and lilting. "Did I tell you that Haven has an eighty percent success rate?" She turned to face Sandra once more.

"Yes, you have," Sandra said solemnly, avoiding eye contact.

"Good!" She sat back in her seat.

Jimmy slowed to a stop after pulling off the highway, and Sandra suddenly raised her head, looking outside the window again, only to discover they were obeying another red light. She was anxious to see Haven. Sandra only knew that Haven was in Anaheim, in Orange County, on Cortelyou Avenue, not far from Disneyland, but hadn't known what it looked like. Peals of laughter suddenly rushed inside the car, coming from a group of little girls playing double Dutch on the sidewalk. Sandra watched them intently until the car drove off, chuckling softly to herself—now she knew how she'd felt: like a little girl, ashamed, being driven off to a school for the wayward, with a chatty mother and much too silent father.

As they continued on their way, Gee rambled on and on about Haven's superior medical evaluation and treatment, psychosocial assessment, alcohol and drug education, group therapy, one-on-one counseling, and relapse prevention. She moved on to how the staff at Haven believed that abstinence from alcohol was just the beginning in the recovery process, that full recovery was obtained by a total lifestyle change, and that the residents at Haven lived comfortably, without the use of addicting, mood-altering drugs or obsessive-compulsive behaviors.

After a few additional red lights, Jimmy slowed to a final stop. "We're here," he said wearily.

Gee quickly unfastened her seatbelt and popped outside the car.

Sandra sat still, looking at the back of Jimmy's head.

"Why, there you are!"

Sandra immediately turned her head toward the other cheery voice that boomed across the stretch of grass.

"That's Lindsay," Jimmy mumbled. "Come, let's get out of the car."

To Sandra, Lindsay looked like a bull of a woman, with a bloated face and squared jaws resembling Ted Kennedy's. Earlier, Gee had explained to Sandra that Lindsay had put on an enormous amount of weight after she'd quit drinking. And judging by her size, Sandra couldn't help but wonder if perhaps Lindsay was now battling a different type of addiction. Lindsay's sandy-brown hair was cut close around the back and sides, but at the crown of her head, hair stood up like porcupines' quills. She wore khaki pants, brown clogs, and a white, man-tailored shirt large enough to house a family.

After Gee and Lindsay released each other from their bear hugs, Gee turned around and grabbed Sandra's hand, leading her toward the Bull. Not only was Lindsay wide as a ship, Sandra thought, she was also tall—outflanking everyone.

Lindsay grabbed Sandra's shoulders. "Hi! Welcome to Haven, Sandra! Gee has told me all about you!"

"Probably not about my better half, " she said dryly.

Gee shot a look at Sandra, then at Jimmy, who was standing a short distance away, hands shoved deeply into the pockets of his jeans. Gee summoned him to move closer with a quick snap of her head, but he remained glued to his spot.

Lindsay's pale blue eyes bore into Sandra's, seemingly trying to size her up.

Right there and then, Sandra decided she didn't like her, and stared back at Lindsay defiantly.

Lindsay dropped her hooves to her sides, and a smirk emerged upon her face. She then moved toward Jimmy. "Jim-Jim!"

Jim-Jim? Sandra thought. Please!

Lindsay and Jimmy hugged each other. Gee moved closer, and the three of them assembled, engaged in small talk.

Sandra placed the suitcase beside her feet, then tucked the white t-shirt inside her shorts. She looked around, and her eyes suddenly opened. Haven was beautiful. Its live-in, on-campus houses were actually bungalows—flamingo-pink, with baby-blue steps, surrounded by white picket fences, gurgling fountains, and lush vegetation. Each house had an airy veranda, and there were many palm trees on the rolling grounds. Not far away, Sandra saw a group of women reclining on gleaming-white beach chairs, tanning themselves around a turquoise pool. Haven looked more like a resort in the Caribbean rather than a rehab in Anaheim! Maybe this place isn't so bad, Sandra thought. She quickly looked in Lindsay's direction, breaking Lindsay's stare. "Nice, isn't it?" Lindsay said.

Moments later, Gee hugged Sandra before heading toward the car. Jimmy bent forward, barely kissing her cheek, and Sandra knew he was upset, disappointed. After they had driven off, Sandra picked up her suitcase, following Lindsay to the front door. She turned before entering, looking across the expanse of greenery, with glimmer of hope. Yeah. Maybe this place isn't so bad.

Chapter 8
TURNING POINT?

"This place is Hell!" a Haven resident declared, sneaking behind Sandra as she walked down the clinically clean corridor to the admissions office. Sandra tripped, nearly dropping her suitcase, then placed a palm flat against her chest. Lindsay spun on her heels, standing in the middle of the gray carpet, hands on her squared hips. "Burly! Watch your mouth!"

Burly's knees buckled, and he dropped to the floor in a quivering heap, laughing hysterically. His index finger shot up at Sandra. "Look at her face! Damn!"

"That's enough, Burly!"

Sandra's heart pounded as the other residents closed in to investigate the commotion: a young mousy woman with blond stringy hair, nibbling on a hangnail, snickering; an older man with thick glasses and a bulbous nose, shaking his head in disgust; and fat, redheaded twins wearing a boa and frilly dresses. Lindsay stretched her neck above the small crowd, looking down the corridor. "Where is Burly's detox counselor?" she yelled. Burly managed to get up on all fours. "Miss Lindsay, I'll go get Mr. Pettis!" a freckled-faced boy said. He seemed to dart from nowhere, and Sandra pressed her body against the wall as he whizzed past her, running frantically down the hall, arms flailing.

"All right! The show is over," Lindsay said, clapping her hands. "Disperse!"

The residents moved slowly, and before the mousy woman retreated through a pair of glass doors, she said to Sandra, "Burly jus' likes attention. That's all. He don't mean nothin'."

A bald, muscular black man marched down the corridor. "Burly! Up!"

Burly jumped to his feet and turned toward the man. "I was just having me a little fun," he said, in a woman's voice. "Cain't a girl have a little fun?"

The man grabbed Burly by the elbow and turned toward Lindsay, "I assure you, this will not happen again."

"Don't let it!" she snarled, through clenched teeth.

Following a detailed medical history, a physical examination, a series of diagnostic questionnaires, and face-to-face evaluations, and after meeting the administration staff, the medical staff, the clinical staff, and detox staff, Sandra was finally escorted to her room, loaded with information. She was given a copy of Haven's monthly newsletter, many brochures describing its facilities and activities, and, most importantly, the daily schedule. "Memorize it!" Lindsay said. "Routine is a way of life here."

Sandra threw her suitcase in a corner and plopped onto her bed, cradling her forehead in her palm. What have I gotten myself into? she thought, tears streaming down her cheeks. Man! Her mind suddenly rested on the proceeds of the business that Les had given her. She really didn't need to stay here or go back to Jimmy's house. She could get an apartment somewhere, start all over. But the thought was fleeting; its wings soon took flight out the window, for Sandra had never lived alone, was deathly afraid of living alone. She felt trapped, succumbing to perceived inevitability: What choice do I have?

She wiped away the tears with the back of her hands, then picked up the schedule. On the weekends, the residents had additional time for themselves it seemed. But Mondays through Fridays were rigid: AA meetings at 7:00 AM, breakfast at 8:30 AM, community meeting at 9:30 AM, exercise from 10:00 AM to 11:00 AM, then fifteen minutes of free time, education group at 11:15 AM, lunch at 12:30 PM, group therapy at 1:45 PM, one-on-one counseling from 3:00 PM to 4:00 PM, then optional activities, dinner at 5:30 PM. Sandra paused, placing the schedule face down on her lap. A long funnel of air escaped her lips. She picked up the schedule again. More optional activities from 6:30 PM to 10:00 PM, then lights out at 11:00. Lights out at 11:00? She always got her second wind around 11:00! Sandra placed the schedule on the bed, staring into space. Burly was right, she thought. This place is Hell!

On the fourth morning of Sandra's stay at Haven, the jitters and irritability kicked in—bad. She could've ripped somebody's throat out for a drink if she had to, without hesitation. How else was she going to cope with all those people probing into her business today? And of all people, Lindsay was her detox counselor, which was unheard of, according to the mousy woman with blonde stringy hair—Libby—with whom Sandra now shared a room. "Lindsay musta takin' a likin' to you," Libby had said. Sandra glanced at the clock as she paced barefoot on the terra cotta tile floor. It was 5:45 AM. There was a noise outside. She stopped and pushed back the pastel curtains, watching a band of Mexicans in the gray morning light as they jumped from their pickup truck, preparing for their day of trimming Haven's shrubbery.

"You still up?" Libby said, rubbing her eyes. She stood in the middle of the dim room. Sandra turned around, then looked back toward the window. She didn't feel like being bothered with anybody today. "Betcha didn't sleep last night," Libby continued. "That's how it is in the beginnin'. Can't sleep. Can't eat. Nervous all the time. They have somethin' for that."

Sandra released the curtains and turned to face Libby from across the room, evil-eyed. "Why don't you just shut up!"

Libby nibbled on a hangnail for a moment, then leaped in bed, snickering under the covers. But Sandra knew what Libby had said was true, because she'd already been through the thirty-day primary phase, now entering the structured phase. Just a day ago Sandra had asked Libby how she could afford it. Haven wasn't cheap! Libby looked at Sandra and pulled the sleeves of her cotton-knit sweater over her hands. "I may seem like white trash to you," she said, with a hint of indignation, "but my daddy is a big man in West Virginia!"

Later that morning, fatigue descended upon Sandra at the AA meeting as she stood in a semi-circle with other residents of her group, preparing for their daily recitation from the *Big Book*, AA's twelve steps to recovery. Their voices lifted in unison; Sandra's droned in monotony, reciting the first four steps only, then stood bleary-eyed, waiting for it to end.

After the group had finished, Sandra plopped onto her chair before everyone else, folding her arms against her chest. Rena, a certified counselor and team leader, looked at Sandra with raised eyebrows. "The rest of you may be seated," Rena said softly. She ran her fingertips through her short-cropped hair, as the sound of shuffling feet and chairs scraped against the shiny wood floor.

Their AA meetings were held in the arts center, where southwestern-style ceramic pots were displayed in glass cases and Georgia O'Keefe's paintings hung on pristine white walls. The group sat in the middle of the room, and the sun from the skylight bathed the residents. Their group consisted of twenty people this morning—fifteen men and five women, all colors and variety—and Rena routinely looked at each person's face before she spoke in her usual pensive manner. For a few seconds, she walked around the room, looking at her feet, with her hands clasped behind her back.

Bored and fidgety, Sandra scanned the face of an Ivy-League-looking man, with blonde hair and a tan complexion, dressed in a white polo shirt. He leaned back in his chair, clasping his hands around a raised kneecap, looking attentively at Rena. Sandra's eyes shifted to the frail woman next to him, who looked like an ordinary, middle-class housewife with a pageboy cut.

Rena stopped in the middle of the semi-circle. "This morning I have a special treat for you," she said, placing her hands in the back pockets of her jeans. "As you all know, Haven has an eighty-percent success rate." She paused, looking at the faces again, her large brown eyes gleaming. "But that's just an impersonal statistic," she said, shaking an index finger in the air. "Today, I want you to meet one of Haven's products of success! Will everyone please give a warm welcome to one of Haven's alumni, Mrs. Stephanie Watkins." Everyone clapped and looked around the room, except Sandra, as a tall, golden-brown woman with a swan neck and clothed in a flowered dress, walked from the back of the room to the front. Rena hugged Stephanie before she took her seat.

Stephanie stood in the middle of the semi-circle, rubbing her graceful hands, slightly bowing her upper body. "Thank you for the warm welcome. Thank you." The room grew quiet. "Hello. As you know my name is Stephanie, and I am an alcoholic, although I have been in remission for five years now." Everyone clapped again, with fervor, and the Ivy-League-looking man put his fingers to his mouth and whistled loudly. Stephanie pressed her hands against her lap and bent forward from the waist. "Thank you so much." The clapping got on Sandra's nerves, and she rested her face in her hands.

After the clapping had died down, Stephanie spoke again, her voice solemn. "About ten years ago, my daily routine included a bottle of vodka and a six-pack of beer—I was a mess." She shook her head. "Now, even though I knew that I was a mess and that alcohol would eventually kill me, what I didn't know," her head bobbed as she emphasized her next words, "was that alcohol was just a symptom." A few people clapped again, and one of the fat, redheaded twins stood up, clapping with her hands high in the air.

Stephanie waited for a while before she continued. "You see, I hadn't understood the cause of my addiction, not until I arrived at Haven. Getting to the root of the cause is the key to sobriety. Haven takes you through a fact-finding mission—don't resist it!"

"Yesss!" a thin man shouted, who was sitting next to Sandra.

Sandra immediately removed her hands from her face, looking at the man in thorough disgust. She placed her hands back to her face, oblivious of Rena's observations as she jotted notes onto a pad.

"Don't resist it!" Stephanie repeated. "Because after I understood the cause of my addiction and I put it in my heart to change, knowing full well that I'd been living a maladjusted life with a disease, I dropped to my knees and asked God for help. Alcohol was too much for me to handle." Stephanie's eyes grew moist, and she put her hands over her heart. "You see, every day I recite the twelve-steps to recovery with my friends at AA. But not one of us has maintained perfect adherence to all these principles. We're not saints!" Stephanie moved deeper into the semi-circle of people. "My point is that the principles of the twelve-steps to recovery are guides to spiritual progress, rather than spiritual perfection. But God is merciful and—"

"Oh, please!" Sandra yelled, dropping her hands from her face. "If God is so merciful, why did he allow any of us to become alcoholics in the first damn place?"

The room was silent. Everyone stunned, looking at each other.

Stephanie looked at Rena, who was now standing. Stephanie then cleared her throat and looked at the crown of Sandra's head. "You forget self-will," she said. "God has given us self-will. People live by this self-will, always colliding into something or somebody. Totally out of God's order. And the alcoholic is an extreme example of a self-will run riot!"

Sandra decided that she hadn't liked Stephanie's tone, and jumped up, determined to whip Stephanie's behind. Stephanie took one look at Sandra's face and moved back, a hand over her mouth. It had taken two male detox counselors and Rena to escort a kicking and screaming Sandra outside the room.

That afternoon, Sandra stood before the Bull, who was sitting behind her desk, snorting, it seemed, as she tapped a pencil on an opened magazine. Sandra paced across the room, agitated, hateful, with red-rimmed eyes. Lindsay's cold stare followed Sandra from one end of her office to the other. Finally, she threw the pencil between the pages of the magazine and sat back in her chair, hands folded on top her bulging belly. "Sit down," Lindsay said, with alarming control, halting Sandra in her tracks. Sandra pondered for a moment, eyes cast toward the pale pink wall. Lindsay's office and many of Haven's rooms were painted in soft pastel colors, supposedly a calming affect on the patients and staff members. "Sit down, I said." Upon hearing these words, something in Sandra's stomach twisted, loathing that some big, fat white woman was telling her what to do! Sandra turned to face Lindsay, both staring at each other like two gunmen at high noon.

"Suit yourself," Lindsay said calmly, reaching for the phone. "I'll call Gee to pick you up. Haven will refund your money." A muscle suddenly flinched behind Sandra's stone face, and a smirk slowly emerged on Lindsay's. "One more time," Lindsay said slowly, holding the receiver beneath her double chin. "Sit down."

Tears rolled down Sandra's face just as quickly as she tried to wipe them away with the back of her hands. She sat on a maroon leather couch against a wall with an opened window, overlooking one of Haven's botanical gardens. Lindsay hung up the phone and walked around her cherry wood desk, sitting on its edge. She extended her hand toward Sandra, handing her a wad of facial tissue. Sandra, who made no attempt to accept the offering, stared at a Navajo painting just above Lindsay's head. Her eyes then moved to a tall cactus plant standing in a corner. Lindsay, exasperated, dropped her extended hand onto her lap.

"You know, Sandra, I'm not your enemy—alcohol is. I'm on your side. And I know what you're going through, all too well. The first week is the worst! But outbursts of anger like the one you performed today will not help your situation, and neither will it be tolerated at Haven. Do you hear me?" Silence. Sandra's eyes now focused on a plaque on a wall: Haven was licensed and certified by the state of California. Lindsay dropped her head, her chin hitting her chest, as she plucked at the tissue she held on her lap.

Out of the corner of her eye, Sandra saw Lindsay's pig-pink face looking a bit saddened, and she felt a twinge of victory. Lindsay raised her head, looking at Sandra again. "You know that Haven has a high success rate. We're very proud of that! But the few who haven't recovered are those who could not or would not completely give themselves to this program." She paused. "Usually it's those who are incapable of being honest with themselves. I hope that you aren't one of them, Sandra."

Lindsay got up and sat in her chair, reaching for a book inside one of the desk drawers. She pushed aside the magazine and flipped through the pages of the book, placing it on the desk. She then folded her hands, leaning forward, and mounds of cleavage rose from her scooped-neck blouse. "The most important step toward recovery, Sandra, is a personal housecleaning, which many people have never attempted in their entire lives. To look inside themselves is horrifying. Haven knows this, but it has to be done." She looked down at the book. Her dimpled index finger ran across a page. Sandra looked at Lindsay, cutting her eyes. "Now see, you haven't submitted your personal inventory for group therapy. You know, the grudge list where you place a person's name opposite your resentment." Lindsay looked up. "Sandra, do your really think that alcohol is really the root of your problem?" Lindsay shook her head and chuckled.

I'd like to rip your face off. You fat bitch! Sandra thought, squirming in her seat, wiping the remnant of tears off her face.

"What do you think is the root cause of your alcoholism, Sandra?"

"What the hell was your root cause?"

Lindsay's face turned red, momentarily stunned. She quickly looked down at the book. "Maybe your father is the cause?" she said icily. "What hell did he give you after Jimmy left home?"

Sandra froze. That's why Jimmy was silent on their way to Haven. He wasn't disappointed, but guilty—the traitor. Tears sprang to Sandra's eyes again, and she sank in her seat, beset by defeat and a hundred forms of fear.

The next several days drifted like dream clouds, dispersed by fierce winds, and the night's air embraced Sandra's cries as her fingertips raked through her own hair for consolation. Pity was a friend. It was also an emotion that Haven deeply frowned upon—self-defeating for the alcoholic, which caused Sandra to mimic the days' activities with about as much conviction as would fill a thimble. In therapy she'd discovered that her tangled feelings were like tamped earth: pressed down to perfectly condensed space, too hard to shovel; thus she conveniently shifted the outer layer of dirt from one place to another, unburying nothing.

But to those around her, Sandra appeared to be making progress; her group applauded whenever she shared a diluted thought. But Sandra's dream-life wasn't diluted. In fact, it flourished at Haven, as she had a recurring dream from her early adult life: Amid thick mist, there stood a male figure. Sandra could never make out the man's features, and he said "come" in a reverberating voice. Sandra, as a child, stood before the man in a white taffeta dress, but she refused to come, crying for Jimmy. Jimmy was nowhere to be found. The man would move closer, and Sandra would run in opposite direction, only to find that the man was standing before her again. "Come. You've run a long race…race…race…"

Sandra shifted in bed, listening to Libby's laborious breathing, munching on a hangnail, no doubt. She turned to face Libby, who was sitting on the edge of a chair. Libby looked at Sandra, her eyes laced with much concern. "Ain't right to be in bed so early in the evenin'," she said, dropping her hands from her mouth to her lap, hunching her back.

"Why do you care?" Sandra said. She turned sideways on the bed and rested her head on her palm.

"Cause alcoholics must support one another, 'specially when we're down."

"You really buy into this Haven philosophy, don't you?"

"Sure do!" Libby sat upright. "Court says I can get my babies back if I get straight."

"Babies?" Sandra sat up, her back resting on the rattan headboard. "Libby, you have children?"

"Uh-huh." She looked at her ragged nails.

"How old?"

Libby looked at Sandra. "Both two years old. Twin boys." She smiled. "That's why I believe in Haven. I got two boys waitin' for me. Keeps me goin'." Libby then looked down at the tile floor, then back at Sandra with tears in her eyes.

Sandra's heart suddenly softened, looking at this ragtag, backwoods, child-like-woman dressed in a yellow t-shirt and denim shorts. "It'll be all right," she said softly.

Libby wiped the tears from her eyes. "Yeah. I know," she said bashfully. She sat upright again. "You got kids?"

Sandra paused, feeling the weight of the question. "No."

"Ever want some?"

Sandra turned her head, looking outside the opened window. She thought of Les. "In another lifetime," she said softly, in a far away voice.

"What's that 'pose ta mean?"

Sandra remained silent, looking at the sun descend in an orange sky. She turned toward Libby. "It means that I wanted kids a long time ago, but not anymore."

"Oh?"

Sandra stared into space. "Feels like I'm going to live the rest of my life alone."

"You ain't never gonna be alone," Libby said, in a child-like voice. "'Cause you got a guardian angel lookin' afta you!"

Sandra laughed aloud. "Guardian angel?"

"Sure do!"

Sandra looked from shoulder to shoulder, laughing. "Oh, yeah? What does he look like, Libby?"

Libby stood up and sat on the edge of Sandra's bed. Her eyes gleamed with the wonder of a child's. "You can't see 'im, silly!" Libby said. "He's spirit. You feel 'im!"

After two weeks of no alcohol and daily exercise, the fog in Sandra's mind had finally lifted. She was even looking forward to Family Day, which was every other Sunday. Jimmy said he would come alone, and that was fine with Sandra, since she was still too embarrassed to look Gee in the face. Sandra sat in a white plastic chair on the veranda, waiting for the only blood-relative she had in the state of California, and this fact caused her to quickly abandon her grudge. Jimmy was only trying to help—she could see that now.

Family members of Haven's residents came in droves on this sunny afternoon, with picnic baskets on the crook of their arms, slamming car doors behind them. Blankets were spread on the grass, oblong tables were crammed with foil pans filled with food, cherished children ran along the grounds, and parents kissed the cheeks of their sons or daughters while copious tears were shed.

In the distance, Sandra spotted Burly with his wife, she being the primary reason why Burly was hauled into Haven. Libby had said Burly was brought in with handcuffs, fighting mad, at the hands of his own brother-in-law, a policeman, and the first person that Burly's wife had called after Burly whopped her one—one time too many. His heavy drinking binges reminded him that he hated all women. They'd become his mother, who'd abandoned him when he was eight years old. "Jus' went to the Laundromat to wash her clothes, and ain't never come back," Libby told Sandra. But luckily, Burly made something of himself, in spite of being shifted to numerous foster homes, and at the age of thirty-five, he was a proprietor of a thriving construction business.

He seemed genuinely happy today, hugging his wife who was half his size, as they sat on a bench. But behind that cheeky smile, at least according to Libby, Burly was deathly afraid of being released from Haven—although he hated coming there in the first place—because the world and its fleshly demons would be waiting for him again. They would turn on him like switchblades. Burly had already relapsed two times, and with his imminent release, he'd be faced with the same dilemma.

As for Libby and Sandra, they spoke about everything, except for the root cause of their alcoholism. Their body language justified the belief that the topic was too painful to broach, so they learned to respect one another's privacy, and, in turn, learned to like one another. Libby was Sandra's guide to Haven, informing her of what was or what wasn't accepted, the people to stay away from, and, of course, any details about Lindsay, which were few. Anonymity was her strength, since no one knew of her weaknesses.

Sandra glanced at her watch. It was 2:00 PM. Jimmy said he would be here around 1:00. Had he changed his mind? She began to worry, looking around the grounds, and then she spotted him. The sun encircled the top of his auburn dreadlocks like a halo. A broad smile spread across Sandra's face. Jimmy held a bouquet of red roses in his hand. He caught sight of Sandra and opened his arms as he strolled along the grass, wearing denim overalls, sandals, and a Bob Marley t-shirt. Sandra placed her hands over her mouth, and her eyes grew misty. No longer able to contain her calm, she bolted from her seat, running toward Jimmy with lightening speed. The daily exercise was paying off! Her embrace nearly knocked him down. "So good to see your face," she said, on the brink of tears.

"Hey! It's all right. You okay?"

"I'm okay now!" Sandra said cheerfully. "I just thought that you weren't going to—"

"Come," Jimmy interrupted. "I'm always here for you. You should know that."

"Always?"

"Always!"

After they made their way to the verandah, Jimmy handed the flowers to Sandra and filled her in on the news at home. Home. The word resonated in Sandra's heart, and she closed her eyes. She, too, would have someone waiting for her when she left Haven. Lawrence was dying to see her, and reminded her how much she'd missed her little man, too. "He's really grown attached to you, Sandy. He really has," Jimmy said. He sat back in his chair, strumming an imaginary guitar, his head bobbing to an unheard tune.

"What's this?" Sandra said, smelling her flowers. "I haven't seen you do that in years!"

Jimmy laughed. "Yeah. I know." He stopped his performance and leaned forward in his chair, looking at Sandra. "You know, I was thinking about playing the guitar again. I mean, nothing professional or anything like that, but for enjoyment. Sometimes I get so bogged down with duty that I forget my passions, dreams, talents." He began playing his imaginary guitar again, singing, "Ole pirates, yes, they rob I …stole I from the merchant ships…"

"Ummm. Marley."

"Yeah." Jimmy folded his hands on his lap. "So, how's it going?"

"It's going, I guess. Been doing a lot of thinking, mainly about my life." Sandra placed the flowers on her lap and tucked her lips into her mouth, gazing at the children running along the campus grounds. She suddenly looked at Jimmy. "Remember when I was a kid, I had this ability to know things before they happened?"

Jimmy sat upright in his seat, "Yeah! And you were right on target, too! You knew Ginger was dead before anybody found her in the doghouse. And what about Mrs. Olsen—remember you said she was going to die in her sleep that night, and she did! I never understood how you did that, though." Jimmy frowned.

"Me neither. All I know is that I get a certain feeling in my stomach."

"You always had a sensitive one. Gut feelings, maybe. Intuition."

"Yeah…" Sandra paused. "I…I want to develop that, you know. Maybe it will keep me out of trouble…before it happens."

"You mean, trouble with alcohol?"

"Yeah," Sandra said, playing with the cellophane wrapping around the flowers.

Jimmy leaned forward and touched Sandra's face. "Develop your special gift if you want, but also let people know what's going on inside, Sandy. Let people know, so that they can help you. Don't keep it inside. After you leave Haven, you must go to your AA meetings faithfully—I mean, faithfully. Tap into that wonderful support group. You can't go it alone—not with alcohol. Trust me."

"But suppose I won't be able to make—"

Jimmy placed a finger over Sandra's lips. "You will make it. Just remember that there will be people to help you, and you'll do fine. I know. Just look at me."

Sandra smiled.

Jimmy sat back in his seat. "Anyway, Lindsay said you're doing okay. First week was a little rough. But now, you're okay, right?"

Sandra shrugged. "I'm not sure. The only real progress I've made, at least as far as I'm concerned, is when I completed my grudge list. I put the same name near every one of my resentments. That was a revelation to me."

"Who?"

Silence.

"Sandra, who? Me?"

"No, silly!"

"Who, Mama?"

Sandra shook her head sideways.

"Daddy?"

"No, but I could have!" Sandra hissed.

"Who, then, Les?"

"No…God."

Always after dinner, before sunset, Sandra and Libby would take a walk through the incredible maze of Haven's botanical gardens, pointing to a flower, tree, or shrub they could identify. It was a game to them, and Sandra—who was a kid around Libby—had come up with the idea of keeping score.

"And what will the winner get?" Libby had asked one evening, slipping her arm around Sandra's bent elbow.

Sandra thought long and hard. "Let me see."

Libby stared at Sandra with a grin on her face. "Well?"

"I'm thinking." Sandra stared at the fading sun, then stopped suddenly. "I got it! The loser will wash the winner's feet!"

Libby had laughed. "Good! 'Cause I like my feet scrubbed with loofah!"

But this particular evening, Libby was unusually quiet, not taking any pleasure in their ritual. Sandra almost wore herself out trying to get Libby to talk. After a few attempts at initiating the game, Sandra suggested that they sit down on a stone bench. Neither one spoke for a while. Then out of the blue, Libby said, "It's Burly."

"What?" Sandra frowned.

"It's Burly." Libby looked at Sandra with tears in her eyes. "Ain't been out of Haven for a good week, and I hear he was arrested."

"Arrested? For what?"

"Killin' a man while drivin' drunk."

Libby's words struck Sandra dumb. That night, she couldn't sleep, tossing and turning, certain Libby was afflicted with the same. Because deep inside, they both had been rooting for Burly, not brouhaha, but in a tiny steady voice. In a sense, Burly was them, his success their success, his failure their failure. The nights that followed were a re-enactment of the same: tossing and turning like a dance with fear. Days were encased in silence.

One morning, after fitful sleep the night before, Sandra lay on her back, forearm pressed against her forehead, seriously thinking as to whether she'd stay at Haven following the primary phase. Of course, she didn't give a hoot about the program! No, Haven was a haven from the outside world, and herself. It was easy being a recovering alcoholic without a bottle staring back at you; but when encountered, Sandra had imagined it would whisper, "Pssst. Just a little nip. A little nip ain't never hurt nobody." She thought of Burly. He couldn't handle that whispering bottle. Sandra shook her head. Killing a man while DWI. How many years would Burly get for that? she wondered. She bolted upright in bed and positioned her back against the headboard. She quickly reached for the telephone, rapidly jabbing the touch-tone buttons with her index finger. Jimmy was ecstatic—Sandra was taking responsibility for her actions, even to the point that she wanted to extend her stay at Haven.

"That's great!" Then he paused.

"What?"

"Well…"

"Well, what, Jimmy?"

"You have to tell Mama."

"Tell Mama? Are you crazy?"

"I can't keep making up excuses. How many times can a person be out shopping, in the shower, working? I can't keep this up another month."

"But—"

"Part of recovery is to let people know the truth, anyway."

"But I—"

"She's even talking about coming to California, Sandra. She knows something's up. She's not stupid!"

Silence.

"Sandra?"

"I can't tell Mama!"

"Why not, Sandra?"

"I can't!"

"Well, if you don't, I will!"

"I thought you said you would always be there for me. Please. Jimmy, I'm begging you."

He breathed heavily into the phone. "I am…but not this…I…I just can't…"

"Forget it, then!"

She tossed and turned the rest of the morning, feigned sick. It was impossible to get out of bed. Tell Mama? She couldn't. She covered her eyes with her hands, swept by fatigue.

Pride outweighed fear. Weeks later, Sandra prepared to leave Haven, and like Burly, her protection would be gone, and she'd be faced with her own special demon. Sandra packed her suitcase, then hugged Libby and vowed that she'd keep in touch. Libby escorted Sandra to Lindsay's office. "Bye. Don't forget me. Ain't never had a gal friend to talk to."

Lindsay faced the window when Sandra entered her office. "Sit down," she said, without turning toward Sandra. She spoke slowly. "Sandra, the primary phase is just a stepping stone. As follow-up, Haven periodically makes contact—either by phone or letter—to all its former residents. Just to make sure that they have joined a local AA group, which is vital." She turned around and sat behind her desk.

Sandra sat quietly in her seat, her suitcase next to her foot.

Lindsay sat back in her chair. "Do you have any questions?"

Sandra looked toward the ceiling, "No, no."

Lindsay stood up, so did Sandra. They shook hands. Lindsay handed Sandra her card. "Call me any time you like."

Sandra stared at the card for a while, a little surprised. She then looked at Lindsay. "Thank you." She picked up her suitcase and headed for the door.

"Just one more thing," Lindsay said.

Sandra turned around.

"My father never loved me. He always wanted a son, you see. I'm an only child, but little did he know he had a son all along—just in a girl's body." Lindsay sighed and looked out the window again. "Just wanted you to know what was the root cause of my alcoholism. Fifteen years ago, I'd decided to no longer deny my sexual orientation." She looked at Sandra again. "Just wanted you to know that."

Sandra stepped outside the office and closed the door. She walked down the clinically clean corridor, past the admissions office, with her head hung low. She was happy to see Jimmy's family standing in front of Haven. They hugged and kissed her, and Sandra cried. It felt good to see their smiling faces again, even Rita cracked a smile. But Sandra noticed that Jimmy was a little distant, standing off to the side.

CHAPTER 9
REALITY

It had been two months since Sandra left Haven; it seemed like yesterday. Her life hadn't changed much. She was back to managing one of Jimmy's health food stores: alfalfa, cat's claw, milk thistle, yucca—senseless names that once again became part of her vocabulary. She called Libby a few times to offset the boredom, but their conversation was punctuated more with silence than with words, too loud to go unnoticed. Their common denominator—Haven—was no longer the focal point, and Sandra often wondered how they ever got along. They were two different people. Even gossip about Lindsay had lost its luster, for Lindsay was no longer a mystery to Sandra. As for Burly, well, Libby hadn't heard anything else. Their conversations dwindled to a drip, then not even a drop. And Libby's face began to fade in Sandra's memory, but not her drawl.

The first week Sandra was home, Mama called daily, sounding relieved when she heard Sandra's voice. But why hadn't you called? Just busy, Mama. Busy doing what that you hadn't called your mother in a month? Sandra had thought quickly, without thinking, now knowing how Jimmy must've felt—trapped. I met someone. You met someone? What's his name? Gary. His name is Gary?

"Gary?" Sandra heard Jimmy say while talking to Mama a week later. Sandra stopped dead in her tracks, like a dog does when it suddenly hears the jingling of the keys at the front door. She squeezed her eyes shut. "Ssshhhoot!" Sandra was in the back of the store, looking for a carton containing bottles of B-12. She set the box on the floor, plopped her back against the wall, and crossed her arms against her chest, listening.

"Well, I don't know about that," Jimmy said tersely, then mumbled a few words.

Sandra strained to hear, but couldn't. Later that day, Jimmy's eyes followed her around the store. He said nothing, and Sandra felt foolish. She could not think of one thing to redeem herself. So, she placed bottles of B-12 on the shelves, then bottles of echinacea...goldenseal...valerian root. Senseless, she thought, senseless. Mama never mentioned the name Gary after that day, and Sandra was certain Jimmy had told Mama the truth.

Lawrence helped Sandra stock shelves from time to time. He was still her darling, and without his presence, Sandra's days would have been twice as long. She could tell by Lawrence's eyes that he had questions about Haven, but had good sense not to ask. Instead, he filled Sandra's ears with all the activities he had done while she was away: "You should have seen me on the court, Sandra...fast." The gleam in Lawrence's eyes made Sandra smile. He was so young, so many possibilities. Sometimes that gleam would extinguish, just moments after it had been there. Lawrence would look to the floor, then look at Sandra again and say, "Are you okay? I mean, really okay?" There was too much concern in this young boy's eyes.

"Course I'm okay!" Sandra would say cheerfully, only half-believing her words. She'd flash a convincing smile. Then to cut the heaviness of the conversation, she'd quickly say, "Let me see those muscles!" Lawrence would smile, push up his short-sleeved shirt, then flex proudly, waiting for Sandra's cue. "Huh, you must have a lot of chicks after you."

He'd shrug, just as he was supposed to, and say, "I got a few babes," which set them both to laughter.

Rita was so sweet, it was frightening, at Sandra's beck and call. Once she'd said to Sandra, slowly and out loud, as if Sandra were deaf or mentally incapacitated, "Do you want me to polish your toenails?" This amused Sandra, but amusement quickly gave way to irritation, because it had sunk in that someone must have told Rita that alcoholism was a disease. To Rita, Sandra was sick, now convalescing, needing to be cared for. The irritation turned into raw anger when Sandra also realized that her name had been the subject of family discussion. Had Rita known her precious father was—and still is—an alcoholic, a drug addict to boot? Or had he kept his past vice private, only airing out Sandra's? In the next room, Sandra had heard Jimmy practicing his guitar, singing a Bob Marley tune, "...not all that glitter is gold, half the story has never been told..." And Sandra thought, how true, how true.

Other events led to building a case in Sandra's mind that Jimmy had turned against her. She'd adopted an attitude, especially after Jimmy had announced he was hiring extra help: "What—you don't think I can handle it?"

Jimmy held up his hands. "Whoa! I didn't say that," and backed off. He didn't defend his decision, an obvious admission of his guilt.

Then came that particular incident in the store when a bottle of wine had miraculously appeared in the storage room, stashed behind a box containing bottles of garlic capsules, which were flying off the shelves. And someone knew—had to be Jimmy—that before long Sandra would venture to the box. It was red wine. French. Her weakness. She expected the wine bottle to at once commence its whispering, but it hadn't. She lifted the bottle that was wedged between the box and the wall, slightly bouncing it in her hand as if weighing it, weighing her decision to drink. Then, in her mind's eye, the wine bottle began to flap its lips. They were sensual, full, glossy. "Pssst. Just a little nip. A little nip ain't never hurt nobody." Sandra quickly put the wine bottle back in its place and stood up, briskly wiping her hand on the side of her jeans as if she'd just touched something dirty. She grabbed a few bottles of garlic capsules and headed out the door, back to the counter to reposition control.

But when the afternoon crowd had thinned, Sandra found herself back in the storage room, resting on her haunches, face-to-face with the murmuring bottle. The bottle's label said that the wine was 100% aged in oak. She loved that "oaky" flavor. Good with game, beef, any kind of cheese, the bottle's label continued. Sandra swallowed the saliva collecting at the back of her throat, licked her lips. She bit into one of her knuckles, tapping it against her bottom teeth. She thought of her job at the store, the jumbled names of herbs she recited each working day—enough to drive anyone to drink. She needed this wine to take the edge off the boredom. The sight of the bottle had stirred excitement in Sandra's chest that she hadn't felt in months. Her heart started to pump faster, stronger, with purpose. Sandra sat on the floor cross-legged and lifted the bottle again. If only she had a corkscrew. She thought of her future again, bleak as it was, no direction, nothing to look forward to. Perhaps she could improvise something that would pry the cork from the bottle's neck. Her head suddenly darted toward the four corners of the room. Nothing. Sandra stood up, bottle in hand, her mind so absorbed with her thoughts that she hadn't heard the jingling of the bell above the glass door. It was Jimmy and Lawrence.

"Sandra, you left the store unattend—" Jimmy stood still, eyeing the bottle, with Lawrence standing behind him. Lawrence stuck his head out from Jimmy's side, peering at the bottle, too.

Sandra turned toward Jimmy, looking at him hard, making sure that her surprise did not register upon her face. What was he doing here? He's not supposed to be here today.

She thought quickly on her feet. "Is this some kind of test!" She held up the bottle.

"What?"

"Oh yeah, right. Now you gonna act like you don't know. I'm stupid. Okay!" Sandra swiveled her body away from Jimmy and smashed the bottle against the wall for effect, putting her whole body into it as if she were pitching a baseball.

Lawrence's eyes widened, covering his mouth with his hand.

"Acting all righteous and mighty, like you never had a drinking problem." Sandra turned toward Jimmy again.

He was speechless.

"Even got the nerve to tell Mama about me!"

Jimmy remained calm. "I don't know what you're talking about."

Sandra laughed dramatically. "Yeah, okay."

"I don't."

Sandra folded her arms against her chest and paced the floor. The winey smell played with her head. She stopped in front of Jimmy and pointed her index finger at him. "Did you tell Mama that Gary doesn't exist?"

Jimmy stepped back. "So that's what this is all about?"

"Just answer me!"

He didn't.

"I heard you talking to Mama, and ever since then she hadn't asked me about Gary. I know you told her!"

The winey smell was strong.

Jimmy shook his head and proceeded to walk out the door. Lawrence moved out his way, then tagged behind him.

Sandra pursued Jimmy. "Tell me!"

Jimmy turned around, stopping Sandra in her tracks. "Tell you what!" he said through clenched teeth.

Lawrence squeezed Jimmy's arm, feeling that something bad was going to jump off. "Let's go, Dad."

Jimmy brushed Lawrence's hand away and looked at him. "Go where? This is my store." He turned to Sandra, his eyes cold and piercing. "Mama asked me about Gary. I had no idea who she was talking about. She was surprised and suspicious that I hadn't heard of him. Then it hit me. So I lied and told her that you two broke up, and that's why I vaguely remembered him. And maybe that's why she'd never asked you again—to save you embarrassment!"

Sandra's face softened. "What?"

Jimmy brushed by her and stood behind the counter, hurt by the accusation. He removed imaginary dust from the register. "That's what you really think of me?" he said softly. "Then you accuse me of stashing a wine bottle in the store as a test?" Tears sprang to his eyes. "Oh, Sandra."

She felt small, watching a tear slowly trickle down Jimmy's face.

They stared at each other in silence.

"I put it there," Lawrence said meekly.

They both blinked and looked at Lawrence, forgetting that he was standing there.

"What?" Jimmy asked. "Why?"

Lawrence looked to the floor, looking as if he were about to cry. "I...I just wanted to make sure Sandra was really okay. I'm sorry."

It had occurred to Sandra—right there and then—what she'd put Lawrence through, the whole family through. She felt terrible, and decided she would join a local AA group. Sandra walked toward Lawrence and hugged him. "Don't be sorry...don't be."

Months later, Jimmy stood in the middle of the glossy, wide-plank pine floors of the dining room, wearing khaki shorts, socks, and construction boots. All summer long, he'd been working on the extension to the deck, so the California sun had baked his milky-white skin into the color of Ritz crackers, painting his auburn dreadlocks with blonde streaks. Now early fall, he was completing the finishing touches. Jimmy's back was facing a bay window overlooking the weeping willow tree in the front yard. The sun behind his back shadowed his face. Still, Gee saw the intensity in his eyes.

"What's that?" asked Gee. She and Sandra just walked in from the patio, sporting colorful swimsuits, sarong skirts, and flip-flops. The stem of Sandra's sunglasses dangled from her lips. Jimmy's eyes remained fixed to the piece of paper. Gee glanced at Sandra, raising her eyebrows. Sandra frowned and removed the stem of her sunglasses from her mouth, sticking it between her cleavage. Both were staring at Jimmy.

Laurence suddenly blasted into the room, bouncing an imaginary basketball, performing some serious moves on the court. He dodged here, dodged there, crouching low in a fancy dribble. He scored a jump shot, and the high pitched sound of his sneakers on the wooden floor forced Jimmy to look up.

"Boy! What did I tell you?"

Laurence immediately froze under his father's hard gaze, his arm standing straight in the air. Slowly, he moved his raised hand forward. "Swishhhh!" he murmured.

"This is fantastic!" Jimmy said, hitting the edge of the paper. "Fannntastic!"

"Mind filling us in, sweetheart?"

"Really," said Sandra, placing her hands on her hips.

"I'm sorry! I got so caught up in Dad's letter." He then jumped high in the air. "Dad's cancer is in remission!" He shot his fist toward the ceiling. "Yesss!"

"What?" Gee and Laurence bolted toward Jimmy, hovering around him.

"Here it is," Jimmy said, reading from his father's letter. "'After one year and eight months, the doctors have told me my cancer is in remission. Hallelujah! Your papa is cancer-free!'"

Gee wrapped her arms around Jimmy's waist, jumping up and down, pressing a cheek against his back. "This is great news!"

Sandra sat down at the round pine table, staring at the crystal vase containing Birds of Paradise. She felt a breeze coming from the ceiling fan overhead.

"This calls for celebration!" said Jimmy, plopping onto the seat of the window's alcove. "I wonder how soon I can catch a flight to Boston?"

"I don't know," said Gee. "The weather is pretty bad in Boston right now." She sat next to Jimmy, resting her elbow on his shoulder, looking at him. The sun illuminated one side of her face.

"Can I go, Dad?"

"No! You're not missing school."

"Ah, man!" Laurence dropped his arms to his sides, dragging himself out the room with droopy shoulders.

"How bad can the weather be, Gee? It's not dead winter yet. It's October. What do you think, Sandy? Want to go?"

"I'll pass." Sandra sat back in her chair, crossing her arms against her chest.

"To everyone's surprise, Jimmy, there was snow last week," said Gee. "The roads are still icy! That's what Mama told me."

"Listen! I have a few things to straighten out at the health food stores anyway, so it'll probably be a few weeks before I'm able to get to Boston. Maybe the weather will be better by then. And I'll make sure I get a good rental car when I drive to Cambridge, just in case. 'Kay?"

"Jimmy!"

"Gee!"

"You lovebirds just kill me," said Sandra, shaking her head.

Gee sat on Jimmy's lap. "So I guess that the extension to my deck won't be completed until you get back, huh?"

"You wouldn't mind, would you, baby? I don't want you to be angry with me;

couldn't bear that." He made gurgling sounds as he snuggled his face in the crook of Gee's neck.

Gee laughed, throwing her head back. "I could never be angry with you. Never."

Sandra stared at them for a while. Gee nestled her head on Jimmy's shoulder as he gently swayed side to side, as if he were listening to the rhythm of a sweet lullaby. Sandra's eyes then drifted past them, looking at the weeping willow tree.

Two weeks later, Sandra watched the interaction with Jimmy and his family, camera in hand. They were playing Monopoly on the patio. It was a lazy Sunday afternoon, and after church, the family relaxed and played games: backgammon, chess, checkers, Clue, Charades, today Monopoly. They attended a nondenominational church. "For the kid's sake," Gee had whispered to Sandra one day. "When they're older, then they'll decide."

"Go to jail!" Rita squealed.

"Ah, man!"

"Say cheese!" said Sandra.

Everyone looked up from the Monopoly board, startled. "Cheeese!"

"Perfect! Let me get another one."

Laurence stood up, "Just in case you haven't noticed, we're trying to play a game here!"

Rita pulled the edge of his t-shirt, "Boy! Sit down!"

"Just one more," Sandra begged. "Everyone huddle closer together." She placed the camera to her face, then quickly moved it to her chest. "Laurence!"

"What?"

"You know what!" Sandra glared at him.

His two fingers were extended above Rita's head like rabbit's ears.

"Okay," he said, grudgingly.

Sandra snapped the picture just before Laurence crossed his eyes. "Hope they stay that way, brat!"

He stuck out his tongue.

They continued with the game when Laurence suddenly declared that he no longer wanted to play.

"Why?" Rita asked, "Because you're a sore loser?"

Laurence clamped his hand on Rita's forehead. "No! I just don't want you to cry too much when I whup your…"

"What?" Jimmy interrupted.

Rita fought to remove Laurence's hand from her face. "Get off me!"

"Stop it!" Gee and Jimmy said.

Laurence sat down, sulking.

"Now why don't you want to play?" asked Gee.

"Just don't."

Jimmy folded the board. "I'm tired anyway."

"Dad!" Rita exclaimed. "Just because he doesn't want to play shouldn't mean we should stop!"

"Too late!" Laurence said, gloating.

Rita stood up. "Pig!" She popped Laurence on the head, then dashed into the house.

Laurence ran after her.

Gee jumped up, running after them. "I need to prevent what's going to happen when Laurence catches up with her."

Sandra sat down and placed the silver camera on the table. It sparkled in the sun. "Were we like that when we were younger?"

"Probably." Jimmy grinned. "But beneath that boiling sibling hatred, there's love!"

They laughed heartily.

Sandra suddenly winced, doubling over.

"Is your stomach bothering you again?"

She nodded swiftly. "It'll pass."

"You should go see a doctor. How long has it been now?"

Sandra kept her eyes closed, trying to tolerate the pain. "Not long."

"Well, what does that mean, not long?"

"I don't know, Jimmy!" She sounded irritated, resting her head on her forearm. "Probably around the time you said that you were going to Boston."

Jimmy looked to the sky. "That's only two weeks ago." He frowned. "And the pain is that severe?"

There was silence.

"Sandy…you…why don't you go see a doctor?"

Sandra raised her head. "It will pass." She rested her head on her forearm again.

Jimmy placed his hand on the back of Sandra's head, rubbing her hair. "I think you should see a doctor."

After a while Sandra sat up. "It's passing. Feels like labor pains." She wiped the sweat from her forehead with the back of her hand.

"So when did you give birth? I missed that one!" Jimmy jibed.

"Funny," Sandra said, feeling her strength come back.

Jimmy grinned.

Laurence returned, plopping in a chair.

Sandra and Jimmy looked at him.

"What?"

"So what happened?" Sandra asked.

"I buried Rita under the weeping willow tree. That's why it's weeping!"

"That's not a nice thing to say, my man."

"Sorry, Dad."

"All right." Jimmy gently shook Laurence by the shoulder.

Sandra looked at Jimmy. "Packed for your trip tomorrow?"

"Yep! Ready to go. Dad is ecstatic!"

Laurence looked at Sandra, sad that he would not be going with his father, although Sandra tried to persuade Jimmy.

Sandra mouthed the words, I'm sorry.

Laurence mouthed back, Don't mention it. Then he rolled his eyes.

They laughed.

What's so funny?" asked Jimmy.

They laughed harder.

"Private joke, huh? Private joke. I have one thing to say about private jokes." Jimmy stood up slowly and walked behind Laurence.

Laurence looked up, staring at his father's upside down face. "What's up, Dad?"

"I'll tell you what's up!" He swiftly crouched down to tickle Laurence.

"No, Dad!" Laurence tried to peel his father's fingers from his belly. "Oh, no, Dad. Please!" he said between giggles. "You're going to make me pee in my pants!" He laughed and cried at the same time, toppling his chair. "Dad, no! Sandra, help! Help me please! Somebody help me!"

Jimmy and Laurence rolled on the ground, as if they were wrestling.

"Sandra, help! Help meee!"

Sandra stood over them, laughing. "Laurence, I didn't know that your face could turn so red. Wow!"

"Help me, Sandra! Please! Oh my God! Dad, I going to pee in my pants! I swear! Come on now!"

"Okay," Jimmy said, jumping up, dusting off his hands. "We don't want any accidents."

Laurence lay on the ground, panting, holding his stomach.

Jimmy walked over to Sandra. "And as for you…"

Sandra slowly backed away. "Get away from me, Jimmy. Get away!"

Jimmy swooped down toward Sandra's thighs, lifting her over his shoulders. "Put me down, Jimmy! I'm not playing with you! Put me down!" She pounded his back. Jimmy laughed and stood above the pool, dumping Sandra in the water, shielding himself from the splash.

Laurence, who recovered from his attack, stood next to his father, pointing a finger at Sandra. "Oh, snap! Oh, snap!" He slapped his father five.

Sandra was bobbing in the water. "Jimmy! Jimmy! I'm going to get you!" She sprouted water from her mouth, shaking her hair like a wet dog. "And what are you laughing at, Laurence?"

Laurence stood by the edge of the pool, bending over. "Sandra, I didn't know your face could get so wet. Wow!"

The following night after the family had driven Jimmy to the airport, Sandra became ill. The pain had awakened her from sleep. She walked into the dark kitchen and opened the refrigerator, pouring a glass of milk to sooth the lining of her stomach. She'd vomited twice, but wine was not the culprit; fear was. A fear she couldn't name.

She sat in the alcove of the bay window. The full moon cast its silvery light into the kitchen and onto the leaves of the weeping willow tree. The tree hung exceptionally heavy tonight, as if it were truly weeping. She sipped her milk. The tree swayed in the night's breeze. It had to be at least one hundred years old, she thought, imagining all that the tree had seen. A sharp pain suddenly stabbed her chest, and the glass of milk fell from her hand, shattering on the hard wood floor. Sandra couldn't breathe. She clutched her throat, thinking that she was going to die, falling to the floor on her hands and knees. A jagged piece of glass cut her hand. Sandra's face twisted, eyes bulged, gasping for breath. The pain stopped, just like that, and calmness overwhelmed her, a feeling of supreme peace. Sandra hadn't felt anything like it, well beyond the scope of her understanding. She sat on the floor, dazed, grabbing tufts of her hair, trying to figure out what had happened. Her hand began to throb, drawing her attention to the gash. Sandra stood up, holding her leaking hand, and rushed toward the kitchen sink. She ran cold water on it for a few minutes, then wrapped it with a clean towel.

Two hours later, the phone rang, startling Sandra. She glanced at the kitchen clock: one-thirty AM. Who would be calling at this time of the morning? "Hello? Hello? Hello? Daddy, is that you? Slow down. What? What? What? Wha—" Sandra slid to the floor. "No…No…Oh, no…No! Not my brother!"

She dropped the phone and managed to crawl upstairs. Gee's eyes were heavy with sleep when Sandra held her by the arms, "Daddy just called! Jimmy's dead!"

For a while, Gee sat still in the moonlight, sheer white curtains blowing in the breeze. The news hadn't registered. Sandra shook Gee's shoulders. "Gee," she said between sobs. "Wake up! Daddy just called! He said Jimmy died in a car accident. His car slid off the road and slammed into a tree. He died on impact. Gee?"

Gee stared at Sandra blankly, then her delicate nostrils began to flare, eyes widening. Bam—she punched Sandra in the face! A flurry of fists hit Sandra's head, neck, shoulders, chest. Sandra fell to the floor, balling herself into a tight knot.

"Gee!"

"Nooo! I don't believe you!"

"Jimmy's dead! He's dead, Gee."

Gee froze, fists still raised in the air. There was silence, like the fluid silence just before a tidal wave. Sandra peeked through her cupped hands, heart racing, not knowing what was going to happen next. Gee snapped back her head, thick veins straining against her throat, and the utterance that forced its way past Gee's lips was more animal than human. Sandra was petrified.

Gee collapsed to the floor, crying out, "No! No! No! Jimmy! Jimmy! Oh God! Jimmy! Why, why, why?" Then she stopped, springing up in the middle of the carpet, looking as if she had just remembered something. She looked to the left, right. "Oh my God! Oh my God! Where are my babies? My babies!" Gee tore at her hair, scratching her face. "My God! Where are my babies? Sandra, what happened to my babies?" Sandra grabbed Gee by the shoulders, kneeling beside her.

"They're okay, Gee. They're okay."

They heard footsteps. "Mom? Mom?" It was Rita, peeking inside the room. She raced toward her mother, dropping to her knees. "What is it, Mom?" Panic grew in her voice. She cupped her mother's face. "Mom, Mom, what's wrong? Please! Mom?" She was on the verge of tears.

Gee leaned against Sandra's bosom, touching Rita's face. "Something happened to Daddy, sweetheart. He's dead, baby." Gee burst into tears as dreadful reality rolled off her tongue.

Rita clamped her ears with her hands. "No! I don't believe you, Mom. Mom? Mom?" She began to cry.

"It's true, baby. It's true," Gee said, pressing Rita to her chest.

Rita moved her head to her mother's lap, wailing, "Mom, what's going to happen to us? Mom? Mom?"

"I don't know, baby. I don't—Oh, God!"

Laurence walked into the room, rubbing his eyes. He focused on the scene. "What's wrong?" His body stiffened, looking directly at Sandra.

She walked toward him, crying.

"What's wrong?"

Sandra tried to hug him, but he pushed her away.

"Tell me!"

"Laurence, come—"

"Tell me, Sandra!"

"Your father is dead."

Laurence swung at her. "Stop joking with me!" He ran toward his mother, squatting on his haunches. He shook her legs. "Mom, tell Sandra to stop playing around. Mom, tell Sandra to stop playing around!" He shook her legs again. "Tell her!" His chest heaved. Spurts of air shot through his open mouth. "Mom? Tell her!" Tears streamed down his cheeks.

Gee touched his face.

"No, no, no, no, no, no!" He jumped up, running out the room.

Sandra followed him downstairs. "Laurence, wait! Laurence!"

He unlocked the front door and ran down the street, barefoot, clad only in pajama bottoms.

Sandra tried to catch him, but Laurence was too fast, running at high speed. Sandra stopped and bent forward in the middle of the sidewalk, hands pressed to her knees, gulping air. She looked up, watching a lone silhouette running in the moonlight. She pressed her fingers to her lips, "Oh my God! Laurence."

Hours later, two policemen brought Laurence home. His face looked old, streaked with dry tears. He walked stiffly into the living room, a blanket thrown over his shoulders, his raw feet bleeding. He spotted Sandra on the couch, placed his head on her lap, and wept bitterly.

The pain was unbearable. Gee had lost a husband. Sandra had lost a brother. The kids had lost a father. Whose burden was the heaviest? Sandra didn't know. Later, Mama provided the answer to the question: "There's nothing worse than the death of a child…nothing worse…"

When Sandra, Gee, and the kids arrived in Cambridge two days later, they all were afraid for Mama. The dark circles under Mama's eyes looked like purplish bruises, and loose skin hung from her throat and collarbone like soggy clothing on a wire hanger. Mama looked as if she'd lost twenty pounds in just a few days, as she sat in a chair, unmoving, staring into space. So Sandra didn't have much time to mourn for Jimmy, too worried about Mama, the living. And she'd pushed her father away anytime he'd try to get close to Mama. "Get away! This is all your fault! Jimmy would be alive today if it weren't for your stupid letter! I hate you!" Then Sandra would surround Mama like a beggar hoarding food. Reverend Hamilton had no choice but to walk out the room, head hung low, terribly grieved. "Mama, Mama," she'd whispered into her mother's ear, "I know you loved Jimmy since the day he was born. But I'm here, Mama. I'm still here…"

The day before Jimmy's funeral, Lilly stood before the kitchen sink, washing dishes. Her voice was lifted high in song, "Amazing Grace, how sweet the sound, that saved a wretch like me. I once was lost, but now am found. Was blind, but now I see…" Lilly's voice slipped beneath Sandra's bedroom door, lifting her head from a pillow saturated with tears. The sweetness of her voice was a stranger to Sandra, like an intruder, and any intruder who trespasses another's territory conjures up fear and alarm. This intruder was a false sense of happiness, that everything was going to be all right. But things were never going to be all right again! Sandra wanted to go downstairs and tell Lilly to stop. Stop giving people false hope. Grace? What grace is there when your family has been rattled by death? Jimmy was never sick a day in his life! There wasn't any warning, no cushion to offset the blow. Grace? "Grace my black butt!" she spat.

Sandra reached over to stroke Laurence's hair. He was asleep, but sleep was not peaceful. He thrashed about periodically, moaning, scratching himself until he drew blood. Sandra would wake him, and his aged face would cry out, "Dad." Sandra turned toward Gee's soft snore. Sleep finally embraced her after several days of wakefulness. Gee's face was surrounded by a tangle of blonde hair as she lay in fetal position. Rita was next to her mother, sucking her thumb, a new activity since her father's death. They were all huddled together on Sandra's queen-sized bed, afraid of being alone, afraid of death. Who would it snatch next? Sandra hoped her father would be the one, but still he strode around like a bull. Her mind then rested on Mama, and she cringed at the thought. She would die if Mama were next, would wrestle death to snatch Mama's life from its black talons, offering her own life as sacrifice instead. She wouldn't survive Mama's death, just wouldn't!

Yet death gripped Sandra anyway, shook her out of sleep sometimes. The feeling in her stomach and chest frightened her. She remembered that night when Jimmy died, the stab in her chest, then indescribable peace. She was now convinced that she'd felt what Jimmy had felt. He hadn't suffered much, and now he was at peace—her body had confirmed it on the floor.

As long as I don't vomit, she kept saying to herself, Mama would be okay. She'd stay alive. I just know it. What Sandra knew, she couldn't find a reason for her knowing, like trying to reason why clouds were white instead of blue.

The other night really scared her, though. Her eyes were playing tricks on her again. This time, people did not appear far away—people disappeared. She was looking through a photo album, at old pictures of the family. She viewed one picture closely. Jimmy was sitting on Daddy's lap. She was sitting on Mama's. Then gradually, the picture began to fade right before her eyes. Mama, Jimmy, and Daddy disappeared, leaving her alone on the couch. Sandra dropped the picture immediately, rubbing her eyes. When she looked at the picture again, there were four smiling faces. Sandra ran into Mama's room after that, checking for her limbs, putting her hand close to Mama's nose to feel her breath. Only then had Sandra's heart stopped racing. Mama was still here.

"He always wanted to be cremated," Gee murmured, sitting in the front pew of Mount Baptist Church. "He couldn't stand the thought of being trapped in the ground." Following the small funeral service for the family, Jimmy's body would be cremated as he wished. Laurence sat between his mother and sister, his arms tightly around their shoulders. He looked old in his black suit, the man of the house now, carefree days long gone. Rita was in another world, her head resting on Laurence's shoulder, sucking her thumb. Behind them sat Gee's parents, a stately older couple, tanned and silver-gray. Lilly sat next to them. Aunt Enid sat alone, stone-faced. Her presence was an obligation to Reverend Hamilton only. Certainly she was not there out of love for Jimmy; she hated Jimmy just as much as he hated her.

Uncle Rufus was a slovenly mess. A wine bottle had fallen out of his back pocket, shattering green glass on the tile floor of the church vestibule. Sandra inhaled and closed her eyes, its smell clinging to her nostrils like an old friend. Mama was shrouded in a black veil, everything black, except for the white handkerchief pressed to her face, sitting in her wheelchair, acknowledging no one. Sandra, teary-eyed, also sat in the front pew, reaching out to Mama, patting her back. Reverend Hamilton sat quietly next to Sandra, her accusation of taking Jimmy's blood still on his hands.

The gray casket was closed, for Jimmy's lacerations were too deep for cosmetics, too deep for family viewing. Reverend Hamilton tried to say a few words, but collapsed, having to be carried out. Reverend Thornhill, an old friend of the family, took over, remembering Jimmy as a young man growing up in Cambridge.

The service was over soon after it began. Everyone was relieved, it seemed, not wanting reality to linger too long, not wanting it to get too comfortable in the pews. As they walked out of church, Gee said, "I'm angry with Jimmy, Sandra. The first time I've ever been angry with him, angry with him for leaving us."

The following month, everyone tried to get back into the rhythm of life, except Mama. "There is nothing worse than a death of a child…nothing worse," she had murmured to Lilly one day. Lilly remained silent as she tucked crisp sheets between the box spring and mattress of Hyacinth's bed. Hyacinth sat on the edge of a chair—still dressed in a nightgown, although mid-day—viewing pictures of her son, her only activity. After Lilly had smoothed the undulating wrinkles of the top sheet, she helped a weakened and frail Hyacinth to bed, plumping pillows to the contour of her concave back.

"There," Lilly said, handing Hyacinth her photo album.

Hyacinth grabbed Lilly's wrist instead. The photo album fell to the bed. "Lilly, promise me you'll look after Sandra when I'm gone."

Lilly removed her wrist from Hyacinth's barely perceptible grip. "Now where you going?" Lilly said, placing her hands on her hips. "Talking 'bout when you gone." But she knew what Hyacinth meant. The life in Hyacinth's eyes had been chipped away like wood, bit by bit, leaving only a splinter.

"I'm not even going to make it to see this Christmas. Promise me, Lilly."

"Now why you talking that way? The doctors say you going to be just fine.

Your heart is a little weak right now. That's all."

"My heart is broken. Promise me, Lilly." Tears streamed down Hyacinth's face.

"Now don't upset yourself." Lilly sat on the edge of the bed.

"Promise me."

"I promise." She smoothed back Hyacinth's hair. "Lord knows you have my word. I've always been a woman of my word."

Sandra, who was standing outside the doorway listening, pressed her forehead to a wall, full of anguish, struggling with maddening thoughts of alcohol. Hyacinth reached for the photo album. "There is nothing worse than a death of a child…nothing worse…"

These words entered Sandra's dreams every night, waking her up in a cold sweat. Then she'd quickly place her feet into her slippers, and knock on Lilly's bedroom door. Lilly had rose as a pillar of strength after Jimmy's death, holding the family together with her unquenchable faith, faith that everyone else lacked. Even Gee was attracted to her light, resting herself at Lilly's feet, her head on Lilly's lap. And in the darkness, Lilly's hand would find its way to Gee's hair, stroking it ever so gently. Lilly never turned Sandra away during those late hours of the night, always receiving Sandra with open arms, pressing Sandra against her ample bosom.

"You got to be strong in the Lord, Sandy. 'Cause He never gives anyone more than they can bear." Although Lilly's words had soothed Sandra's heart, they did nothing for her mind. Her mind was a soldier marching off to war, preparing itself for the enemy. Sandra could smell the enemy. It was near. And who was the enemy? Death, of course. This was only the beginning of its havoc. Sandra just knew it. When she tried to explain her fears to someone else, it was a different story, like grasping for fog. Lilly would listen, then smile indulgently, as if she were listening to the tall tales of a child. "Just keep your eyes on the Lord, baby." Sandra would look at Lilly and nod solemnly while her mind burrowed itself in the trenches.

Each night Lilly prepared meals, and everyone tried to eat, except Mama. Sandra attempted to place a spoonful of morsels inside Mama's mouth, but she'd shake her head in vehement protest like a two-year-old who had just discovered newfound autonomy. Then Mama would press her head against the pillow, exhausted, her infantile fight proving to exert much energy. After dinner, Reverend Hamilton would lock himself inside his study, focusing on sermons. Sandra would lock herself inside her bedroom, struggling, hands cupped around her elbows, rocking back and forth on bent knees, with a bottle of Scotch before her.

After a month and a half, Gee and her family flew back to Santa Monica to resume life without Jimmy. Gee thought she was strong enough to stay in the house on Stanford Street, but she was wrong. Jimmy's personality was stenciled on every nook and cranny, and Gee eventually put the house up for sale. She and the kids moved into her parents' home, a refuge until she could stand on her feet.

The enemy was here. Sandra could smell its stench even in sleep. She twisted and turned, entangling herself in her long yellow nightgown. She heard Mama's scream echo from a dark chamber. I'm coming, Mama! I'm coming! Sandra felt herself run, but stopped. Where was she running? Pitch black darkness pressed against her on all four sides. Mama, Mama, where are you? Mama's screams became more persistent. Get away from her! Mama! Sandra suddenly bolted upright in bed, sweat pouring from her brow. She realized that she had been dreaming, and relief enveloped her breast, allaying her fears. Sandra took deep breaths as she reached for the light, the house silent, except for thumping in her ears.

She placed her back against the headboard and closed her eyes, listening to her heart slow to normal pace. Then Jimmy suddenly appeared in front of the curtain of her eyelids, looking the same way as he had in life, not one bloody furrow slashed across his body. Sandra clapped her hands to her chest, feeling her cheeks rise with laughter. She marveled at the sight of him—he looked so real! In her mind's eye, Sandra reached out to touch Jimmy, but her hands went through his chest like vapor. Her smile faded.

She opened her eyes, thinking that the sight of Jimmy was now odd, for this vision of him was not a memory from the past—there was no backdrop of familiar objects, no particular time or place she could recall. Then Sandra's stomach began to churn, saliva rising in her mouth. She quickly cupped her hands to her lips, but before she could release her feet from the tangle of her gown, she had spewed vomit on the floor.

Sandra crouched in a corner, knees raised to her chest, hands draped over her head like a cape. She wept silently, a thin yarn of mucus dangling from her nose. She was dressed in the same yellow gown she'd worn two nights before, dried vomit caked in front. Lilly, also wounded by the news, managed to clean the bedroom with pine disinfectant, but it was impossible to clean Sandra—no one could get close. The sour smell would not leave the room, burgeoning with the rise of Sandra's body odor.

Finally, Lilly suggested professional help, but Reverend Hamilton, who was broken and battered, objected weakly. "No," he said, fighting back tears, "they may give her medication or, worse, lock her up. She's all I have left, Lilly." After he said these words, he tried to coax Sandra to eat, pushing a plate of rice and chicken near her feet. Sandra cowered at the sight of him, squeezing herself closer to the wall, "Mama, tell him not to hurt me. Mama?" Reverend Hamilton's face caved in, and he cried, leaving the task to Lilly.

Lilly put the spoon to her mouth, feigning she was eating rice. "Um huh! This is good. Sure is tasty, Sandy. Here, try some." She moved the spoon toward Sandra, but she quickly backed away, as if Lilly had just handed her a snake. Lilly left the plate of food in the middle of the floor.

Hours later, the food disappeared, and Sandra was curled in a corner asleep, exhausted. Grains of rice stuck to her cheeks. The sight was pitiful, forcing even Lilly to break down, crying a torrent of tears. Lilly's hands moved along Sandra's matted hair. "Oh Jesus. Jesus, Jesus."

She removed the soiled gown, then sponged-bathed Sandra. Afterward, she dressed Sandra in clean pajamas, guiding her to bed. Lilly tucked her beneath the sheets and sat on a nearby chair, looking at Sandra's lifeless eyes, so flat and black. Her hands traced the curve of Sandra's face, reciting Psalm 23:

The Lord is my shepherd;
I shall not want.
He makes me to lie down in green pastures.
He leads me beside the still waters.
He restores my soul;
He leads me in the paths of righteousness
For His name's sake.
Yea, though, I walk through the valley of death,
I will fear no evil;
For You are with me;
Your rod and Your staff, they com—

"Mama?" Sandra sat up.

"Baby," Lilly said, gently pushing Sandra on her back. "Your mama has gone and met the Lord."

"Mama?" Sandra sprang up again, her head darting left to right. She placed an index finger to her lips. "Shhh! Don't you hear it?" she whispered. "Don't you hear it?"

"Hear wha—"

"Mama?"

Lilly shook her head, tears in her eyes, realizing that this poor child would not make it to her own mama's funeral.

-PART TWO-

CHAPTER 10
LIFE AND DEATH

People were at the mercy of the harsh wind: hands clamped down on hats and tightly grasped coat collars, skirts lifted, and pieces of paper twirled in the air like tornadoes, tossed to and fro, blown off course like the lives of Sandra and her family. The wind's onslaught belied the fact that it was April 1992—rather than billowy March—five months following Mama's death, which neither Sandra nor her father had fully comprehended. For Sandra, it was because she heard Mama's voice, wafting through the air with eerie fluidity. For her father, it was his belief and disbelief. He had often quoted from Ecclesiastes: "As fish are caught in a cruel net, or birds are taken in a snare, so men are trapped by evil times that fall unexpectedly upon them." Now disbelief that evil times had unexpectedly befallen his family had gotten the best of him. He preached less, cried more, growing thinner by the day. But this had given Reverend Dexter the opportunity to take on more responsibility, permanently. All agreed he was a handsome young man, with large quiet eyes, but had a voice to ignite a revolution.

It had been a while since Sandra had stepped foot outside the house, and only due to Lilly's prodding, as well as the bright sun that peeked through the slats of the blinds each morning, reminding her that life must go on—no matter what. As Sandra walked, she took note of Cambridge amid the forceful spring air. For months, her mind had been so absorbed with the past that she hadn't realized winter passed them by. She spotted two sparrows on the ledge of their house, looking like tiny lovers. Sandra swore they were communicating: one chirped, the other responded with a shrill. She watched their quick, darting movements as they flew across the street, landing on another house. Her heart sank, because like Mama, she too had become preoccupied with birds.

Walking along Massachusetts Avenue, she stopped and took in the magnificent view of City Hall, a stately example of Romanesque architecture. The city's Latin Motto, when translated, meant, "Distinguished for Classical Learning and New Institutions," which Sandra always thought befitting, since Cambridge harbored MIT, Radcliffe, and Harvard. But she hadn't gone to any of these schools. She attended Boston University, earning a Bachelor's Degree in Business Administration. Yet scholastic achievement dominated her household as well as the city's population, black and white.

She caught glimpse of herself in a shop's window and stopped. She looked tired, and the concealer didn't hide those dark circles. Sandra suddenly pressed her forehead to the glass, peering at the display of liquor bottles stacked neatly in the shape of a pyramid against the backdrop of royal blue cloth. She glanced at the sign: Andy's Wine and Liquors. She was tempted to walk through the door, but stopped in its threshold, remembering the last few times she'd placed a bottle to her lips and how she'd ended up throwing half of its content against a wall. For she had heard Mama's voice, and a thought had occurred to her: If hearing Mama's voice was not a symptom of insanity, then possibly there was something more to death. And if there were something more to death, then there must be something more to life. Perhaps it had a purpose, that she wasn't dropped here by accident, and maybe, just maybe, there was a reason why she was still alive. Sandra had a moment of clarity.

"May I help you?" the bald man from behind the counter asked Sandra, who was still standing in the doorway.

"No, no, thank you," she said, backing away.

She plunged her hands deeply into the pockets of her sweater coat, fingering a card Lilly had placed on her dresser that morning. Sandra's thoughts rested on their encounter, and she sensed Lilly had something on her mind when she entered her bedroom.

"Lilly, is Daddy all right? Is the nurse with him?"

"Oh. Sure. Sure." Lilly had folded her hands on her lap. Her eyes fixed to a fragment of sunlight on the rug.

"So what's wrong, then?"

"Oh. Nothing. Nothing."

"Lilly, this is Sandra, remember?"

Lilly got up from her chair and looked outside the window. "Thank you, Lord, for this glorious day."

"Well, are you going to tell me?"

Lilly spoke to the window. "You know, Sandy, when my Raymond died, I thought I was going to lose my mind. It was something awful! But I didn't, with the grace of God. The Lord told me to seek out people who were going through the same thing I was going through. So I joined a group of people who lost loved ones, too. Every Tuesday night we met and talked about our sorrow. It made the burden lighter, and I got stronger. It helped me cope." Lilly paused. "I met some mighty fine people. To this day, I keep in touch with them. I hear Reverend Dexter holds similar meetings. I think you should go, since you won't talk to me. 'Cause whether you believe it or not, Sandy, you've been going through some trying times! And before your mama died, I told her as long as you living in this house and there's breath in my body, my job is to take good care of you. And I'm a woman of my word. Well, that's all I got to say."

Lilly had left the card on the dresser and gently closed the door behind her, humming "Amazing Grace" as she'd walked down the corridor.

Sandra removed the card from her pocket. Its bold red letters said: Just when you think there is nowhere to turn or no one to turn to, come join our family of friends. Together we will see you through. God's Grace Community Center. Sandra placed the card back into her pocket and turned the corner, toward Janet's house, bracing herself against the persistent onslaught of the wind.

Now that Sandra had been in Cambridge for months—and looked as if she'd be staying for a while, since she had nowhere else to go, no place of her own—she thought to seek out childhood friends, which were few, and probably not really friends at all. But her mind had rested on Janet a few nights ago. She was the closest to a true friend, although the paths of their lives, once parallel, were now miles apart. Yet Janet would be able to bring familiarity to Cambridge, a place Sandra once knew, but now a stranger. Sandra had flipped through the phone book, and there it was. She dialed the number, then felt stupid, about to hang up, but she heard Janet's voice on the other end.

"Hello?"

Sandra hesitated. She couldn't speak.

"Hello?"

Sandra cleared her voice. "Janet?" Her voice sounded meek like a small child's.

"Who's this?"

"Sandra."

"Who?"

"Sandra. Sandra Hamilton."

"Oh. My. God."

After a few awkward moments of silence, their conversation was easy. Sandra spoke of her breakup with Les, her time spent in California—but not of

Haven—and the deaths of Jimmy and Mama, which had brought her back to Cambridge.

"Yes. I heard. I'm so sorry. I was meaning to send a condolence card but...Oh, I don't know."

"It's okay."

Janet spoke of her family, of being a wife, the joys and demands of motherhood.

"Two kids!" Sandra exclaimed. "I only knew about Maureen."

"Well, we have little Terrence now."

"My goodness."

Then Janet had invited Sandra over to her house. "I would really like to see you," she said. "Really, I would."

Janet Bowen Garnett, Sandra's childhood friend since grade school, smoothed the cotton ball saturated in deep cleanser over Sandra's terribly oily skin, in preparation for the clay mask treatment. Even as a teenager, Janet had an interest in cosmetology. Now that she was thirty-four, it provided her earned cash and independence while her husband Carl—a successful certified public accountant—brought home the bacon for his wife and their two children, Maureen and Terrence.

"There." Janet examined the cotton ball. "Been a long time since you gave yourself a deep cleansing, I see."

"Yeah. Can I open up my eyes now?"

"Sure. Go ahead."

The vapor from the cleansing solution stung Sandra's eyes. She quickly shut them, blinking several times. The blurred vision soon gave way, and she focused on Janet's face, a beautiful face. Janet was as dark as a Hersey bar, but had naturally straight hair and fine features like people of Ethiopia. And she was still Sandra's friend. They both dived into their same way of conversation—outspoken always, combative sometimes—feeling as if there were no lost time.

"And then we're going to do something with this hair." Janet stood up, grabbing Sandra's wooly locks with her fingertips. She examined Sandra's head from side to side, picking through her hair like a primate during grooming.

"What's wrong with my hair?"

"You need a perm."

"I don't perm my hair."

"Did when we were in college."

"But that's before I…I…"

"Before what?" Janet held tufts of Sandra's kinky curls in her hands. She pulled her head backward, making eye contact as Sandra sat in her seat.

Sandra looked away, her eyes moving along Janet's red t-shirt, stopping at the Indian beaded belt inserted in the loops of her faded blue jeans.

"I was going to say, 'That's before I decided to go natural.' But then I stopped." Sandra frowned. "It wasn't my decision."

"Well, whose decision was it?"

"It was Les's decision." Sandra brushed Janet's hands away from her hair. "And it wasn't my decision to perm my hair either. Just following everybody else."

"Well, most did. So what?" Janet shrugged.

"So what? Janet, when people you love are dying like flies, it causes you to examine your own life. For the first time, I'm taking personal inventory. For the past month, I've been trying to remember the last time that I made my own decision. Me! And I can't."

Janet sat down, looking at Sandra's hair standing in different directions. With her forearm, she moved the hair appliances and beauty jars to one side of the kitchen table and folded her hands. "Well, weren't you the one who decided to go to New York?"

"No. Not really." Sandra shook her head. "Just wanted to get away from my father. That's it. I was driven away. I didn't decide to go New York. There's a difference."

"Sandra, you always did complicate things. Listen, you decided to go to New York."

"No, I didn't. Even my move to California wasn't really my idea. It was Jimmy's." Sandra placed a hand over her eyes.

Janet heard Terrence's cry over the monitor. "Excuse me," she said, placing her palms flat on the table, "but I have to check on Terry."

Sandra sat still in her chair, sullen, thinking of all the decisions people had made for her, up until adulthood. Buying the clothes shop. No. No. Les's decision. Brownstone. Nope, his. Just went along with it. Even my photography. His idea.

Sandra dropped her hand from her eyes and folded her lips into her mouth, disgusted. Thirty-three, soon to be thirty-four, and she hadn't navigated her own life. She thought of the trips to Africa, but quickly dismissed the idea as being hers. Clearly, those trips were Les's dreams to visit the Motherland. Yes, Sandra discovered a part of herself in Africa, no doubt, discovering a pride of her ancestors, her people. But as teenagers, she and Janet had always dreamt of the romantic English countryside.

"Too many of Jane Austen's books!" Les had scoffed.

So Sandra had studied Africa, eventually knew her better than Les. He wasn't laughing then. She remembered all those dates, names, events. "Seems like Africa is in my blood more than she is in yours," Sandra jokingly said one day. But Les retorted, "Oh! Yeah! Well, why are you still straightening your hair, if you love Africa so much?" That's when she decided—or really Les decided—to go natural.

Sandra sat at the kitchen table, running her fingertips across her clean, tightened skin. She thought of Jimmy, Mama, about death without having lived life. She thought about herself. Who was Sandra? she wondered.

"Well, to perm or not to perm? That is the question!" Janet entered the room with little Terrence in her arms. "This boy doesn't want to go back to sleep!" Terrence, who was seven months old, had tufts of Janet's hair in his tiny tight fist, slowly moving it toward his open mouth. "Oh no you don't!" Janet gently removed her hair from his hands and sat down. "I said, to perm or not to—"

"I heard you the first time."

"Ooh! Snippy, aren't we?"

"Janet, don't play with me, okay?"

"Okay." Janet shrugged. "Do you want to play with me, Terry?" She lifted the chocolate baby, with a mass of giant curls, in the air. His little legs dangled. "Do you want to play with Mama?" Terry belted out a happy squeal, moving his arms rapidly back and forth, as if a rattle were in his hands. "Oh! You do want to play with Mama. You do!"

Sandra looked on, head cocked to the side.

"Yes! You do want to play with Mama, don't you? Mama's little baby wants to plaaay! Mama's little baby wants to plaaay!" Terrence babbled with delight. "Mama's little baby wants to—Ooh! You bad boy!" A thin, long, strand of drool dribbled on Janet's face. "Well, that's enough playing for one day." Janet wiped the baby's mouth with his bib and wiped her face with a cloth.

"Janet, are you happy?"

"Very happy." Janet didn't look at Sandra. She was running the tip of her index finger over Terrence's open mouth. His head was in the crook of her arm, trying his best to get at the tasty finger. Janet looked up. "Carl and I couldn't be any happier. We enjoy our life, our family, our home, and that's enough for us." Janet paused. "And…and we pray for your happiness."

Two months later, Sandra was back at Janet's house, recalling old memories: "But it's my birthday, Mama!" Her mother was weaving Sandra's mass of wool into two heavy braids. Early that morning on Sandra's tenth birthday, Hyacinth painstakingly pressed Sandra's hair with a smoking hot comb, making a bouquet of Shirley Temple curls on both sides of her head. By mid-day, each bouquet turned into a bush, and with swiftness of hand, Hyacinth had woven them into two bulky braids, with pastel ribbons at the end. Janet never had that problem, Sandra recalled. Her hair was always silky smooth. For Sandra's party, Mrs. Eunice Bowen had parted Janet's hair across her head from ear to ear. She then made a fancy bun perched on her head. The rest of her hair fell to her shoulders with just a hint of a flip. So no matter how hard Janet had rumbled with the boys, her hair did not give telltale signs like Sandra. And Eunice did not gasp like Hyacinth had done when she looked at Polaroid snapshots of her daughter.

Jimmy's job was to supervise the kids. He made sure the little boys didn't trample his mother's grass with their Buster Brown shoes. He shook his index finger at the little boys who would pull the hair of the little girls in cotton candy dresses. He assembled the children around the oblong table draped with a disposable tablecloth with "Happy Birthday!" printed all over it. Sometimes he made sure kids wouldn't pop the confetti balloons taped to the walls or glass sliding doors leading to the backyard. But his greatest task was to calm the children as they anxiously awaited for Bozo the Clown to appear. Then her mother had entered the den with a three-layered birthday cake, with white icing and eleven pink candles. Ten candles for her age, one for good luck. All the kids with pointed hats sang "Happy Birthday." Sandra blew out the candles after she had made her wish, and Jimmy had said, "May all your dreams come true." Life was so much simpler then.

Much simpler than now: the 30th of June, twenty-four years later. Sandra stared at the carrot cake with cream cheese frosting and two candles shaped in a three and four placed on top. She looked around Janet's living room—no Jimmy, no Mama—with tears in her eyes. But Jamie, who was Janet's brother, was sitting next to Sandra on a floral couch with plastic covering. Maureen, a small replica of Janet, was sitting on the shag carpet near Sandra's feet, looking intently at Sandra's face. Carl was in his easy chair, looking more distinguished than his thirty-seven years, and Janet was carefully cutting triangles of cake.

"Why you look sad, Sandra?"

Janet's head sharply turned toward Maureen, the knife in her hand frozen in the middle of the cake.

Maureen looked at her mother apologetically, "I mean, Miss Sandra."

"That's better," Janet quipped. "But you shouldn't ask Miss Sandra personal questions, Maureen. It's not polite."

"I'm sorry," Maureen said in her slow drawl, fiddling with her fingers.

Sandra wanted to cry. Maureen's big shiny eyes were filled with much concern. Maureen was eight years old. So lucky to be that age, Sandra thought. She motioned Maureen to come closer.

Maureen stood on her knees, placing each hand, palms down, on Sandra's lap.

"I'm sad because I am not a cute little girl like you," Sandra said softly. She pulled one of Maureen's pigtails cascading down her back.

Maureen smiled.

"She's old! That's why she's sad!" Jamie blurted out.

Maureen, not knowing that Jamie was joking, seriously replied, "You not old, Miss Sandra. You pretty."

"Why, thank you, Maureen." Sandra kissed her on the cheek, then sharply nudged Jamie with her elbow. "Old?"

Jamie smiled. "Just kidding."

Janet passed around slices of cake on small plates. "After you finish this, Maureen, I want you to go upstairs and get ready for bed."

Later that evening, after Maureen was put to bed, the adults sat in the living room. "So how's Reverend Hamilton?" asked Carl, adjusting his heavy rimmed glasses.

"He's hanging in," Sandra said dryly, before scooping the last piece of cake into her mouth.

"He's sorely missed, but Reverend Dexter is a good man, too. Great orator." Carl stiffened then slowly relaxed, reclining again in his easy chair. He folded his hands, placing them on top his flat stomach. "Cake was good, honey."

"Thank you." Janet walked over to Carl, slipping her slim body next to his. Sandra noticed that their bodies fitted nicely together, like perfect pieces of a jigsaw puzzle. Carl handed Janet the remote to the television nobody was watching.

"So how are you doing financially? Are you working yet?"

"Carl!" Janet said, raising her head from his shoulder. She tugged at his navy blue polo shirt.

"Listen, we are all friends here, practically family. Right, Sandra?"

Sandra cracked a dry smile. Carl always thought about numbers, dollars, and cents. The numbers tell the story, he always said. And it was true: they'd grown up together in Cambridge, went to the same high school together, the same church together, practically family.

"I'm still living off the money Les gave me, and the money I'd earned working for Jimmy. Work? Well, I haven't even considered what I'd like to do. Retail is what I know best, but I don't know if I want to continue in that business. I don't know what I want." Sandra placed the empty plate on the nearby table and rested her head on the back of the couch. "At thirty-four, I don't have a clue about my life and where I'm going."

The room grew quiet.

Finally, Jamie rested his hand on top of Sandra's. "Just remember we're always here for you."

"Yeah," Carl and Janet said.

Sandra nestled her head deeper into the comfort of the couch and closed her eyes. Although Jamie's words were soothing to her ears, they rattled the rusty tin can inside her heart, its lid sealed shut, a storage of unfulfilled promises. For Jimmy had said that he'd always be there for her. Mama had said that too, even Les. Now they were gone. No, she couldn't risk pleasant thoughts that people would always be there for her—it hurt too much. Sandra opened her eyes, looking around. Her eyes rested on Janet, envying all that she had: love, security, fulfilled promises. She was present years ago when Carl, on bent knee, had promised Janet that he would marry her after college and make her happy. And he had. They'd even produced two children. Sandra had always wanted to get married and have children. Now looking at her life, it would probably never happen, she thought.

Her eyes shifted to Carl, then Jamie, who were now watching television. There wasn't anything more to be said. What else could they say? Her life was crumbling. A feeling of separation suddenly surrounded her like a fence. She was part of this family once, but many years ago. Now they were no longer kids, but adults, changed. And although they had not seen it, Sandra was changed before she'd become an adult—changed by the myth that childhood was bliss, changed by the comfort of strong drink. It occurred to Sandra that their shared connection through childhood was a lie. They'd never known about her struggles: suicidal thoughts, hangovers at the age of twelve. To Carl, Jamie, and

Janet, childhood was wonderful. To Sandra, it was a wonder that she'd survived.

"Sandra, did you hear Carl?" asked Jamie. "Sandra?"

"What? Excuse me."

"I said, 'Now Jamie and his friends don't have to worry about Reverend Hamilton standing at the doorway anymore, yelling at them to stay away from you.'" Carl grinned.

"Yeah. Reverend Hamilton was something else. He scared all the boys away from Sandra," Jamie said. "I can hear his big booming voice now, sounding like Paul Robeson. You expected him at any moment to belt out, 'Ole Man Riv-er!'"

Everyone laughed, except Sandra. She was weary of their reminiscing. She stood up and said it was time to go home.

Carl and Janet looked at each other.

Jamie said, "What did I say?"

When Sandra got home, she placed her presents on a chair in the corner of her bedroom: a sundress from Janet and family, a pair of sandals from Lilly, a silver bracelet from Gee and the kids. She placed the vase of red roses from Jamie on her dresser. Sandra sat on the edge of the bed, cradling her forehead in her hand. She felt alone, lost, as she wiped the tears from her cheeks. She needed someone to talk to. Sandra spotted the white card Lilly had given her and picked it up, placing it on her open palm like a jewel. She looked at her watch, too late to call at 12:00 AM. She thought of Lilly, but knew she'd be asleep. She thought about calling Gee, but changed her mind. Gee would just be getting in from work. "Why you look sad, Sandra?" Too bad Maureen wasn't there, she thought. Maureen seemed most concerned, sensed that Sandra's condition was grave.

The following day, Sandra slammed the car door and walked through the entry gate, passing headstones, until she found Mama's. Sandra's hesitant fingertips slowly moved across the cool granite. She looked at the stone angel with broad wings hovering over Mama's grave, hands in prayer, with a cherubic face like Cupid's. The sun shone high and bright above Mount Auburn Cemetery. Sandra bent down, placing the bouquet of pink Gladiolus on Mama's resting-place. She sat down on a granite bench. The grass was green, tender, and young, marking the end of the bitter winter. Sandra remembered Mama's words long ago: "Sometimes endings are beginnings, Sandra. It's just that we hold on to the ending, because sometimes we are afraid of the beginning. The newness of it all doesn't seem to fit right. You know what I mean?"

Sandra shook her head and wiped tears from her eyes. She hadn't attended Mama's funeral, hadn't said her last good-bye. Sandra wasn't even present when Mama had died. Lilly told Sandra that Mama had called out her name with her last breath: Sannndraaa. Said it sounded like air let out of a balloon. Lilly did not know that Mama's voice had been calling Sandra ever since.

CHAPTER 11
VISITATIONS

His hollow eyes greeted her. They were the only part of Reverend Hamilton that appeared to be alive. Sandra recalled looking into those eyes as a little girl, so they were somewhat recognizable. The rest of him she couldn't recall. Her father was always a big, strapping man. Now he didn't talk much, too weak. His vocabulary had dwindled to a "Yes," or a "No," or a feeble nod of the head, and he'd dropped from two hundred fifty pounds to one hundred fifty—a weight much too stingy for his generous six-foot four frame. But those eyes were alive, talking. Yet still, they had not said, "Please forgive me."

Recently, Sandra had understood that sometimes people's eyes faltered. Their eyes allowed her to read what they wanted her to read. That's when her nose stepped in. Sandra's nose had become an auxiliary function, a cane that aided her when people's eyes left her groping in the dark. Once she had read the pain in Aunt Enid's eyes while standing over her father's bedside. Her pain moaned in such a sorrowful way. But in flash of recognition, Aunt Enid had known that Sandra was reading her eyes, so with great skill her eyes changed face. They were so full of hope for the future. "He'll be all right," she'd said confidently, patting Sandra on the wrist. "Just all right." Sandra was certain Aunt Enid had smelled the decay, too.

Sandra first stumbled on the aid of her nose after her father's bone marrow transplant. Soon following Mama's death, her father was told that his latest scans revealed abnormal nodules in his lungs. His face dropped. A transplant was his only viable option, the doctors had said. After the transplant, Reverend Hamilton smelled different to Sandra. She couldn't put her fingers on it. It was a subtle smell, like creamed corn. The doctors had said that it was the preservative the bone marrow and stem cells were stored in, and his lungs released the smell of the preservative. Then followed the liver problems, kidney problems, all kinds of problems. Each day her father grew smaller, his face thinner, and his cheekbones rose up like newly formed mountains, and he never did smell the same. The scent of cherry tobacco long since gone.

But this morning, his smell wasn't too bad to Sandra. Reverend Hamilton's eyes beckoned her to sit down on the edge of his bed. He liked the way she smelled, like scented soap, Hyacinth's scented soap. Sandra sat beside her father, but during times like these, she separated her feelings from her body, casting them off like clothing, and taking on characteristics of stone. She assured herself that this was for his safety. Otherwise, she would have stormed the kitchen, fingering the points of knives.

It was almost a year since Reverend Hamilton last preached at Mount Baptist Church. He had been pastor for forty-something years. Now Reverend Dexter fully relieved him of this duty. Lilly said she believed Reverend Dexter was moving the church in a whole different direction, recruiting many young people. He even spoke about necessary job skills: "Yes! Young brothers and sisters, I'm here to feed your soul! But it is up to you to feed your head! Stay in school! Learn the necessary skills to compete in this forever-changing world we live in!"

As her father grew weaker, Reverend Dexter visited him frequently, sitting by his bedside reading Scripture. "You know his wife died a couple years ago I hear. Seems like he's eligible," Lilly had whispered to Sandra one day, and Sandra wanted to know, why? For the fire in her womanly soul had been extinguished a long time ago. Only trails of smoke remained.

Still, Lilly's comment had intrigued Sandra—his wife dying so young and all—so during one of Reverend Dexter's visits, she'd watched him through the small opening of her bedroom door. Her father's room was just across the hallway. Reverend Dexter was spoon-feeding her father, as the nurse stood behind him looking on, moved to tears by his gentleness. Even Sandra's feelings were stirred a bit, because Jimmy could not have loved their father more. After that day, Sandra wanted to know more about this Reverend Dexter. Who was he and where did he come from? Neither Lilly nor Janet provided many answers, other than the fact that his wife had died and he had no children. Does he have any other family? Don't know, they had said. Well, when did he become associate pastor of my father's church? About three years ago, they had answered unequivocally—and that was the extent of what they'd known about the young minister's life.

After Sandra spent her morning avoiding her father's touch, she jumped into his car and headed toward the library. She often told herself that there had to be a reason why she heard Mama's voice. So while everyone was either at work or living life, she spent many days searching books for answers. Today she stumbled across a book about parapsychology. Sandra had heard about the subject, but hadn't known much about it; and apparently, other people did not know either—for it had nothing to do with Bigfoot or any of the crazy things they had said. The book said that parapsychology was the study of psychic phenomena. Sandra looked toward the ceiling, mouthing the words, physic phenomena. Her heart raced, for she believed she was on the verge of finding an answer. Her eyes dropped back to the book. She read on:

> *There is a long-held, common-sense assumption that the worlds of the subjective and objective are completely distinct, with no overlap. Subjective is "here," in someone's head. Objective is "there," out in the world. Parapsychology, then, is the study of phenomena suggesting that the assumption of strict separation between subjective and objective may be wrong, that human experience suggests that some phenomena occasionally fall between the cracks, not purely subjective or objective.*

Huh? Sandra sat back in her chair and pondered what she'd just read. It was complicated, so she read it again. Her fingernail moved slowly across the page, beneath each word. Okay. What it's basically saying is that some experiences are not strictly inside someone's head, like Mama's voice, that experiences like these are just as real as the experiences out in the world. Sandra thought that she'd grasped the understanding, so she read further.

From a scientific perspective, the book continued, such phenomena are called anomalous because they are difficult to explain within current scientific models. Some of these occurrences include telepathy, precognition—which Sandra believed she had a touch of, for how else could she explain the things she'd known beforehand?—near death experiences, reincarnation, and haunting. Sandra's eyes stopped at the word haunting. According to parapyschologists, it meant recurrent phenomena reported to occur in particular locations that included apparitions, sounds, movement of objects, and other effects. Yes, she heard Mama's voice, but not in any one particular location. She heard Mama's voice everywhere, even in the rush of the wind, raindrops descending on the roof. So this wasn't a classic haunting. Mama wasn't haunting her, Sandra assured herself. What was it, then? She couldn't find any neat categories. Why did she hear Mama's voice, but not Jimmy's? Did

Mama have something specific to say?

Sandra knew of many cultures that believed in communicating with the dead. For after all, she'd traveled numerous parts of Africa. But now she wanted documented cases, scientific proof that she was not bordering insanity. She wanted to tell someone, but knew that she'd couldn't. She almost told Janet one day, but quickly changed her mind. Janet, with her earth-bound practicality, would've said, "Listen. You need a doctor!"

Sandra pushed the book away. She sat back in her wooden chair. It creaked with each of her movements, echoing throughout the cavernous corridors. She rubbed her eyes, then collected her purse and car keys. This is crazy, all of it, she said to herself, heading toward the door.

She drove down Massachusetts Avenue, then decided to leave the tan Subaru in a parking garage to walk the brick sidewalks of Harvard Square. She stopped at the Globe Corner Bookstore, and had lunch at an Indian restaurant on JFK Street. Afterwards, she walked around, peeking into shops. It was a beautiful July day: sunny, clear skies. Many people were in the square: tourist taking pictures of Harvard campus, long-haired musicians playing on street corners, young boys with spiked green hair and pierced body parts huddling in front of The Coop. Further down, a young woman with two long braids was selling her charcoal sketches spread out on the sidewalk. Opposite her stood a small group of people rummaging through used books on a tabletop. Young lovers walked hand-in-hand with knapsacks on their backs, licking ice cream cones. Sandra sat on a bench and soaked in the sun, watching a golden retriever chase a fluorescent Frisbee, and fearing that her search would not yield an answer, something to make sense of it all. She put her purse beside her and sat forward on the edge of the bench, placing her face in the cushion of her hands.

"Is life that bad?" a small voice asked.

Sandra's head popped up, looking into the wizened face of a white woman. Sandra quickly looked around. Where did this lady come from? She had to be at least ninety years old, Sandra thought. Her skin was cracked with many wrinkles, like land parched from drought. She held a cane, and her stockings sagged around her elephantine ankles.

"Are you talking to me?" Sandra asked meekly.

The woman smiled. She had a full set of false teeth. "May I sit?"

"Sure." Sandra shrugged.

The woman, with curvature of the spine, grasped the back of the wrought-iron bench and proceeded to sit, very slowly, so for a moment her bony behind seemed suspended above the seat.

Sandra offered to help, but the old lady declined, waving her free hand, the handle of her cane straddled around her thin wrist. She groaned when she finally sat down and said, "Ursula."

"Excuse me?"

The woman extended her skeletal hand. "Ursula. Ursula McKeon!"

"Oh! My name is Sandra."

They shook hands.

Ursula smoothed her flowered dress against her small lap. The skin on the back of her hands looked like crepe paper.

"Is life lickin' ya, Sandra?"

Sandra glanced at Ursula, then stared at the open space before her. Finally, she answered mechanically, "Yeah. Guess so. Licking me bad." She wedged her hands between her lap and looked at Ursula. Despite her snow-white hair styled in a neat bun and wrinkles, Ursula's eyes were youthful, twinkling emerald green. They stared at each other; Ursula's eyes did not tell Sandra any tales. Sandra examined every line on Ursula's face, understanding that she would never see Mama grow old. Tears sprang to her eyes.

Ursula tapped Sandra's knee. "Don't! Laughter is a better remedy." She reached into her purse that dangled from the crook of her elbow and pulled out a plastic bag of breadcrumbs, scattering them on the ground. Soon pigeons were around their feet.

Sandra wiped the tears with the back of her hands, watching pigeons' heads bob, scooping Ursula's gift into their mouths.

"Someone dear has died," Ursula said. She quickly frowned and looked toward the trees. "No. No. More than one, but dear." She continued to scatter breadcrumbs. "And there is someone else that ya need to make amends before it's too late. Death is very near. I'm afraid."

Sandra sat upright, amazed. "Yes. Go on."

Ursula did not continue. She was concentrating on the brood of pigeons that were now fighting for territory, wings flapping. "Oh, my!" She shook her head. "What have I done?"

"Ursula?"

The sharp tone of Sandra's voice broke Ursula's focus. She looked intently at Sandra.

"What else do you see?"

"I see that you're impatient." Ursula stuffed the empty plastic bag into her purse.

Sandra rested her back against the bench. "Sorry."

"Stop searching for life's answers and let them unfold. The world is more than what we see, so much more that it can't be found in books."

Sandra's mouth dropped. "Who are you?"

"I'm Ursula. Ursula McKeon!"

Sandra picked up her purse and pressed it against her chest. All of a sudden, she felt afraid of the old woman. She felt like running, but instead frantic words gushed from her mouth. She told Ursula about her childhood, that she hated her father, that she hated him even more since Mama and Jimmy were dead, that the hate overwhelmed her at times, and she thought about killing him, but the cancer was doing a fine job. He was the reason she'd become an alcoholic, that she spent one month in a rehabilitation center, only to discover that she blamed God too, blamed him for allowing this to happen to her. She was just a kid! Now she was going crazy, because she heard Mama's voice, which no one else could hear. Why?

Ursula folded her hands on her lap and sat quietly, then she leaned toward Sandra. "Everything is revealed in due time," she whispered. "Take courage. Know that ya have a guardian angel."

"Someone once told me that before, that I have a guardian angel looking after me!"

Ursula raised a gnarled index finger. "Ah! But ya do!"

When Sandra parked in her driveway later that afternoon, she still had Ursula on her mind. She was a strange one. But thoughts of Ursula soon gave way after Sandra spotted her next door neighbor, Mrs. Wheats, and Aunt Enid talking on the sidewalk in front her house. They huddled closely together, whispering, conspiring, and Sandra knew something was up. She said a curt "hello" as she walked passed them to the front door. Inside the house, Sandra heard muted voices in the living room and walked toward its entrance. She saw Lilly and Reverend Dexter sipping tea, having a discussion about the Bible, she supposed. They looked up. Lilly placed her cup on a tray, then stood up and said, "Here is Sandy!" She walked toward Sandra, placing her arms around her shoulders, leading her toward Reverend Dexter.

He stood up. "Finally, I get a chance to meet you, Sandra. I was beginning to think you were just a figment of Lilly's imagination."

They shook hands.

"Nice to meet you," Sandra said softly. He was much taller than she'd expected.

"Nice to meet you, too," Reverend Dexter replied, then smiled.

His teeth were dazzling, Sandra thought. He gazed at her for a second, but too quickly to read his eyes.

"Sit down, Sandy," Lilly said, taking her by the hand. "Want some tea?"

"No, Lilly, I'm fine."

They sat on the sofa. Reverend Dexter sat across the room, sitting in her father's wingback chair.

Sandra placed the car keys and purse beside her on the couch.

Lilly shook Sandra's thigh. "Reverend Dexter was just telling me about the summer recreation hall at God's Grace Community Center. His way of keeping kids out of trouble." Lilly beamed.

"Yes," Reverend Dexter interjected, "Lord knows I wish I had a recreation hall when I was growing up." He picked up his cup of tea and took a sip.

Sandra folded her arms against her chest. "And where did you grow up?"

Before Reverend Dexter could reply, the front door slammed, and they turned their heads toward the entrance of the living room, staring at Aunt Enid's grief-stricken face. She brusquely walked inside and plopped on the couch and, without warning, barked, "Where are you from?" Reverend Dexter glanced at her, sipping his tea, legs casually crossed. Lilly and Sandra gave each other a look. Lilly was appalled because it sounded more like a command rather than a question. Anyone who had accepted Reverend Dexter as pastor would have never spoken to him that way—then again, Aunt Enid attended another church. So she asked with great authority, "Where are you from?" She waited impatiently for an answer. Reverend Dexter took his sweet time, setting the empty teacup on a tray.

Finally, he said, "Oh, here and there. To and fro."

Aunt Enid snapped, "What kind of answer is that?"

Reverend Dexter's eyes narrowed into piercing black slits. "My answer. That's what kind of answer it is."

Aunt Enid's eyebrows raised. Lilly looked at her as if to say, "Enid! You better leave this man alone!" After Aunt Enid left the room in a huff, Reverend Dexter looked to the floor. His hands were between his knees, apologetic.

"You must excuse me," he said, "but I just hate ugly ways. The devil is working overtime."

"Amen to that!" said Lilly.

Reverend Dexter looked at her and smiled. He sat back in his chair, reaching into the pocket of his shirt for a slim cigar. "Do you mind?" Lilly and Sandra shook their heads sideways. Reverend Dexter lit it, then sighed deeply. He crossed his legs in leisurely fashion again, holding the cigar between his index finger and thumb. Sandra knew he needed to say something, but he didn't know where to start. She knew because she saw it in his eyes.

"Just say it," she said softly.

"What?"

"Just say what you have to say."

Reverend Dexter shifted in his chair. He spoke slowly at first, soon picking up momentum. "I grew up in a beat-up tenement in Harlem with my mother. Never knew my father. My mother—God rest her soul—is the reason I changed my ugly ways. I was a bitter young man with no direction, no love for myself or anybody else. I sold reefer all up and down 125th Street to adults as well as children. Graduated to heroin. Stole fancy cars, loved another man's woman. You name it, I've done it. I'm not too proud to admit it." Reverend Dexter stopped, looking at Sandra and Lilly, checking their faces for any expression he could read. Their faces offered no signs, but their ears were eager for information. He flicked cigar ashes into the ashtray. Sandra sat still. Lilly leaned forward, resting her face in her palms.

"Do you know what can change a young criminal's heart? The death of the only person he truly loves—his mother. That's right! Ain't nobody gonna love you like your mama!" He uttered a small laugh. "My mother was struck by a bullet meant for me. Talk about being at the wrong place at the wrong time. One minute she was sitting on the stoop with other women and their children. The next minute she was at the bottom of the steps with a trickle of blood in the middle of her forehead. Her eyes wide open, staring up at Heaven. When I approached her casket, I was barely fifteen years old. Her spirit rose up. I tell you! It rose up! She looked at me, shaking her index finger, saying, 'Boy! You better change your ugly ways 'cause God don't like ugly.' I turned around and said to the people, 'Don't you see her? She's not dead! Can't you hear her?' They thought I was delirious. Two men on each side carried me out of the church while I yelled, 'Don't you see her? She's not dead! I tell you! Mama's not dead!' Old ladies shook their heads, saying, 'Poor boy!' But I know what I saw. I know what I saw. My mother led me to the path of righteousness!" Reverend Dexter suddenly laughed and shook his head. "You're probably saying, 'What is this all about?' I don't really know myself. But I think it's the answer to the question, 'Where are you from?' I think I owe it to you ladies."

The third Saturday of July was designated "Annual Fundraising Day" at Mount Baptist Church, a great event for the ladies in the congregation. Always the night before, Lilly and her friends stood up late, preparing fish and chicken dinners. Later, they would bake cakes, pies, and breads. Somebody's kitchen— Lilly's this year—would be filled with frenzied activity and lots of women's talk. Sandra stood in the doorway, unnoticed, watching Lilly, Adele, Ruth, and Sadie—stout, God-fearing matriarchs on a mission.

"Sadie, throw some smoked neck-bones in them greens, will you?"

"Chop more boiled eggs in that potato salad now. People like it with boiled eggs."

"My Lord, Adele, you pretty heavy-handed with that black pepper here."

"Girl, don't tell me what to do! I been cookin' for years!"

The scene produced a smile on Sandra's face, a genuine smile that stretched her lips after long absence. The connection that these women shared was no different from the connection among women Sandra had seen in Africa, pounding yam, cooking alongside dirt roads. Different lands, customs, languages, yes, but a universal connection. The more Sandra pondered her life and life the common thread was visible. Just the fact that these women laughed while their former pastor was dying upstairs was another pattern of the common thread—that life and death were of the same coin, only two different sides.

The woman had spoken about Annual Fundraising Day all week, hoping that the proceeds this year would go toward building the recreation hall of God's Grace Community Center. They wholeheartedly believed in Reverend Dexter and his vision. Sandra wasn't certain as to whether she believed in the man, but she certainly believed in the man's story about his mama. Reverend Dexter was her documented case. What surprised Sandra most was that he'd talked about it with conviction! He truly believed there was a reason for the experience. Sandra wanted to know more, but hadn't known how to go about it. It had to be subtle, not drawing too much attention to herself. So she decided she would participate in the fundraising event this year. Surely, Reverend Dexter would attend, but she wouldn't say anything to him. She would watch him first before she made her move.

"Well, look who's here," Sadie said, nudging Lilly on her hip.

Lilly turned around, gazing at Sandra.

"Now what is a young gal like you doin' home on a Friday night?" Adele asked.

Young? Sandra thought. She hardly thought of herself as young. She smiled, not knowing what to say.

"Girl, when I was your age," Adele continued, "I had plenty dates knockin' at my door."

"Leave the child alone, Adele," Sadie said. "She ain't missing nothing. Ain't too many good young men in the world these days."

"What about Reverend Dexter?" Ruth chimed.

"He ain't in the world," Sadie shot back. "He's in the Lord."

"Yeah, that's the God's truth," Ruth conceded.

The statement finalized the conversation, and their heads suddenly dropped toward what they were doing. After a few seconds had passed, Lilly raised her head from her duty of chopping onions. With her chin, she pointed to an apron draped on the back of a chair. "Get that, Sandy, and grate some cheese for the macaroni."

Sandra washed her hands at the kitchen sink, then tied the apron around her waist. She sat down at the table, staring at a block of sharp cheddar cheese. She rubbed it against the grater like a washboard, until curls of cheese dropped onto the plate beneath. "I'm going to the fundraising event," she announced.

The women's heads swiveled on their necks toward her.

Lilly dropped her knife next to the hill of chopped onions and reached for a nearby dishtowel. She wiped her hands, then rushed over to Sandra, taking a seat. "That's a good idea, baby, give you a chance to be around people, church folks. That's what you need." The other women had forgotten what they were doing and crowded around Sandra, peering at her as if they were witnessing a car accident.

Lilly touched Sandra's wrist. "It a good idea, baby, good idea. Can't just keep yourself cooped up in the house most of the time."

"Ain't healthy," Sadie interjected.

Sandra looked at the ladies gathered around her. She stopped grating and took in their faces of deep concern. They looked liked women who'd served hot lunch in cafeterias of public schools: dressed in white aprons tied around their expanded waistlines, hairnets on their heads. Ruth rubbed Sandra's shoulder. Sandra knew that to these women her announcement was akin to a confession of turning her life to the Lord. It had nothing to do with the Lord; it had all to do with Reverend Dexter.

The thought made Sandra laugh aloud, startling the women. They laughed too, not knowing what they were laughing about, looking at each other uneasily. Sandra laughed harder, covering her face. The women grew silent. Sandra kept laughing, thoughts clamoring to the surface of her mind. She couldn't stop. She laughed about the tragic turn her life had taken, laughed about the irony that her father was still alive and Mama and Jimmy were dead, laughed that she heard Mama's voice and didn't know why. She laughed that she was desperate enough to tell her whole life story to some crazy old lady. Tears streamed from her eyes. Hell! Maybe she was crazy, too! Lilly stood up and bent over, hugging Sandra. She whispered, "God is good, Sandy. He'll find a way when you think there's no way." God? Sandra thought. Her laughter heightened to a cackle. She sat back in her chair, tears rolling down her cheeks. She laughed until her ribs hurt. Lilly wiped Sandra's face with the edge of her apron. "Laugh, baby. Let it out. Laughter is part of the healing, just like prayer."

Later that evening, Sandra hadn't known what had gotten hold of her. She only knew Lilly's eyes remained fastened to her, as if at any moment she would come undone.

CHAPTER 12
DIRECTIONS

Two weeks later, Sandra recalled that the fundraising event had proved successful. Woman of all shapes and sizes stood erect like soldiers behind rows of oblong tables in front Mount Baptist Church, which were laden with cakes, peach cobbler, apple pies, cookies of all assortment, fried chicken, biscuits, and collard greens. The ladies' foreheads sweated in the sun, as did their hands that exchanged goods for cash. They hastily stuffed dollar bills placed between their fingers into pockets of aprons. Sandra too had stood behind a table, keeping one eye on the mounds of potato salad she scooped onto paper plates, the other intently fixed on Reverend Dexter. He was easy going among the crowd, approachable, stopping now and then to greet various clumps of people.

Around mid-day, Sandra had entered the empty church, tired, needing to rest her feet. She was surprised to see Reverend Dexter sitting in a front pew. His back was facing her, but the slant of the sun streaming from a nearby window illuminated the side of his face, so she could see his jawbone working rapidly. He heard a stir and quickly turned around, with specks of pie crust scattered around his face. To this day, Sandra had not known where she'd gotten the boldness to say, "Huh! I thought that gluttony is a sin!"

He threw back his head, his laughter echoing throughout the church. "You're right!" he finally said, catching his breath.

Sandra, feeling easy, pointed to her cheek. "Crumbs," she said, moving closer.

"Oh!" Reverend Dexter quickly reached for a napkin and wiped his mouth. "Thanks."

"No problem. May I sit?"

"Sure! Go ahead." He patted the pew.

Sandra sat down and rubbed her calves.

Reverend Dexter looked on, then quickly averted his eyes, his attention back to the slice of apple pie. He had examined it in his hand and shook his head, a serious look on his face. "Women can cook!" he had said, before taking another huge bite.

Sandra smiled, folding her hands on her lap. Right there and then, she'd decided that she liked him. He was real.

From that day on, she had made it her way to speak with Reverend Dexter during his daily visits to the house, with the intention to lead him into discussions about his mother so that, in the end, she'd get her answers.

But today, no answer could possibly pull Sandra out of her funk. She'd tried to shake it off, but couldn't. She paced the floor, looking at the number, once, twice. Finally, she picked up the phone.

"Hey! How are you?" Reverend Dexter suddenly paused, his voice taking on a cautious tone. "Sandra, is everything okay?"

"My father is still alive if that's what you mean."

"Good." Reverend Dexter emitted a sigh of relief. "So what's going on? This is the first time you called me at home…must be important."

Silence.

Reverend Dexter waited. "I'm listening, Sandra."

Still silence. Then, "I don't know where to begin."

"From the beginning."

"The beginning?" she said meekly. "I don't even know. All I know is that I feel lost…like…I lost my place in the world." Sandra laughed softly. "Who am I kidding? Like I ever knew my place in the world."

"I see. Sandra, this may sound strange to you, but sometimes the position that you're in is not a bad place to be; I call it brokenness. God can use that. You realize you are lost. This makes you ripe for change, a new direction."

"Reverend Dexter, the reason I called is because I'd like to come to God's Grace Community Center tonight. Lilly had given me a card a while ago. Are the meetings still held on Saturdays?"

"Most certainly," he said seriously. "In fact, I am driving over there later. The meeting begins at eight-thirty and lasts about two hours. Sometimes we finish a little earlier. Sometimes we don't. It's only five o'clock. We can go together if you'd like. I will introduce you to our counselors. Most of the people are from the church, but some are not. It's a very healing place, Sandra. I'm glad that Mount Baptist Church let me start the program. With God's grace, we helped many people with everyday problems—job loss, loss of a loved one, loss of one's faith, loss of self—you name it."

"I'd like to go with you, Reverend Dexter."

"Good. Sandra, have you had dinner yet?"

"No. Why?"

"Listen, every Saturday night I take the time to prepare dinner, and Lord knows I never can eat it all. Would you like to join me? I'm about to make a salad, but after that, I can pick you up. What do you say?"

"Okay."

"Good. I'll see you later."

After Reverend Dexter hung up the phone, he watched clear water cascade over the head of iceberg lettuce in the sink, thinking about Pauline, his former wife, her similarities with Sandra. Over the course of their numerous conversations, he'd observed Sandra carefully. Like Pauline, Sandra also appeared to be a woman desperate to unbraid her life and set it free, desperate to glean meaning from life's dizzying journey. It had been months since he last thought about Pauline. Now the thought of her—or was it Sandra?—caused him to think of his earlier years.

Reverend Dexter pulled alongside the curb a little after five-thirty. Sandra climbed into the navy-blue van with Mount Baptist Church printed in white letters on both sides. He closed the door behind her and walked around the vehicle to the driver's side. Across the street he caught glimpse of Enid getting out of her car.

"Oh, boy."

"Well! Hello Pastor," Enid said mockingly. "May I speak with you?"

Reverend Dexter glanced at his watch as Enid approached him. "Sure. I have a second."

"I know what you are up to, and you are not going to get away with it!" She pressed her index finger hard against Reverend Dexter's collarbone.

His eyes widened. "Sister Enid, the devil always has his way with you. I have no idea what you are talking about."

"Sure you don't!" Enid placed her hands on her wide hips. "Like I'm stupid!"

"Goodnight, Sister Enid." Reverend Dexter climbed into his vehicle. He closed the door and sped off.

"What's that all about?"

"I don't know." Reverend Dexter looked serious. "Sandra, have you heard any rumors about me? I mean, your aunt thinks I'm up to something."

Sandra looked toward the roof of the van. She shook her head sideways. "No…no…not really. Well…"

"What?"

"Well, people want to know why you haven't remarried, being so young and all. According to Lilly, female enrollment at Mount Baptist Church has gone up. Sky-rocketed, in fact."

"Now that's an overstatement, Miss Hamilton. Don't you think?"

"Not according to Lilly. The number of those young sisters keeps growing all the time."

Reverend Dexter smiled and shook his head. "That Sister Johnson," he said lovingly, "she is something else. So what else did she tell you?"

"Well," Sandra paused, then said solemnly, "she also told me that your wife passed away. If you don't mind my asking, how did she die?"

Reverend Dexter stiffened. Sandra looked at him, waiting for an answer.

He kept his eyes forward, fast to the road.

Sandra looked down at her lap.

After a moment Reverend Dexter said, "My wife isn't dead. I'm divorced."

"Oh?"

There was a very long period of silence—like eternity. Sandra looked outside the window, watching the elms speed by. But her thoughts were speeding faster. Why had Lilly believed his wife was dead? Remembering the day when Lilly had approached her, "You know his wife died a couple of years ago, I hear. Seems like he's eligible." She wanted to know why Lilly was telling her this, because she'd never seen any desire in Reverend Dexter's eyes. His eyes were always warm and honest, clear of any sexual innuendoes. But she wasn't dead! Reverend Dexter was a good-looking man. Squared jaw. Cleft chin. Nice eyes. Definitely nice eyes, large and innocent.

The stretch of silence continued.

The mention of his wife caused Reverend Dexter to think of her again, the soft way she'd called his name just above a whisper, "Samuel." After his mother's death, he remembered how he had packed his belongings and moved to Laurelton, Queens to live with Uncle Troy, his mother's brother, and there he met Pauline. There were many hot summer nights with Pauline, sitting on her porch. He did the talking, Pauline the listening. He had never talked so much in his entire life! The life he'd formerly led on the hard streets had meant living virtually in anonymity. One had only talked about the events in the neighborhood: the raw sex you had the night before, the best corner to sell drugs, where the next party would take place. Never did any man talk about himself, especially about his feelings—this would have left him wide open for sabotage, an exposure of his weakness. But with Pauline, his feelings flowed, and she listened. This was her gift. The life he once led had fascinated Pauline.

". . . and after my moms died, I promised I would make somethin' of myself, you know. Wished I could've done it when she was alive."

This particular night, he had squatted on his haunches, looking at Pauline sitting in a white wicker chair, with a rose print cushion, her cotton dress almost matching its print. Her hair was combed into a ponytail high at the back of her head. It was hot and humid, and fireflies flickered above the grass and perfectly trimmed hedges. Pauline placed her glass of soda on the small, white wicker table. He absent-mindedly cupped his crotch, then shot a squirt of spit from the side of his mouth. Pauline shot a look at him.

"Sorry."

He sat cross-legged on the bare porch, leaning his back against the side of Pauline's house. It was a well-kept house of white aluminum siding and forest-green, French-style shutters.

"Last night, Uncle Troy said he knew my pops. Said he remembered what he looked like. Said he looked like a important man, big, strong—like a chief of police or somethin'. If that's true, my moms never told me. Fact she never said nothin' 'bout him. Chief of police. Man, can you believe that? One thing I know for sure is I ain't never gonna be some chief of police!"

"Why not?"

"'Cause the stuff I did! I stole, lied, cheated, got a juvenile record a mile long."

"Samuel," Pauline leaned forward in her chair, "God forgives all our sins. You should know that by now. How long have you been going to my father's church? Almost a year, right? You can become anything you want to—chief of police, teacher, engineer, even a minister and a good one. That's if you really want to, and put God first."

A current of emotion had coursed its way through his body. Again, Pauline made him believe he could achieve just about anything. Anything.

"Reverend Dexter?" Sandra touched his elbow.

"Huh?" He glanced at Sandra.

"Are you okay?"

"I'm okay. Sure. I'm okay." He licked his lips. "Sandra, what…what…what type of relationship did you have with your father? What was he like when you were growing up? Was he a good father?"

"My father? What was he like when I was growing up? Oh, I don't know," she said, in a slight tone of irritation.

"What do you mean, you don't know? What was he like?" Reverend Dexter pulled into the graveled driveway.

"You want the truth?"

"Yes. The truth." He turned off the ignition.

"Reverend Dexter," she said, looking into his eyes, "my father was a conniver!"

His head snapped backward, and the skin between his brows crinkled. "Wow."

"It's the truth, and when I think about some of the things he's done, I hate him." She fumbled to open the door.

Reverend Dexter jumped outside the vehicle. "Wait! Let me help you."

Sandra stepped outside the van, face-to-face with Reverend Dexter.

"At least you knew your father. I, on the other hand, didn't have that luxury. It plagued me most of my life."

"Well, you're probably better off!"

"What could he have possibly done to make you so bitter?"

Sandra cupped her forehead in frustration and looked toward the sky. Tears sprang to her eyes. She suddenly dropped her arms to her sides and looked at Reverend Dexter, stone-faced. "Look. I'm hungry. Can't we go inside and eat?"

Sitting at the dinner table, Sandra took another sip of iced tea. "Dinner was great."

"Want more?" Reverend Dexter pushed his chair from the chrome and glass dining room table, about to get up.

"No. No, thank you." Sandra looked around. It was a typical man's place: spartan. Plenty of books stacked high against the walls. There was an awkward silence. Sandra thought hard for something else to say, then finally, "I guess your wife appreciated your cooking skills, huh?"

Reverend Dexter looked at Sandra in surprise. "I guess." He wiped his mouth with his napkin.

"You guess?"

"Well, yes, she did. She did," Reverend Dexter said shyly, stabbing the chicken on his plate with the tine of his fork. He looked at Sandra. "In fact, I was a better cook than she was, and she knew it!" He laughed, staring into space. "Memories," he said, shaking his head. "Memories."

"Do you ever think about remarrying?" Sandra poured a little more iced tea into her glass.

"Boy! You are full of direct questions tonight, aren't you?" He laughed again.

"Sure, I'd like to remarry." Then he suddenly tapped the handle of his fork on the table. "Now for my question. Why don't I see you in church? You believe in God, don't you?"

Sandra sat upright, placing her elbows on the table. Her face grew serious. "When I was a little girl, I believed in God."

"Well, what about Jimmy?"

"Jimmy believed in himself! Like I should believe in myself!"

"You should believe in both! Let me tell you one thing, Sandra, if you don't have spiritual guidance, it's hard to find yourself. Take it from me. I know. I was lost before He came into my life. He's a loving God."

"Now that's the thing!" Sandra slapped a palm on the table. "I never viewed God as a loving God. All I remember is God's wrath. Practically scared me to death! It's not easy when you are a minister's daughter. You can't imagine!"

"Don't be so sure," he said solemnly. His eyes were cast downward, stabbing the chicken on his plate again.

"But how can you, Reverend Dexter?"

"Don't be so sure." The clang of his fork against the plate permeated the room.

"But how can you?" Sandra slapped a palm on the table again for emphasis.

"Because of my wife, Pauline. That's how! Well, ex-wife." Reverend Dexter poured himself a glass of water. "I know more than you think, Pauline—I mean Sandra!" He placed the pitcher of water on the table. He looked embarrassed, placing his hands over his face. "I'm sorry." He dropped his hands onto the table. "I must confess, Sandra, you remind me so much of my former wife. You both have the same upbringing. She was also a minister's daughter. She also felt the weight." He slumped in his chair. His mind had taken him back to that night on the porch with Pauline.

Reverend Dexter remembered how he had reached into the pocket of his dungarees and pulled out a package of cigarettes.

Pauline looked at him sternly.

He tapped the side of the box and pulled one out, placing it between his lips. "Oh! I ain't gonna light it!" He twirled the cigarette in his mouth, looking at the full moon and bright stars. The neighborhood was silent. He wrapped his arms around his upright knees, rocking back and forth. "Anyway, Pauline, what you want in life? What you wanna do?"

The question had stunned Pauline. She was accustomed to listening, not accustomed to answering questions about herself. What did she want in life? Pauline had to think. She didn't know. Pauline only knew she'd wanted to get married, to have children. But sometimes even this seemed remote, never to come to fruition. Pauline had many dates. Yet when she had made it clear she wasn't going to have sex before marriage, men ended the relationship, never to be seen again. She was twenty years old, with no prospects of marriage, and still a virgin. Was there something wrong with her? Her mother always spoke about virtuous women, but her mother was born during a different time. Young men didn't care about a woman being virtuous—even the young men who had attended church. They seemed to care about their own sexual desire.

"Well, ain't you gonna answer the question?" He had removed the cigarette from between his lips. He leaned forward, tucking one hand underneath his chin.

"Well…maybe…maybe I'd like to become an executive secretary. I…I went to secretarial school and learned stenography…Dictaphone. I can type pretty fast and—"

"You ain't real right now, Pauline. Ain't no passion in what you tellin' me. What is it you really wanna do? Listen, baby, I been on the streets so long I can sniff out bull miles away. What is it you really want to do? Seriously!"

"I don't know! Okay!" Pauline looked like a bewildered child, fixing her eyes on an imaginary target just above his head. Her eyes didn't move from that spot for a long time. "All I know is that I really want to get married to a wonderful man, to have children—plenty of children—and be happy."

"Ain't nothin' wrong wit' that."

"That may not even happen."

"Why? Shoot! You beautiful!" He shot up on his feet, standing directly in front of Pauline. He looked down at the crown of her head.

"Because men want sex first, marriage later!" Pauline had blurted out. "I wasn't raised that way."

"I'll marry you then. I'll wait!"

"Samuel, you are only sixteen years old," Pauline said had sweetly.

"Sixteen goin' on sixty! Pauline, I dated women ten, fifteen years older than me. I don't care 'bout age. All I'm sayin' is, if I make somethin' of myself, I marry you. That's if you wanna, and I'll wait. You worth waitin' for."

Pauline had looked at his face. His face looked serious and much older than his sixteen years. Pauline knew that he was much older than she was when it came to life experiences.

"Okay, Samuel, you will make something of yourself, then we will see. You will finish high school, then go to college. Then, we will see."

Reverend Dexter now rubbed his face wearily. "I loved that woman so much," he finally said, "but when I truly found God, she started to move away from Him…and me." He smoothed his hair from front to back, seemingly talking to himself. "Pauline believed she hadn't experienced a lot in life. I was the only man she had ever been with. So when I was busy trying to establish my career in the church, Pauline was busy…well…busy getting…well…you know." Reverend Dexter gulped down his water.

"I'm sorry."

"Don't be," he said in an icy tone. "The Lord knows what's in my heart. He'll send the right woman along. I'm confident." Reverend Dexter stood up and collected the plates for the dishwasher. When he returned, he placed his palms on the table. "Well, are you ready?"

Sandra stood up. "Certainly."

God's Grace Community Center was a renovated warehouse. It had a small soup kitchen, a large meeting room, and an administrative office. During the summer months, when the children were out of school, the meeting room was transformed into a recreation room during the day. It was a sure way to keep the young people out of trouble. Due to the proceeds from the fundraising event, the church had enough money for the expansion of a real recreation hall. Reverend Dexter was proud of God's Grace Community Center.

"And this is where we conduct our administrative work." Reverend Dexter extended an arm outward as if he were giving a grand tour.

Sandra looked around the well-kept office, which contained four gray metal desks, computers, fax machines, a copier, and a television perched high on a shelf near the ceiling. There were posters of places around the world: a Kenyan Safari, the snow-capped mountains of Switzerland, and the Arc de Triomphe illuminated by the City of Light.

"Take a seat, Sandra. I'd like to check my messages."

Sandra sat on a gray metal chair, watching Reverend Dexter behind one of the desks.

"My! You're early, Pastor Samuel!"

Sandra turned around and set her eyes on a young lady standing in the doorway. She looked about twenty-nine or thirty, and very attractive. A cascade of curly dark hair fell to her shoulders, and she had a clear olive-toned complexion. To Sandra, she had a Latin-American look.

Reverend Dexter turned toward the voice. He excitedly jumped up. "Hey, Camille! I was about to check my messages, but it can wait." He stepped from behind the desk and walked toward the young lady. He gently pulled her toward Sandra.

"Now, Sandra, this is the lady you want to meet. This is Camille. She is my right-hand wo-man!" Reverend Dexter laughed.

"Oh! Stop it, Pastor Samuel."

Camille placed her cup of coffee on a desk. She extended her hand toward Sandra. "Pleased to meet you."

Sandra stood up and shook her hand. "Same here."

Reverend Dexter placed one of his arms around Camille's shoulders. "What do you mean, 'Oh! Stop it, Pastor Samuel?' You know it's true." He turned to Sandra. "Camille is modest. Let me tell you, this woman has been by my side since the creation of God's Grace Community Center. Camille is an attorney and a member of Mount Baptist Church. Her function here is to handle our legal affairs, and Lords knows she has been a great help to us all!" Reverend Dexter walked back to his desk.

Sandra sat back down.

"You're probably thinking, Wow! A Christian lawyer—now that's a concept!" Camille said, slipping off the jacket of her beige pants suit. She carefully placed it on the back of her chair. She turned toward Sandra. "Lord knows the legal profession needs a great deal of moral disinfectant!" She laughed.

Sandra nodded her head in agreement and smiled, watching Camille roll up the sleeves of her white blouse. The smart tortoiseshell eyeglasses Camille placed on the bridge of her slender nose made her look intelligent, sexy. Her apparent ease and confidence made Sandra feel uneasy. Attorney, huh? Sandra thought. I have about five, six years on this girl. Obviously she knows her place in the world. What have I done? What have I achieved? Nothing!

Watch out for the destruction!

"Mama?" Sandra was surprised! This was the first time she heard Mama say more than just her name.

"Excuse me?" said Camille.

Reverend Dexter raised his head from the desk.

"Excuse me!" said Sandra.

Reverend Dexter fastened his eyes on Sandra for a long while. "Camille," he finally said, "this is Sandra Hamilton. Reverend Hamilton's daughter."

Camille looked at Sandra over the top of her glasses, tapping a pencil on the desk. She shot up from her seat. "Do you want something to drink? A cup of coffee, tea maybe? Let's go into the kitchen." She grabbed her cup of coffee and motioned Sandra to follow her. Sandra observed her free-spirited stride. Camille abruptly stopped in the middle of the meeting room bustling with activity. The counselors were setting up chairs for the meeting, others were back and forth in the kitchen preparing refreshments, and the director pored over the night's program. Camille waved to them.

"Now that's Thomas. He's the director. He's wonderful! You are going to like him. And, oh yeah, that's Ron. He's the counselor for our boys ages fifteen through eighteen. Over there is Sara. Sara counsels our girls within the same age group. You will get a chance to meet them all. This place is a redoubt for anyone who has lost his or her way, Sandra. This place is the reality of Pastor Samuel's vision." Camille rubbed Sandra's upper arm and shoulder. She went on to say that she was sorry to hear about Reverend Hamilton's illness, the deaths of her mother and brother. Camille recounted Reverend Hamilton's achievements and his impact on the religious community, and on Pastor Samuel's life. She said that her father, Roy Sanders, was also a man of purpose.

She told Sandra that she was raised in Roxbury, how her father was a tall, big black man who read books about Marcus Garvey and Malcolm X. Although his level of education hadn't gone beyond the eleventh grade, he was a self-taught man and socially conscious. Her mother, Marina Sanchez, half-Mexican and half-Puerto Rican, worked hard as a domestic since those jobs were off the books and hadn't interfered with her ability to collect welfare checks to support her and her brother, Santos. Marina was a quiet and reserved woman, who burned white candles and hung rosary beads on the pictures of Jesus, and she spoke little English, with less education than Camille's father. Yet somehow her parents got along.

She said she became familiar with successful women of color with the help of her father, and Shirley Chisholm was one of his favorites. It was customary for her to recite to her father excerpts from Shirley Chisholm's speeches. He particularly loved "Who Speaks for Us? Women and the Political Agenda." She'd recite the speeches loudly and proudly, looking down at the piece of paper in her hand, and her father would smile and kiss her on her cheek, saying, Yeah, that's my baby girl, gonna be somebody, gonna be somebody.

"One thing I am truly grateful for," Camille said, her voice now quavering, eyes misty, "is that my dad lived to see me graduate from law school. That day was the proudest day of our lives. Although my dad has been dead for a long time now," Camille's voice began to strengthen, "he is with me always." She gently tapped her fist against her chest. "I hear his voice everyday!"

"You do?"

"Yes, I do—especially when I'm not feeling my best." Camille's eyes began to mist again.

"Your father meant a lot to you?"

"More than life itself."

"So how did you deal with the loss?"

"With the help of my other father. God is good all the time. But I still have *mi madre*. She's alive and healthy. Now! What would you like to drink?"

"A cup of tea with lemon and honey would be nice."

"Coming up! Take a seat, Sandra. The meeting will begin in about fifteen to twenty minutes. I'll be back."

Meanwhile, back at Sandra's house, Nurse Pavony, a middle-aged, heavy-set woman, who wore orange lipstick and combed her gray hair into a bun at the nape of her neck, handed Lilly and Enid a copy of a pamphlet with the message: "Lasting is the song, though the singer passes." Enid and Lilly looked at each other, knowing what this meant.

"I knocked on Sandra's bedroom door, but I don't believe she's home," said Nurse Pavony.

"No, she's not." Enid said.

"Well, I must say Reverend Hamilton has put up a valiant fight for life. I have never seen anyone so determined to live in my twenty years' experience." She sat down on the couch. "Take a seat. I'd like to explain some things to you. First, I've already called Doctor Albright. He's on his way. I am going to be frank. It would be a miracle if Reverend Hamilton makes it through the next forty-eight hours." She stopped to look at Lilly and Enid.

Lilly shook her head. A tear streamed down her face.

Enid remained frozen.

"His blood circulation is decreasing. So you will notice that his skin will be cool to the touch. There is also swelling of his arms and legs. I assure you, though, that this is a natural part of the departing process, and he will not feel any discomfort at all." Nurse Pavony had said this as if death were as pedestrian as breathing air. "You will also notice he'll have less ability to swallow. This may cause saliva to remain in the back of his throat," she touched her neck, "making somewhat of a gurgling sound. Often, changing the patient's position can relieve this. If it gets very bad, Doctor Albright can prescribe medication to dry up the saliva, but I don't think that this will be necessary. The rate of his breathing pattern is slowing down. Eventually, as everything else in the body slows down, the breathing rate also slows down. Sometimes there may be a lapse of fifteen to twenty seconds between breaths. When this very slow breathing pattern continues, you will know that death is near. Do you have any questions?" There was no response. "Well, if you do, you can always call me or Doctor Albright." Nurse Pavony slapped her knees before getting up from the couch. "Well, I believe my job is done."

"Our job is done when we have reached out and brought as many people as we can to the Lord," said Reverend Dexter. "Our mission is done when everyone we encounter has discovered and utilized the talents God has given him or her. We all have a purpose in life—whether we acknowledge God or not!"

"That's right!" Someone in the audience interjected.

"But first we have to discover what our purpose is. When we discover our purpose, we must energize ourselves. God said, 'Be fruitful and multiply!' One doesn't become fruitful by sitting down! The word 'fruitful' means producing results! And once you know your purpose, stay focused! Don't get caught up in the little things of this world—they'll just sidetrack you from achieving your goals. Romans, chapter twelve, verse two says, 'Do not conform any longer to the pattern of this world, but be transformed by the renewing of your mind...' And that's what God's Grace Community Center is all about. It's about renewing your mind to achieve success in a godly manner. Isn't God an intelligent god?"

"Yes!" the audience replied, as if in a military drill.

"Say what?" Reverend Dexter cupped his ear. "I can't hear you!"

"Yes!"

"And can you be successful in life and still love God?"

"Yes!"

"And can you be rich and still love God?"

"Yes!"

"But what must we do?"

"We must put God first!"

"Yes! That's right! We must always put God first so our success in life will not become our master!"

Wow! Sandra felt the electricity in the room, amazed to see how many young people were in attendance on a Saturday night. Love and respect emanated everywhere. Sandra looked at Reverend Dexter. Camille had said that God's Grace Community Center was the fruition of his vision, and her respect for him grew even more. Reverend Dexter had found his purpose in life, and he was helping others to find theirs. Sandra didn't know her purpose, but she was never more willing to find out.

CHAPTER 13
ENDINGS

Hey, Babe, sorry to hear about your father...

Sandra's eyes raced to the bottom of the letter—Les. She sat down at the kitchen table and pulled a tissue from the pocket of her terry cloth robe, pressing it against her lips.

> *I guess you're probably wondering how I know. Gee told me. I know that things have been tough for you within the past few years, Jimmy and your mother. I'm sorry. Babe, whether you believe me or not, I really mist you.*

Funny how you detect a misspelling even in mourning, Sandra thought. It seemed so trifling. Yet she remembered that Les was always a terrible speller. He'd write things like: "I want to come see you, butt I'm afraid I can't." With all his worldly knowledge, the man still didn't know the difference between but and a butt. And now he mist her. This was just one of the endearing qualities Sandra remembered after Les was out of her life. What endearing qualities would Sandra remember of her father? She did not know—but this she did know: She didn't have any more tears to cry. They'd been exhausted. There was a drought, although people had expected a monsoon. Yet death had different ways of affecting people. Lilly waxed her father's desk a million times a day, and when her tears splattered on the glossy surface, she'd wax it again and again and again. Enid was unusually quiet, but her face was still a rock. Uncle Rufus was in a drunken stupor, sitting in a corner with his head between his hands. And Reverend Dexter stood in her father's bedroom long after the coroner removed the body. Now it was the body—not her father.

. . . the boutique is still making good profit. I hired several people to keep up with the pace. Still things are not the same without you. Why do people realize a good thing after it's gone?

Sandra folded her lips into her mouth.

Gee said she was going to drive to New York after your father's funeral. We were talking about hanging out in a jazz club or something, just to capture the good old days. Why don't you come along? It would be good to see you. I know that I messed up big time, but that doesn't mean we have to say goodbye. Goodbye is too final...

Goodbye is final, Sandra thought. She had said goodbye to her father three days ago. Nurse Pavony had said her father might be able to hear her, encouraging Sandra to say all that she needed to say. She slowly approached her father's bedside. Stony death was on his face, and Sandra grimaced, covering her mouth to keep from screaming. Love, hatred, pity rose in equal measure inside her. The little girl's love for her father counteracted the grown daughter's hatred, and the ravages of death provoked her pity. She slid to the floor, holding her father's skeletal hand. Sandra gradually stood on her knees, pressing her lips close to her father's ear: "Daddy, I...I . . I know Jimmy loved you, and you took very good care of us. We were never with want. Mama once told me that. And Mama? Oh, how she loved you with all her heart."

With all my heart.

Reverend Hamilton immediately stirred, opening a weak eye. His mouth labored to form words.

Sandra snapped upright on her knees. "You hear Mama! Don't you, Daddy? Don't you?" His mouth moved, but words did not come forth. Small bubbles collected at the corners of his lips. Sandra laughed uncontrollably. "You do hear Mama! You do hear her!"

Nurse Pavony had rushed into the room, concern in her eyes, touching Sandra on her shoulder.

"Are you okay?"

"Oh! I'm okay! Goodbye, Daddy, goodbye!" she had said, choking on her laughter.

Heavy footsteps approached the kitchen fast and furious. Sandra quickly folded Les's letter, stuffing it into the pocket of her robe. She looked up. Enid was standing in the doorway looking like Satan in a flowered muumuu.

"I know that you, your brother, and your mother never liked me! But I'm your aunt, nonetheless, and at the rate that this family is dying, I think we had better learn how to get along before it's too late!"

Sandra was perplexed. "What exactly are you talking about, too late?"

Enid plopped in a chair, its legs groaning under her weight. "I'm talking about family—real family members sticking together—not some outsider infiltrating the family circle for his own ulterior motive!"

"Again, what exactly are you saying, Enid?" Sandra cradled her forehead in her palm, trying her best to maintain composure.

"Don't act stupid with me! You know exactly what I mean and who I'm talking about!"

"Enid, if you are referring to Reverend Dexter, I don't want to hear it. Daddy—your brother—is barely cold, and you're starting some mess!"

"Don't talk to me like I'm some junkyard dog! I'm just trying to protect you!" Enid jumped up from her chair.

"Protect me? Protect me?" Sandra frowned. "Protect me from what?" She stood up.

"From that false-faced, God-forsaken con artist. That's what! You think he cared about your father? Cares about you? Huh! He's just after the money he thinks your father left you—that's all!"

"What? What? What?" Sandra walked in small circles around the kitchen, with both hands pressed to her ears. "What are you saying? Who told you this? Claudia Wheats?" Sandra stopped and stood directly in front of Enid. "You want to know something? You want to know something? You are one miserable, man-starved hag!"

"So now I'm a miserable hag, huh?" Enid threw her hands in the air. "I'm a miserable hag. Well, if you don't believe me, ask him! Ask him about his mama!"

Sandra felt Enid's hot breath on her face. Enid bolted out the door, and Sandra heard Enid's voice echo down the hallway, "You sorry excuse for a woman!" Those words hung in the air, and the water that quickly sprang to Sandra's eyes was contrary to the belief that she did not have any more tears to cry.

Later that day, news spread of Reverend Hamilton's death. People were combing their closets for their best black suits, the phone was ringing off the hook, flowers, sympathy cards and fruit baskets were being delivered, and funeral arrangements were being made. Yet all Sandra thought about was the gun shot from the hip, "You sorry excuse for a woman!" Enid had hit the mark, the soft underbelly, and doubt that can bring one low was starting to take root.

Well, he did lie about his wife. Told people she was dead. Was this the same with his mother? Why did Enid say, "Ask him about his mama?" Was she in on the scam too? He did say he had led a con artist's life. Had said he was a bitter young man with no direction, no love for himself or anybody else. Sold reefer up and down 125th Street to adults as well as children. Graduated to heroin. Stole fancy cars, loved another man's woman. You name it, he'd done it. Came straight from the horse's mouth. And why was he talking about being rich and serving God? Shouldn't his primary concern be about serving God? It seems like money is on his mind. Coming around here trying to make his way into people's hearts: Lilly's, Daddy's, mine—where did that come from? That mine part. Maybe that's his plan—get to the father so to get to the daughter. Saving souls is big business. Acting like he wants to save the poor little lamb, then turn her upside down and shake every coin from her pocket. Is that how it worked? That's probably how it worked! But...but...what about this mine part? Making his way into my heart? He's not in my heart! Les was in my heart, and I got rid of him. Shook him out of my system! Well, he did invite me for dinner. I mean, when a man invites you for dinner he must have some interest. I mean, I could see myself with him, but that's before all this happened! Before I knew about this scam. Got to be a scam! He can get any woman he wants. That's why they are all flocking to Mount Baptist Church, and most of those women are doing something with their lives. They got it together! So why else would he want to spend time with me? Got to be a scam, got to be!

Sandra's head ached. Fragmented thoughts raced across her mind, bumping up against one another, causing confusion. She lay on her father's bed and closed her eyes, looking down a long tunnel of darkness.

She heard Lilly fumbling in her father's closet. "Sandy, I think your father wanted to wear this suit, right? Sandy?"

"Lilly, what did you say? I'm sorry." Sandra propped herself up on her elbows.

Lilly held two of her father's suits in the air, one navy blue, the other charcoal gray. "I said, I think your father wanted to wear this suit?" Lilly raised the navy blue suit a little higher.

"Yes, that one."

"Lord, Lord, I still can't believe I'm doing this." Lilly put the suits on Reverend Hamilton's bed before wiping her eyes, but the tears kept coming. "Lord, Lord, Lord."

On the day of Reverend Hamilton's funeral, it rained buckets, torrents. Each raindrop was pregnant with power, flattening the grass and parting it in the middle like hair. The sun that morning was not in a position to negotiate a ray, to muscle its way through the clouds. Yet many people on route to Mount Baptist Church wore dark shades. Lilly said the rain was a good sign, but just the opposite for a wedding. Sandra sat in the front pew in a black dress. Her face was calm, but her hands underneath her black handbag were trembling. Alongside her right sat Enid and Uncle Rufus, while alongside her left sat Gee, Laurence, Rita, and Lilly.

The church was filled with dignitaries of the religious community and the entire congregation. There were also firemen, policemen, and people of the medical profession, all of whom were touched by Reverend Hamilton's generosity of volunteer work. No doubt, he was deeply loved and respected.

Since the church pews were filled to capacity—and Mount Baptist Church was ample indeed—others sat in the overflow room downstairs, a room designed specifically for situations like this. The overflow room in the basement contained a multitude of chairs and surrounding large speakers so that the ceremony in the sanctuary could be heard. Still, the overflow room was filled to capacity, and scores of others stood outside the church. There was a sea of people stretching as far as the eyes could see. Raindrops, like stones, raced down the landscape of their black umbrellas, dripping off the edge in long linear patterns.

Surrounding the altar, with its red backdrop and large golden cross, were standing wreath arrangements of yellow and orange roses with red carnations, and baskets of pink and white Gladiolus. A cherry wood casket with brass handles wasn't far from the pulpit. The casket was made from the same wood as the magnificently carved rails that separated the altar from the pews. Inside the casket rested an emaciated Reverend Hamilton, wearing an altered navy blue suit, and his hands were gently placed across his chest. Enid demanded a closed casket funeral, but everyone else disagreed. People would remember Reverend Hamilton as he was not as he is, they reasoned. But Enid would not give in, demanding a closed casket. Finally, Sandra said, "Enid, you are overruled!" And that was that.

Sandra looked at the program of her father's funeral, believing that Good Faith Funeral Home had done a wonderful job. Its cover said, "In Loving Memory of Reverend Dr. Trevor Hamilton Jr.," and below was a handsome picture of her father. Underneath the picture were the words:

February 12, 1922–September 10, 1992
Saturday, September 15, 1992,
Eleven o'clock AM
Mount Baptist Church,
174 Marlborough Street,
Cambridge, Massachusetts 02138
Reverend Samuel Dexter, Officiating

Sandra's hands shook as she held the program. Laurence touched her wrist. His warm fingertips were soothing, and her hands stopped shaking momentarily. Laurence now looked like a grown man: six feet tall, muscular, with a goatee, and auburn dreadlocks down his back. Sandra looked into his deep mature eyes and smiled. He smiled too, brightening Sandra's sullen space. That same smile greeted her several days ago when she had opened her front door.

"May JAH be with you, Aunt Sandra!"

"Laurence? Naw! Can't be! Look at you. Damn!"

"Me in the flesh!" His arms were wide open. Sandra slipped into the open space until she hit his chest.

"Move aside, Laurence!" It was Rita, who was still petite like her mother, but husky in personality. "Greetings, Aunt Sandra." She kissed Sandra on the cheek.

"Greetings to you too," Sandra said between laughter and tears. "Where's your mother?"

"Ta da!"

"Gee!"

"How are you doing under the circumstances?" Gee said softly.

"Best I can, Gee. Best I can. It's so good to see you all."

They hugged each other.

"Well, the next time we get together," Rita said, "I hope it's for a graduation or something."

"I hear you, Rita. I hear you," Gee had said. "Let's get our bags and come inside."

At the church, someone gripped Sandra's shoulder. She looked up and saw the face of an elderly white woman, wearing an enormous black hat cocked to the side, covering one of her eyes.

"Are you Trevor's little girl?"

Sandra was startled. "Yes. Yes. I am."

"I knew you when you were this high." The woman placed her hand knee level. The rings on her wrinkled fingers were dazzling. "I'm Loring Brownstone. I met your father at a Christian conference back in the 70s. He was a marvelous speaker." The woman placed her fingertips on her chest upon saying this. "Since then, we've been fast friends. I'm so so sorry for your loss—and ours."

"Why thank you, Ms. Brownstone. I appreciate it."

The woman slowly walked away.

It went on like that for some time, except the names and faces changed. A little later, Janet, Carl, Jamie, and Maureen walked up to the front pew to pay their respects. Janet hugged Sandra tightly, and little Terrence, nestled in Janet's arms, slapped Sandra's face. "Ooh! You bad boy." Sandra was exhausted, and the service hadn't even started yet. She caught glimpse of Reverend Dexter. He was talking to Reverend Thornhill near the altar. He looked at the front pew and nodded. Everyone nodded in return, except Enid. She rolled her eyes and sucked her teeth. The gesture didn't seem to bother Reverend Dexter, but the sight of him agitated Sandra, and a terrible heaviness settled in her stomach, sweat dripping between her breasts. So she closed her eyes, listening to the organ, wanting peace of mind.

Yet her mind roamed, cutting into her want of stillness. Buried thoughts rose with urgency, seemingly from nowhere. Her mind was taking her to places she didn't want to go. The mournful sound of the organ pressed against her soul—heavy, burdensome, like his weight had pressed against her twelve-year-old body. Sandra had found herself on her knees in the middle of her bedroom floor, trying to hide his stains in the middle of her sheets with talcum powder. It was washing day. She balled them up and quickly stuffed them at the bottom of the baby-blue lattice basket, heaping layers of her bobby socks, jumpers, t-shirts, and shorts on top. She ran down to the laundry room. Her mother was sorting the colors from the whites when she spotted the bird fluttering near the window. "Oh, look, an Eastern Bluebird! How rare in New England." The bird looked like any old bird to Sandra. But her mother was so excited that she grabbed a handful of sheets, pressing them to her face. She suddenly frowned, sniffing rapidly. They were Sandra's sheets. Her mother's eyes flung open.

The white walls moved toward the middle of the room, closing in on Sandra. Her mother snapped the sheets open and examined them carefully, scratching something with her fingernail. Sniffed again. Her eyes—like evil slits—had slowly landed on Sandra. "Go clean yourself!" she barked. Sandra looked down at her navy-blue Keds in a pool of yellow water.

The organ rose to a crescendo, startling Sandra, and it suddenly occurred to her, mouthing the words, Mama knew. A tear rolled down Sandra's cheek followed by a series of them.

Gee reached over to hug Sandra as she sobbed uncontrollably, her shoulders heaving up and down. "Don't worry. All of this will be over soon," she said softly. Sandra let out a mournful wail, remembering the words of her mother's poem:

> *I know as well as you, but try to forget, and make conversation of simple grain. And all the while listening to myself not really speaking at all…*

Gee rubbed Sandra's shoulders. "It's okay, Sandra. It will be all over soon. I'm here, just remember that. I'm always here."

Sandra rested her head on Gee's shoulder, burying her face in Gee's blonde hair.

"Shhh," Gee said, as if hushing a baby to sleep. "It's going to be all right. Just take deep breaths, Sandra. Deep breaths."

Sandra took deep breaths like she had never taken before: inhaling, exhaling, inhaling, and exhaling, slowly, deep from her belly.

"That's it, Sandra. That's it. Concentrate on your breathing," Gee said in a soothing voice. "Concentrate like your life depends on it. In and out, in and out, in and out, slooowly. That's it. Feel the rhythm?"

Sandra nodded her head, and gradually the thoughts in her mind began to fade. Her mind became still, maybe momentarily, but Sandra didn't care. She closed her eyes, still inhaling and exhaling, slowly, concentrating on her breathing. And then her spirit seemed to float, as if it were leaving her body. She fell asleep—a deep sleep Sandra had been robbed of for several days.

When Sandra awoke, Reverend Dexter was at the altar, visibly shaken. Sweat was pouring from his brow, competing with the rain outside. His tears joined in, making way through the competition. Sandra heard Enid murmur, "Crocodile tears." She then heard Lilly's weeping, other people sniffling, and a "Yes, Lord" here and there.

"…and I never knew my daddy as a young boy growing up in the streets of Harlem. I knew my mama, certainly, but not my daddy. But when I entered young adulthood, however, I became acquainted with my Father—the Lord." Reverend Dexter paused. "The one who had been there all the time without my knowing, even before the sun's rays cast shadows upon the earth. Then many years later I was fortunate—like all of us—to have met Reverend Hamilton. Although he was gravely ill, I saw the powerful light beaming from his eyes." Reverend Dexter wiped a tear from his cheek with the back of his hand. "And we were also blessed to have first seen this powerful light manifest in his healthy body and earth-shattering voice." There was a stir from the pews. "But when he was ill, he spoke just above a whisper, then eventually not at all. He moved to writing on pieces of paper, then eventually not at all. But I say to you today that the light in his eyes was still blinding! And I knew I made a profound connection with this man—likening him to be the earthly father I had never known growing up. The father I yearned to play basketball with, to take long walks with. But I only learned about this yearning when I met Reverend Hamilton. I didn't know that I yearned for a meaningful father figure when I was a boy. I thought I could handle things myself. But nobody can truly handle things him or herself. We need God—Amen!—or someone who can guide us to Him. And looking at this large congregation, I realize that Reverend Hamilton had done a lot of directing, a lot of shepherding. I am humbled before him." Reverend Dexter took a long look at the casket. "He will be missed, oh, Lord. He will be missed. But not for long, Lord, not for long. We look to your promise, Lord, that Reverend Hamilton will once again rise—and walk!"

"Oh! Yes! Lord! We look to your promise, Lord," a weeping woman cried out. "We look to your promise."

"Jesus said, 'I am the resurrection and the life. He who believes in me, though he may die, he shall live. And whoever lives and believes in me shall never die.' Do you believe in this promise from God, my brothers and sisters?"

There was an unwavering "Yes!" in the church.

"Then let us wipe away our tears and rejoice! Because this man, Reverend Hamilton, who had touched all of our lives, will come back to us in the glory of God. Yes! He has discarded his earthly body. Yes! He has left this earthly realm. Yes! He'll no longer walk among us! But his spirit—Oh! Lord!—his spirit will live! Forever!"

The rest of the ceremony was a blur to Sandra. She only remembered the procession of cars on Fresh Pond Parkway en route to Mount Auburn Cemetery, the cars passing through its Egyptian Revival entry gate, slowly approaching her father's resting place next to her mother's resting place, and other notable people buried there. Later, she remembered the mountains of food shoved in people's mouths while they reminisced about her father. Sandra stretched her arms and yawned, happy the day had ended. She closed her eyes and pulled the covers over her shoulders. She took deep breaths, inhaling, exhaling, inhaling, and exhaling, slowly, deep from the belly.

CHAPTER 14
BEGINNINGS

Reverend Hamilton was gone, settled among the dust, but the smell in his room had not. The smell grew stronger weeks after his demise, of decay and shoe polish. Although Sandra and Lilly had stripped the bed and changed the mattress, the odor clung to the walls like a layer of sweat upon skin. Sandra even swore the walls now had sheen to them, dragging her fingertips alongside the coolness of the paint, rubbing her fingers together. Sure enough, there was residue that had not been there before—his spirit was present.

Lilly couldn't attest to all that. Certainly, she couldn't deny the smell of decay, that of his dying flesh, and she knew the smell of shoe polish derived from his life-long standing of dignity. Reverend Hamilton, though he looked mummified during his last days, refused to see any visitor before being propped in a chair, wearing a starched white shirt, perfectly pleated trousers, and a pair of spit-shine shoes. But his spirit present? No, Lilly couldn't buy that. She reminded Sandra that perhaps her father's spirit was in her memory rather than in his room. Sandra had not said a word after that. She knew what she knew, didn't need anyone to validate it. So she kept her thoughts to herself, as everything else— like her hearing Mama's voice that arose each morning with the distant chirping of the birds, then blossomed into a swelling sound.

Since Sandra couldn't get rid of her father's odor, she was bent on getting rid of his clothes. The less of her father's belongings in the house, the better, she thought. She wiped the dampness from her forehead with the back of her hand, kneeling over a pile of her father's woolen slacks. Although she was dressed in a white tank top and khaki shorts, she was sweating profusely during this spell of Indian Summer. "Hey Rita, turn up the air conditioner, will you?"

"Sure." Rita carefully removed one of Reverend Hamilton's jackets from a hanger, a tweed jacket with suede patches at the elbows. She dropped it into a box, then walked across the room. Her sneakers made sharp squeaky sounds on the shiny hardwood floor, and the additional blast of air that swooshed through the vents traveled up her denim jumper.

"That's better. Thanks. So! You didn't answer me the first time, Rita. Do you have a boyfriend?"

Rita remained silent for a moment, thinking about what her mother had said before she jumped into a rental car headed toward New York to visit Les: "You be good to your aunt while I'm gone, you hear?" Rita smiled, walking back to the closet. "Why do aunts always ask that question?"

Sandra looked up and shrugged. "I don't know. Guess we don't know what else to ask."

Rita giggled. "I do. I do. His name is Jarod. He's seventeen and nice people. He goes to my school. Mom likes him a lot! She said his personality reminds her of Dad." Rita reached for a gray metal box on the closet shelf and opened it. "Aunt Sandra, what do you want me to do with this? Looks like small toys and a picture."

"What? Let me see that." Sandra reached for the box. "Now why in the world would he keep this?" she said underneath her breath. Sandra sat down on her father's bed.

Rita sat next to her, folding her hands on her lap. "Do these toys belong to you?"

"Well, the red ball and jacks are mine. I had to be about...I think about...twelve years old." Sandra's eyes widened. "Well, I'll be damned," she said softly.

"Are you okay?"

"I'm okay, I guess." Sandra placed the ball back into the box. "Just wondering why he kept these things?"

"What else is in there?"

Sandra reached for a neatly folded cloth. "Oh my God. My two front teeth?" She rested her palm on the side of her face, shaking her head. "I was only seven years old. I never knew he was so sentimental!"

"Well, Mom says the dead cough up a lot of secrets." Rita stood up, then bent forward with her hands on her knees, peering into the box. Her dreadlocks fell to her face.

Sandra looked at Rita. "Your mother is right!" She placed the small teeth on the white bedspread. "Wait a minute! Wait a minute! This is your father's blue and white whistle he'd gotten from Cracker Jack!" Sandra laughed out loud, throwing her head back. "Jimmy loved this whistle! How Daddy got his hands on this, I'll never know! And look! Jimmy's yo-yo."

Rita grabbed Jimmy's toys and held them to her chest. "These are my father's toys! Can I have them, Aunt Sandra? Please."

"Sure."

"Thank you!" Rita placed them on the bed, fondling them. Sandra looked on, grinning ear to ear.

Rita glanced into the box. "Aunt Sandra, who's that?" She pointed to a black-and-white picture of a small boy. "Can't be my father."

"I don't know who this is, Rita." Sandra frowned. She picked up the picture and turned it around. There was handwriting on the back: Just in case you want to know what he looks like. That's all it said—no date, no name. The little dark boy with wild hair looked about two years old, wearing a striped t-shirt, overalls, and high-top shoes. Sandra looked at the picture closely. "Beats me." She threw the picture on the bed.

Rita picked it up. "He's cute, though."

"Yeah, cute."

Sandra suddenly needed air. She grabbed her father's car keys, her handbag, the picture, and headed for the door. "Rita, I have to pick up my clothes from the cleaners. I'll be back!" She had lied to Rita—twice. She didn't have any clothes in the cleaners, and she knew who that little boy was. Her stomach confirmed it. He was her little half-brother. The little boy she and Jimmy had never known, kept hushed over the years, a secret swept underneath the rug. Mama never spoke about it. Her father only whispered about it, because the little boy was another one of his mistakes, a mistake he'd prayed to God for forgiveness.

But hadn't God brought the little boy into this world? Sandra thought. Then why should God have to forgive His unique creation? How could this little boy with shiny button eyes, two bottom teeth, and dribble on his chin be a mistake, anyway? Well, mistake or no mistake, Sandra reasoned, this was her half-brother, the only brother she had left in this world. She was going to try to find him. He would be close to her age by now. His mother's name was Trudy—that she knew for sure. Trudy had been a member of her father's congregation years ago. That's all she had to go on. She would talk to Lilly first. Yes, Lilly had known what went on in Mount Baptist Church, what was still going on in Mount Baptist Church.

Sandra drove around the block for the fourth time, in circles like her mind. She thought again and again how her father had thrown a tight rope around people, innocent people—Mama, Jimmy, herself, this little boy and his mother—like rustled cattle, for the sole purpose of inflicting pain. People's lives were scarred, and now he goes to the grave unpunished, a respectable man in the memory of his congregation. Sandra couldn't stand him. He was dead, yes, but her disgust was alive, had grown fat by the fuel of hatred. Huh! He didn't want anyone to know about his so-called mistake. Yeah, well, she was going to find him—her last act of defiance!

Sandra grew weary of circling the same territory, on the road and in her mind. She parked in front her house and pressed her head against the steering wheel. She really didn't want to go back inside, certainly didn't want to touch his clothes. Sandra sat in the car thinking, what was the purpose of this life? Things seemed to just happen, no rhyme or reason, to good people. No, there wasn't a purpose—to anything. Sandra lifted her head from the steering wheel. Well, there had to be a reason why she heard Mama's voice. There had to be a purpose in that—but what? Still she hadn't known, frustrating.

A tap of her forehead on the steering wheel led to another, when an old but familiar thought crept inside her mind: A drink. I could use a drink. She quickly gunned the engine, heading for a trendy watering hole in the square.

Sandra parked the car, then walked along the sidewalk crowded with tourists, glancing around for a bar. It was late afternoon, but the September sun was beaming, glistening on the heads of tourists. Why were they so fascinated with Harvard Square, anyway? You can't walk one inch without stumbling on a damn tourist! she thought. Sandra shoved her way through the people, parting them like the Red Sea, and walked ahead, occasionally bumping a shoulder or two. She pulled out the picture from her handbag and continued to walk along the sidewalk, looking at that chubby little face—not looking anywhere else. The deep pool of sadness in his shiny large eyes drew her. Perhaps he had been crying just before the picture was taken, then someone pulled out a camera, a snap of the flashbulb, blinded by the light, his sadness immortalized.

When Sandra looked up, she was not standing in front of a bar, but a store she had not seen before, named ART N FACTS. There was a sign in the shop's window. Wanted: Manager. Sandra quickly shoved the picture back into her handbag and, to her surprise, walked in. The store contained many African photographs, paintings, sculpture, instruments, clothing, and books—the books were the FACTS, Sandra guessed. The store reminded her of Nubia, the African boutique she had once owned. The familiarity of the place soothed her. She picked up a black-and-white photograph and examined it closely. It was a silhouette of a woman standing near an open door looking out to sea. The bottom of the picture included the inscription: "Door of No Return in the House of Slaves. Dakar, Senegal."

"Does the picture interest you?" A deep voice asked.

Sandra turned around, looking into the face of an elderly baldheaded man with a white beard. He was wearing a dashiki made of Kente cloth.

"Yes. It does. Reminds me of the time I was there. House of Slaves on Goree Island. Africans were kept there before being herded to sail the Middle Passage. It's a national museum now."

"That's correct." The man drew closer. "Where else have you been in Africa?"

Sandra carefully put the picture back in its place. She turned to face the man again. "Oh, Ghana, Nigeria, Ethiopia, Morocco, Kenya, and, of course, Senegal."

"Most memorable sight?"

"The eleven churches in Lalibela, Ethiopia—all hewn out of the solid rock of mountains. Breathtaking."

"Oh! Yes! Yes! Spectacular, indeed! I've been there, too! If I'm not mistaken, I believe the Church of Emanuel is the largest."

"I don't think so. I think the Church of the Savior of the World is the largest. It measures one hundred ten feet long, seventy-seven feet wide and thirty-six feet high. Facts about Africa stay in my head. Don't ask me why." Sandra placed her hands on her hips.

The man looked into the air. "Are you sure? I could have sworn—Come!" He motioned to Sandra, and she followed him. He picked up a book a few feet away and thumbed through the pages. His eyebrows raised. "Impressive! You're right! Oh, you must excuse me. My name is Winston Maxwell. I am one of the owners of this place." He extended his hand.

"My name is Sandra Hamilton."

They shook hands.

"So how can I help you today, Sandra?" The man snapped the book shut and placed it on a nearby table. "Are you looking for anything particular?"

"Well, actually, I want to inquire about the manager's position." Sandra was astonished when those words tumbled from her mouth, but maintained composure.

"Have you worked in retail before?" The man clasped his hands behind his back, bouncing on his toes.

"Sure. I was co-owner of an African boutique in New York a few years ago. I also worked in various department stores here in Cambridge. I was born and raised here, but I lived in New York for a while."

The man's eyes brightened. "You don't say." A small crowd of people entered the store. The man quickly glanced at them. "I'll be with you in a moment." He looked at Sandra again. "Listen! Can you come back next week? I'd like you to meet my wife. She is the other half of this business, and I can't hire anyone without her approval."

"I can come back."

The man handed Sandra his card. "Call to set up an appointment. Bring your resume. My wife needs to look at a resume."

"Okay."

The man clapped his hands. "Now! I must attend business. Good day, Sandra." He bowed his head.

"Good day, Mr. Maxwell."

"Winston," he whispered. "Call me Winston."

Sandra approached Lilly later that day, handing her the picture of the little boy. "I found this in Daddy's closet. I believe he's my half-brother. Turn the picture around. Read what it says on the back."

"My Lord! That's Trudy's handwriting!"

"Do you remember Trudy?"

Lilly sat back in her chair at the kitchen table. "I remember Trudy, all right. We all—meaning the ladies at church—called her Trudy 'cause she kept intruding in people's business! Yes, Lord. That was Trudy! Always in somebody's business."

"What happened to Trudy? Do you know?" Sandra folded her hands on the table.

"I don't rightly know." Lilly looked puzzled. "Seems like she just disappeared off the face of the earth. Didn't tell anybody where she was going!"

"Well, what's Trudy's real name?"

"Don't know that either, but I can find out. You see, Trudy didn't come to church much. I just knew her as Trudy. Now you're talking many years ago, but somebody will be able to tell me something." Lilly paused, placing her hands flat on the table. "Why all the questions, Sandy?"

"I want to find my half-brother."

"Lord, have mercy. Why?"

"Because he's the only brother I have left. I need to find him, talk to him. He's part of this family, and I want to be connected to the remaining family members—well, except Enid." Sandra smiled faintly. "And you are a family member too, Lilly, because you've not only been a close friend to me, but a mother as well. And I want you to stay right here in this house. There's so much room, and I don't want to sell it. I plan to settle in Cambridge for a while. And like a daughter, I want to take good care of you for a change. You've been taking good care of us for so long now." Sandra clasped Lilly's hands.

"Well, I'm mighty grateful, Sandy. You know I'll stay and support you in whatever you want to do. 'Cause you sure are the daughter I never had, but always wanted." Lilly's eyes grew moist.

"Thanks. So you'll ask the ladies in church about Trudy?"

"Sure."

"Do you want to take this picture?"

"Can't hurt." Lilly took the snapshot and placed it next to her. Her face turned serious. "And speaking of church, Sandy, Reverend Dexter been asking about you. He said after your father's funeral he's been trying to talk to you, but you've been avoiding him. He's a little worried. So he asked me to talk to you. What's the matter all of a sudden?"

Sandra really didn't know what was the matter. She only knew Enid's words had snagged on her insecurity, like a sweater on a fence, and hung there. Why would Reverend Dexter want to spend time with her if it weren't for some scheme? Especially with those women he could choose from, professional women, too. They made her feel inadequate. "Daddy's dead!" she blurted out. "There's no need for Reverend Dexter to talk to me now."

"What? The man cares for your well being. You know that."

"No, I don't know that. How do you know that? How much do you know about Reverend Dexter, Lilly?"

"What? Why you so quick to say that? Lord, Lord, something has gone wrong here! Who you been talking to? Enid? Yeah, smell like Enid had a hand in this one!" Lilly smacked her lap. "Tell me what disease Enid been spreading now?" Lilly stood up with her hands on her hips. "'Cause Reverend Dexter is God's gift to Mount Baptist Church!"

"Lilly, don't get yourself upset. Sit down. Please."

Lilly looked at Sandra's pleading eyes and sat down, flattening the creases in the front of her dress with her hands.

"Are you calm?"

"Oh! I'm calm!"

"No, you're not."

"Am too!"

"Okay." Sandra placed her hands flat on the table. "Remember you told me Reverend Dexter's wife was dead?"

Lilly nodded her head.

"Where did you get that information?" Sandra drew closer to Lilly.

"Well, the sisters at church told me Reverend Dexter himself said so. Why?"

"His wife is not dead. He's divorced, and he told me so. Don't you think it's strange that he would lie?"

"Well…well…"

"And, Lilly, if it's so easy for Reverend Dexter to lie about something so simple, don't you think it would be easy for him to lie about other things as well? I mean, he just worked his way into this family like he had a purpose in mind."

"I thought he was just being respectful since your father was the pastor of the church. I don't see nothing wrong with that. That's the only purpose I believe he had in mind, truthfully." Lilly pursed her lips.

"Lilly, you have a good heart, but sometimes a good heart may be in the wrong place. I just think Reverend Dexter is up to something."

"Just be careful of what Enid says, Sandy. She's always been full of vinegar and venom. You know that. Maybe Reverend Dexter had good reason for not telling the truth about his wife to the women at church—but he told you, didn't he? He didn't have to do that!"

Silence.

Lilly reached for the picture on the table before heading for the door. "Anyway, I'll see what I can find out about Trudy."

"Thank you, Lilly. I'd appreciate that." Sandra rubbed her face and sighed, wishing she had as much faith as Lilly. She stood up from the table and headed for her father's study; perhaps there was some liquor inside. Sandra approached the door, then stopped, with a hand resting on the doorknob, thinking about her action, now that she was calmer compared to the earlier part of the day. She stepped away following a few moments, and turned around, headed toward her bedroom. She didn't need the liquor, she thought, didn't need to go to the place it would take her.

The next morning Sandra opened the front door to take out the trash, surprised to see Jamie, with his finger poised to press the doorbell. "Jamie!"

"Hey!" A broad smile emerged on his face. He leaned against the doorway, plunging his hands deeply into the front pockets of his jeans. He wore a white t-shirt, with the words "Ain't Nothin' But the Blues!" written on the front. His eyes traveled toward the trash can and he quickly removed his hands from his pockets. "Let me get that for you!"

Sandra watched him as he placed the trash can at the curb, noticing that he wore brown loafers without socks. As he turned and made his way toward the house, she made note of the rhythm of his gait, that happy-go-lucky step since childhood, walking on the balls of his feet. Sandra smirked, crossing her arms against her chest as she leaned against the open door.

"Why are you smiling?"

"None of your business!"

Jamie rushed forward, standing close enough for Sandra to smell his cologne. "What do you mean, none of my business?"

Sandra pushed Jamie away. "Please. I am in no mood to play. Where's Janet?" She stuck her head out the doorway.

Jamie's face dropped. "Where's Janet? Can I visit you without my sister? We go way back too, you know. I wanted to see how you were doing? Maybe go for a walk or something."

Sandra looked at Jamie sideways, as if he were suspect. "A walk?"

"Yeah. A walk. You know, when you use both your legs to get around. A walk." He flashed a grin.

Sandra grasped the front of her pink robe, wrapping the material closer to her body. "I...I...I don't know, Jamie. I just—"

"Just what? Made plans to stay home and be miserable. Is that it?"

Sandra's face turned to stone. "Excuse me?"

"You heard me."

"Listen! You rang my doorbell, Jamie, at ten o'clock in the morning, talking about taking a walk. So don't get cute with me." She was about to slam the door.

"Okay! Just one question!" Jamie held up a finger. "Just one."

"What?" Sandra yelled through the crack.

"When was the last time you've been out with a man for dinner, relaxed?"

Sandra thought about her evening with Reverend Dexter, the dinner he prepared, how pleasant the evening had been. She flung the door open. "Why? Why would it matter to you?"

Jamie slumped against the brick wall of the house, looking across the street at the row of other brick houses, with white shutters and two colonial-style lights on both sides of the front doors.

"You are a woman. A woman needs pampering now and then," he said softly. "I mean you've had some tough breaks. If I could take some of the pain away—if even for one night on the town—I would, you know." He looked at Sandra.

Sandra's eyes did not meet his stare. She looked toward her feet. "Well, for your information, it's been awhile."

"Then how about a walk? Maybe dinner later on," he said. He moved to face Sandra, placing a raised arm on the doorway.

"Listen, Jamie, there are too many things going on with me right now. You won't understand."

"What makes you think I won't understand? I didn't have any problems understanding you before, when you were younger."

"But that's the thing. I've changed!"

"I know you've changed! You were once fearless—not fearful!"

Sandra's eyes met Jamie's.

And he gauged the intelligence behind hers: She was thinking, weighing, realizing that perhaps there was more to him than she had given him credit for.

Sandra tied the belt of her robe and shoved her hands into its front pockets, head down, pacing the vestibule like a lion in a small cage: two steps, turn, two steps, turn. She heard Jamie say something else, but she'd wandered too deeply into the hinterland of her mind, the remote regions, where only his voice was heard, not his words.

He was right. There was a time when she was fearless, a time when she dared to do anything. She was fearless once—when she was very young, a long time ago—and it had taken Jamie to remind her. Now she was fearful of being herself, afraid to let people know of the turmoil inside, afraid they may turn their backs on her. She was afraid of her feelings, for they were too unstable, and fearful of what she might do. Then coupled with her experience with Les, who would dare to love again?

"Sandra!" Jamie grabbed her hand. "Are you in there?" His question was a speed bump, slowing down Sandra's mind.

"What?"

"Listen." He held her hand gently. "I'm only asking for a walk and dinner, not to be joined at the hip, but if you have to deliberate this long, maybe it's not such a good idea."

Sandra shook her head. "No...no...it's not that...it's..."

"It's what, then?" Jamie sounded a little impatient.

Sandra removed her hand from his and folded her arms against her chest. She was weary, longing to be fearless again. "It's just that there are a lot of things I am going through right now. Nothing that concerns you."

"Hey, I understand," Jamie said softly. "I'll catch you around."

Sandra watched his back as he made his way down the brick pathway leading to the sidewalk. She parted her lips to call his name, but couldn't, hard as she tried. She felt fear nuzzle its wet nose against her, preparing itself for a comfortable position, and she thought, no more. "Jamie!" she yelled.

He turned, with a puzzling look on his face, standing in the middle of the sidewalk.

Sandra motioned him with a forward wave of her hand. "Listen...I...I would love to take a walk with you and have dinner," she said, her voice trembling. "Please. Come inside."

CHAPTER 15
SECRETS

Although it was 1992, an election year, no one spoke about the presidential campaign until now, in early November, close to the countdown of the race. To Lilly, it was a time of hope or grieving, depending on which political camp one belonged. She was one of those staunch democrats, who was deeply disgusted by the past years of Reagan's trickle-down-economics, touching peoples lives like an unlucky flip of a coin—favorable for a few, unfavorable for many—and now there was that George W. Bush. Lilly huddled over *The Boston Globe*, then looked up at Sandra, who sat across the kitchen table.

"You know I just find these articles so amusing. One day it's this, the next day that. Dan Quayle can't keep his words from stumbling into trouble. There's Ross Perot with his little self and big ole mouth. And then, there's this Governor Bill Clinton from Arkansas." Lilly's face grew serious. "Lord, I love to see a Democrat in the White House."

"Well, we soon shall see, Lilly. We soon shall see." Sandra reached for the container of cream on the table, stirring some into the steamy mug of coffee.

Lilly gently folded the newspaper on the table and placed her hands on top. "I made Belgian waffles."

"No thanks. Coffee will do."

Lilly looked intently at Sandra.

"What?"

"Oh, nothing." Lilly sat back in her chair, smiling. "Just seem you been in a good mood lately, at least for the past couple weeks."

Sandra placed an elbow on the table and raked her fingers through her hair. "I guess getting the job at ART N FACTS has something to do with it."

"It was meant for you, baby." Lilly touched Sandra's wrist. "And I been praying for you, too. Lord knows that's the truth."

Sandra removed her hand from her hair and wrapped a fist around the handle of the coffee mug, taking a sip. She gently placed it on the table, then folded her hands on the red-and-white checkerboard placemat. "I know you have. Thanks. It's just feels good being back in the world again, you know? Making a contribution again. It's not about money. Daddy took care of that." Sandra sighed and stared into space.

"What is it, Sandy?" Lilly leaned forward.

"It's just that I didn't really want to get back into retail, but I only have experience in retail. I guess it has to do for now. Hopefully, something else will come along. Who knows?" Sandra shrugged, taking another sip of coffee.

"The good Lord knows, baby. The good Lord knows. So, you been spending time with that Jamie fellow, I see. Came in late again last night."

Sandra smiled. "Now, Lilly, have you been spying on me?"

"Who, me?" Lilly pressed her palm flat to her chest, as if she were reciting the pledge of allegiance.

They laughed.

Sandra traced her finger around the rim of the mug. "Jamie is a good guy. Sometimes it takes someone else to make you see yourself clearly." Sandra paused. "You know, Lilly, I've been wanting to talk to you about something for a long time, but I was too afraid."

"What is it, baby?" Lilly looked concerned. Her eyebrows moved closer together.

"You know, it's amazing how you can live with people and still not know them. I mean, Daddy was so cold I had no idea he was so sentimental. I only found out after finding those things in his closet. He even kept my front teeth! He was a man full of secrets you can't imagine, Lilly. So full of contradictions." Sandra suddenly looked at Lilly. "Did you get anything on Trudy?"

"Not yet. Give it a little time, honey. It's just been a couple weeks."

Sandra looked to the table. "Yeah. You're right. You're right. Anyway, I knew Mama's secret before she died. Did you know that Mama wrote poetry?"

Lilly nodded her head. "Sure, I did. Your mama shared a lot with me, Sandy. She was a special woman. Strong in her own way—took a lot. God rest her soul."

Sandra placed her elbows on the table and looked at Lilly. "You know, when I was growing up, Mama always seemed weak to me. Since Daddy overpowered her, I never thought her to be strong, but she is."

"Yes, she was."

"No. Is, Lilly."

"Sandy, I know I'm not a English teacher, but I think 'was' is correct since your mama's dead."

Sandra chuckled, covering her face with her hands.

"What I say?"

"No, nothing at all, Lilly." Sandra placed her fingertips on Lilly's wrist and smiled, but her smile gradually faded, replacing itself with a tight-lipped posture.

Sandra's face grew too serious for Lilly to handle. "What's wrong, Sandy?"

Sandra sat back in her chair, looking at Lilly's anticipating eyes. "I said 'is' because Mama's not dead to me. I…I hear her voice all the time."

"Child! There's nothing wrong with that!" Lilly slapped her thick palm on the table. "I always hear my Raymond's voice."

"Lilly! Listen to me." Sandra drew closer, her face grim. "I really hear Mama's voice, not a memory of her voice. I really hear it. Daddy heard it too, just before he died, and then I knew I wasn't going crazy. I've been hearing Mama's voice for a long time now, Lilly. She's been directing me in a way I don't quite understand. Like…like she's trying tell me something, but I don't know—" Sandra stopped and looked into Lilly's eyes. They were blank slates. "Well, say something. Anything!"

"Lord, have mercy."

Lord, have mercy? Is that all she could say, Sandra thought, testing the temperature of the water with her foot before jumping into the shower. What did that mean? Lord, have mercy. Did it mean, Lord, have mercy, she's going crazy? Or did it mean, Lord, have mercy on your soul? Like the Lord have mercy on your soul in the way her father had said it years ago when she had told him that she was going to live with Lester Ricks. Oh, for crying out loud. Now Les says he wants to see her, had told Gee he wants forgiveness, her forgiveness. Well, she was not forgiving like Gee, could never be as forgiving as Gee. After all he had put her through. Umph! Sandra was going to write Les a letter, tell him where to go.

Sandra looked at the clock on the bathroom wall. It was 7:30 AM. She had time to linger in the shower since her hours at ART N FACTS were from 10:00 AM to 8:30 PM, but sometimes she stood longer. Sandra enjoyed talking to Winston and his wife, Meridian. They were advancing in age, and were looking for a responsible person who was able to manage the store so they could have a little more fun during their golden years.

Sandra knew she would need to hire additional people once Winston and Meridian stopped working. ART N FACTS was a very busy place. Many Harvard students perused the books and examined the artwork, with knapsacks on their backs and free cups of coffee in their hands that Meridian made in her back office. Fun time at ART N FACTS was on Zora's or Langston's night, when the store stood open until 1:00 AM. It was Meridian's idea, and she had fully explained her vision to Sandra during the interview.

Meridian's office looked like a large apartment behind ART N FACTS. It contained a burnt-orange, saddle-leather sofa, with a leopard-skin rug thrown over its back, a large coffee table with books about African art on top, and two side chairs made of wicker. Meridian sat behind an oak desk. "Please, have a seat," she had said. Sandra sat down on a brown leather chair. A stream of sunlight poured through the sheer white curtains from a side window. Meridian was a golden-brown, tall thin woman—Sandra guessed about fifty-five or sixty—with white hair cut close to her head, revealing her scalp. Long earrings made of cowry shells dangled from her lobes, and a large ring made of malachite was perched upon her index finger.

"So, Sandra, tell me about yourself. I know what your resume says, but I like to hear it from you." Meridian sat back in her seat. Her elbows were placed on the chair's armrest. Her fingers were interwoven and clasped underneath her chin.

"Well, I grew up in Cambridge. After college I—"

"Now you mean…" Meridian leaned forward, looking at Sandra's resume, "Boston University, majoring in Business Administration."

"Correct."

"How was that?"

"Okay, I guess. Seems so long ago to tell you the truth."

Meridian laughed. "I know all about things seeming so long ago. Go ahead. Continue."

"So after college, I moved to New York. At first, I worked in several retail department stores in a salesperson capacity then as department manager. I was a buyer for a while."

"I see. Now why did you decide to become co-owner of an African clothes shop? Why not, say, a bridal shop, for example?"

"Well, quite frankly, Mrs. Maxwell—"

"Meridian."

"Okay, Meridian. Quite frankly, I grew up ignorant of our culture. Don't get me wrong. I believe I had a good education. I just lacked the understanding and contributions of our people. When I arrived in New York, I met young men and women who were immersed in our African heritage. To make a long story short, I found a part of myself. When I became co-owner of an African clothes shop, my partner and I had one objective in mind: to educate. Yes, we sold clothes, but my partner and I had traveled to Africa for the materials and articles of clothing. We were able to educate the buyer about what part of Africa the clothing came from, what language the people spoke, about their customs, beliefs."

"Good answer!" Meridian pointed an index finger at Sandra. "Because that's what ART N FACTS is all about—to educate. And you think that you were ignorant of our culture! When I was growing up—" Meridian stopped and removed a box of green tea from the desk drawer. "It's tea time for me. Want some?"

"Sure. Why not."

"Now when I was growing up in Florida—I was born in 1932—colored folk didn't know nothin' 'bout nothin', as my daddy used to say. He didn't want his children to be ignorant. So he started collecting any information pertaining to black history, black literature. And I got hooked. I can still remember the first time I read *Their Eyes Were Watching God*. For the first time, I fell in love with the beauty of our people—poor, broke, humorous, sometimes ignorant, but blessed with innate wisdom. Beautiful! It still pains me to think of how Zora died, destitute and on welfare. She was the most memorable figure of the Harlem Renaissance. Florida girl born and raised! How could a Barnard graduate, author of several books and an anthropologist, be reduced to that? I'll never know!

"That's why, out of commemoration, each Friday night at ART N FACTS is Zora's night. Young women come to recite their poetry or excerpts from their books. For balance, each Saturday night is Langston's night when young men get up and do the same. We get to hear some fine young voices, too." Meridian stood up and slapped the front of her long African-print dress. "Now let me prepare this tea. Excuse me."

"Well, Meridian," Sandra yelled loud enough to be heard in the next room, "I'm quite sure I will enjoy both nights if I get the job."

Meridian poked her head in the doorway: "Oh, honey, you got the job!"

The thought suddenly pierced Lilly's brain, causing her to wince, praying it wasn't an aneurysm. She was assured it couldn't have been her high blood pressure since she'd been taking her medication faithfully. Lilly groped for the back of the bench before she sat down.

"Ma'am," the young girl said, "are you okay?"

Lilly nodded her head. Yet the young girl was hesitant, looking at Lilly's forehead glistening in the sun and the large stain of sweat in the middle of her pink dress like a cummerbund.

Lilly tried to assure the young girl that she was okay, waving a weak hand, as if she were saying goodbye. "Go 'head, darling. I'm just fine."

The young girl bent down and picked up a picture near Lilly's foot. "Is this yours, ma'am?"

"Why, yes, it is. Thank you. You're mighty kind."

After Sandra had proclaimed she heard her mama's voice, been hearing her mama's voice for some time now, later that day Lilly got dressed to meet the church ladies for their bi-weekly luncheon. As usual, the ladies quarreled over what they'd eat. Adele suggested West Indian food, but Lucinda reminded Adele that West Indian food had given them heartburn and that their digestive systems were well past sixty.

"Spicy foods are for young people," Lucinda said.

Adele quipped, "That's why I like it! It makes me feel young!"

Lucinda shot a look at Adele as if to say, You silly old woman!

Lilly looked at Adele in the rearview mirror, watching the expression on her face change. It looked like Adele had suddenly been reminded of how the curry chicken two weeks ago tore her stomach up. How she'd sucked on Rolaids to kingdom come followed by Phillips' Milk of Magnesia straight up.

"Well, how about Chinese, then?" Adele said.

"Naw, too greasy!" said Ruth.

"Listen!" Lucinda said, "Why don't we just go to a restaurant that serves plain, old-fashion American food. Our stomachs will appreciate it, because it won't cause a rumbling—if you girls know what I mean?"

There was silence, which everyone took as agreement. So Lilly parked alongside an American restaurant. It was times like these when Lilly did not connect with these women. They acted like old hens, loved to squabble—no matter how small or insignificant the subject. But Lilly knew that the squabbling had kept their hearts pumping, and that's what mattered to them! Sometimes they'd have a serious discussion about the accurate way to carve a turkey, as if they were sitting in a boardroom.

Of course, Lucinda had to be chairman. She had the loudest voice. Lucinda was a thin high-yellow woman, and she was always quick to let everybody know she was a descendant of one of the oldest, Cantabrigian black families. Lucinda had boasted that her great-great-great-great-great grandfather had rubbed elbows with Prince Hall himself—the first Grand Master of the colored Grand Lodge of Freemasons. Now Lilly had never heard of a Prince Hall. He sounded more like a fictitious character to her and, since the information was coming from Lucinda, she was certain that he wasn't real. So, Lilly combed the history books for verification. To her amazement, he had existed. Prince Hall was born free in the British West Indies. In 1765, he worked his passage on a ship to Boston.

Later, Prince acquired real estate and was qualified to vote. He also pressed John Hancock to let him join the Continental Army, one of the few black men who had fought at the battle of Bunker Hill. To add to his achievements, Prince became a minister in the African Methodist Episcopal Church and fought for the abolition of slavery. But to the ladies, Prince Hall was most renown for his friendship with William Bowen, a Freemason, a free man himself, and Lucinda's great-great-great-great-great grandfather.

Prince had met William during the War of Independence when Black Freemasonry began. According to legend, Prince took a liking to Lucinda's great-great-great-great-great grandfather and they became closer than Siamese twins and Prince affectionately called him ole Willie. And as if the women hadn't enough of the boasting, Lucinda had enumerate the long line of college professors, doctors, lawyers, journalists, judges, and God knows what else in her family—all except Indian chief. And being Indian chief herself, Lucinda now directed the young waiter to where they would be seated: "Oh! No! Not there. Here." She then patted the neat bun at the nape of her neck, staring defiantly at the young waiter, with his hair parted in the middle and in a long ponytail. The young man, who was probably a Harvard student, and not yet in the position to snub his nose at Lucinda, graciously obliged, "Sure, madam, we want our customers to be happy. Please follow me." Lucinda followed the young waiter. Then Ruth, Adele, and Lilly followed Lucinda. The arrangement of the procession was appropriate to Lilly. She believed herself to be the last in the pecking order. Each one had some family legend to tell—although nobody topped Lucinda's. Lilly could not forget her humble beginnings, but she knew the Lord looked at how one lived and not one's lineage.

"Whew! Sure is good to sit down," Ruth said.

"Why! Ruth, you were sitting in the car all along," said Lucinda.

"Yes, but now I can stretch my legs."

"Just make sure you don't stretch your legs this way, scuffing up my shoes."

"Oh! Lucinda, you're so—"

"So what?" Lucinda yearned for her blood to be pumping again.

"Oh! Nothing. Nothing at all."

The fire of anticipation in Lucinda's eyes lost its sparkle, and Ruth knew she had won. This was the only way to deal with Lucinda McCray.

After the young waiter had taken everybody's order, Lilly reached into her bag and pulled out the picture of the little boy. She explained to the women that she thought the boy was Trudy's child. All remembered Trudy, whose real name was Edith Langston, but no one knew what had happened to her. Lilly was in the middle of swallowing a mouthful of white rice with chicken gravy when Adele slipped a note underneath her plate. Lilly almost choked on a runaway grain, excusing herself from the table. Adele followed her in the ladies' room.

"Are you sure, Adele?"

"I'm sure. Sure as my name's Adele. I know who that child is."

Lilly looked at Adele in disbelief. This was much bigger than she thought. Reverend Dexter needed to get involved.

"Air. I need some air," Lilly suddenly said, heading for the bench outside.

Adele was the last one to be dropped off at her doorstep. Neither Lilly nor Adele said much in the car, conversing back and forth in fragmented sentences.

Lilly began: "Lord. Lord. What a tangled web we weave here."

"Ummm, uh, uh."

"Lord has got to be coming soon."

"Yeah, coming like a thief in the night."

"People best to get their business in order."

"Sure 'nough."

"Lord, we don't have much time now."

"No. No time at all."

"But we know that the time is coming soon."

"Yeah, we see the signs."

Lilly squinted at the street signs. "Adele, what street you live on again?"

"Girl! You been driving me back and forth for how long now?"

"You going to tell me or not. 'Cause if you don't tell me, I'm going to let you off at the next street corner."

"Worcester Street. It just coming up here."

Chapter 16
VOICES

Sandra sat in Janet's living room on a Saturday night, eating pizza, and playing Scrabble, amazed that Jamie seemed so light-hearted, full of jokes, laughing loudly, when just last week she had sprung the news. She recalled how Jamie had ordered two tumblers of Scotch, downed them back to back, shaking his head violently as the liquor had burned a pathway down his throat. He quickly motioned the waitress for another.

"Ghosts?" he said.

"Jamie," Sandra whispered, leaning forward, "I didn't say ghosts. I said voices." The flickering candle on the table made shadowy patterns on her face.

Jamie glanced at the nearby table, then pressed his lips to Sandra's ear. "What do you mean, you didn't say ghosts? Your mother's dead, ain't she? We're talking ghosts!" He sat back in his chair, screwing his face. "This is plain...just plain ..."

"Crazy!" Sandra whispered in controlled anger.

"Well, yeah!" He had said this too loudly, and people heads turned toward their table. Jamie covered his face. In seconds, his hands slid from his eyes to his mouth, resting there.

"Listen, you can back off if you want. I knew you wouldn't understand!" Sandra pushed her chair from the table and stormed out the restaurant. When she had looked back at Jamie, he was eagerly reaching for his third glass of Scotch.

Later, Jamie had told Sandra he'd stumbled home that night and drank some more, which wasn't like him. He had sprawled out on the couch, with his forearm pressed across his face, thinking of the few times they had spent together—candlelight dinners, movies, long walks, and on several occasions when she cooked for him. To his surprise, she was a good cook, too. He'd heard about New York women who preferred take-out food rather than standing behind a stove, but not his Sandra. She added a little flair to her dishes, mixing in spices she'd discovered during her travels to exotic places he had only dreamt of. He hadn't traveled beyond the boundaries of the United States, and so Sandra's spices not only added a strange and wonderful taste to her food, but also to her conversation. She spoke about the brotherhood of monks that lived in cave dwellings near the twelfth-century rock churches in Lalibela, Ethiopia, while preparing her version of Kay Watt, an Ethiopian dish of chopped beef simmered in garlic, onions, fresh ginger, with hot and thick berbere sauce. The sauce had set his mouth ablaze, and also lit his passion. Sandra was interesting! So how could she be crazy?

Two days later, he had appeared at her doorstep, giddy, in fever-pitch agitation, said he hadn't slept a wink. He hadn't waited until Sandra said to come in—he barged in, talking about he'd done research. He was rambling and pacing the floor, making it hard for Sandra to keep up, mumbling something about autonomous psychic contents deep in the unconscious and how these contents produced visions, sensations, even voices. He suddenly stopped in front of Sandra. "Probably because you've been under a lot of strain…that's all…doesn't mean you're crazy!"

"Uh huh," Sandra had said calmly, watching Jamie pace the floor again like a lunatic.

"And then I read about psychic phenomena, the unexplainable." He shook his fists in the air. "Dreams that foresaw the death of certain people, clocks that stopped at the moment of death, glasses that shattered at that critical moment, people sensing the spirits of the dead—I don't know. I just don't know." Jamie took a deep breath and had plopped onto a chair. "Look. All I know is that you're not crazy. Can't be crazy!"

"Hirsute?" Janet suddenly yelled. "That's not a word, Jamie! Carl! Look it up!"

"Is too a word!" Jamie stood up, feigning he was insulted by the challenge. "Hirsute! Like your legs!"

Carl sighed, throwing the paperback dictionary on the table. "It's a word, honey. It means hairy. He's killing us."

Janet slapped Jamie's kneecaps. "Do you see hair on these smooth things?" She kicked up a leg.

Jamie turned to face Sandra. "Are you going to let her get away with this?"

Sandra shrugged and casually reached for another slice of pizza. "Hey, I don't get involved in family matters."

"See how you women stick together!" Jamie slapped his thighs and sat down. "I can't win." He snuggled close to Sandra.

"Let's call it quits, honey. They're winning. No way we can catch up."

Janet threw her tiles on the board. "Hirsute," she snickered. "Whoever heard of the word hirsute?"

"An ed-u-ca-tor! That's who!" Jamie laughed. "I was born to be a teacher!"

Janet rolled her eyes and waved her hand in Jamie's face. "Carl, help me clean up the kitchen."

Jamie looked at Sandra. "You're beautiful when you have pizza juice sliding down the side of your mouth."

"Beautiful! Jamie, please!" Sandra wiped her mouth with a napkin before grabbing the remote.

Jamie jumped up from the couch, "Why can't you just say thank you when I pay you a compliment, huh?" He cocked his head to the side, grinning.

Sandra looked up at him. "You're blocking the TV."

Jamie shook his head. "There's no winning. I ask you a question, and you're talking about the TV." He plopped on the couch next to Sandra again, looking at her.

"What?" she said, without a glance, flipping through the channels.

"You 're beautiful."

"No, I'm not."

"See! There you go again!" Jamie grabbed the remote from Sandra.

"Jamie!"

Jamie turned off the television. "The TV can wait. I'm serious now. Look at me."

Sandra placed the half-eaten pizza on a plate and folded her arms against her chest, looking at the blank television screen.

"Oh, I see." Jamie chuckled. "You're playing difficult." He slipped the remote in the back pocket of his gray trousers, stood up, and grabbed Sandra by her hands, trying to pull her off the couch.

"Stop it! Will you stop it. Stop it, Jamie!" Sandra struggled to release herself, twisting her wrists from his grip.

"No!" He yanked Sandra on her feet, pinning her hands behind her back.

She growled through clenched teeth. "Okay! What do you want?"

Jamie stood calmly, looking at the crown of Sandra's head. "First, I want you to look at me."

Sandra sucked her teeth, then raised her head, resting the point of her chin on Jamie's chest. "How's this?"

He laughed, watching Sandra's nostrils pulsate. "You're a real funny lady tonight, aren't you?"

"Yep." She flashed an exaggerated smile. "Now let my hands go!"

Jamie released her hands, then quickly pulled her close to him, locking his arms around her waist. "You're a beautiful woman," he said slowly, "and it doesn't matter what you think, because I love you, anyway. Always loved you, since we were kids."

The seriousness on Jamie's face unnerved Sandra, causing her eyes to quickly move from his face to his chest. The heat from his body issued the scent of woodsy cologne.

"Did you hear me?" Jamie's voice was low, sultry.

"I heard you," she whispered. She looked up at him, taking in his long girly eyelashes and razor sharp features like an Arabian.

"You turn me on, Sandra. You're creative, smart, sensitive, playful, well-traveled, sassy…"

Sandra burst into laughter. "Sassy!"

"Yeah. Sassy," he said softly, looking intently at her face. "And beautiful."

"No, I'm—"

Jamie quickly covered her mouth.

Sandra's eyes widened.

"Just say, thank you—just two little words, thank you. See, easy. Now you try it." He slowly removed his hand from her mouth, then raised her chin with his index finger. "Go on."

Sandra tucked her lips into her mouth, staring at Jamie. He wasn't smiling. "Thank you," she murmured.

Later that evening at Sandra's house, she confided in Jamie. "The last time I felt beautiful was when I was eleven years old. Ummm, that feels good."

"Like it, huh?"

"Uh huh. I never had a foot massage before." Sandra snuggled on the couch, her feet on Jamie's lap.

"Never? Surely, you're joking, Miss Cosmopolitan."

Sandra snatched her foot from Jamie's grip. "Don't get cute, Mr. God's Gift to Women!"

They laughed.

"So…so the last time you felt beautiful was when you were eleven. Why eleven?" Jamie continued to knead Sandra's foot.

"'Cause that's when everyone in the house was happy—or at least appeared to be happy. Jimmy and my father had arguments from time to time, but everything was relatively okay. Jimmy always told me I was beautiful, so did my father. And I believed it."

"Did that Les fellow ever tell you that you were beautiful?"

Sandra sucked her teeth. "No!"

"Idiot!"

Sandra grinned.

"Well...you...you were always beautiful to me. But yeah, you were exceptionally beautiful at eleven, with those nappy pom-poms on the side of your head!" Jamie quickly grabbed Sandra's feet.

Sandra raised her head from the pillow. "Okay, get off me! That's it!"

Jamie laughed. "Aw, come on! You know I'm just kidding!"

Sandra stared at him for a while, smirking. "How do I know that?" she said with a pout.

Jamie wagged his head. "Now you know you were the finest thing struttin' 'round Cambridge!"

Sandra plopped her head on the pillow, giggling. "And you say I'm funny."

"So what happened after eleven?"

Sandra emitted a long sigh. "Things in the house got ugly. So I felt ugly. Jimmy left home to live with Uncle Rufus for a little while. After that, my mother slept in Jimmy's room. She said my father drove Jimmy out the house." Sandra raised herself on her elbows and said in wonder, "The funniest thing is that all of a sudden I remember the night before Jimmy left home, as if it all happened yesterday."

Jamie poured additional lotion onto his palm, then proceeded with his massage. "Well, I once read that humans never really forget anything. Contents of memory are stored in the unconscious, but given the right stimulus, those memories rise to consciousness again. That was a good book."

"Yeah. That must be it." Sandra plunged on her back. "That night, Jimmy and my father had a terrible argument. I don't know exactly how it started. All I know is that Jimmy said there wasn't a God, and my father cuffed him—hard. To me, my father's raised hand looked like an ax, and before I knew it, "Jimmy went crashing to the kitchen floor like a pine tree. His body was straight when he fell. Bam! To the floor, like that." Sandra hit her open palm with a fist.

"Whoa."

"Yeah." Sandra looked at Jamie, then back to the ceiling. "Then Jimmy was on the floor in a fetal position, trying to catch his breath. I tried to help him, but he pushed me away."

"Where was your mother?"

"Crying hysterically. She loved Jimmy, but was afraid of my father, I think. The next day, Jimmy left home. He was only sixteen. My mother and father weren't speaking for months after that, only around company. I was mad with Jimmy for leaving me. I wanted to live with Uncle Rufus, too. But my father wouldn't allow it. He didn't even want me to go near Jimmy. After that, Jimmy really changed, was heavily into drugs, alcohol. The next thing we knew, he took off to California."

"I remember the day when you called me on the phone and told me that Jimmy left home."

"I did?" Sandra raised herself with her elbows again, frowning. "Wow, I don't remember that. I remember telling Janet."

"Well, you did. So, since the age of twelve you haven't felt beautiful. Wow, that's a long time."

There was heavy silence.

Sandra lay down, covering her eyes with her forearm. "Yeah," she said soberly. "I haven't felt beautiful since then."

Sandra suddenly sprang up in bed one night, causing Jamie to jump out of sleep, raising his head above the pillow. "What is it?" He sounded afraid.

She didn't respond, rubbing her elbows as if she were cold.

Jamie sat up and placed his arm around her shoulder. "You hear it?"

Sandra nodded. "Sounds like she's wailing," she whispered. "Something's wrong." Then Sandra yelled, "Mama!"

"Shhh! What the hell is wrong with you? Damn!" Jamie jumped out of bed, placing his palm flat across his chest. "You scared me!" He quickly groped for the light switch. He reached for a pile of folded clothes on a chair, threw them in a corner, and plopped heavily onto the seat like he had just unloaded a truck. He rubbed his hand repeatedly from the crown of his head to the nape of his neck, and even from where Sandra was sitting, she saw the worry on his forehead ripple like waves. He was considering whether he had the stamina for this, jumping out of sleep every other night, his stomach churning with unnamed fear. If things kept up like this, it would permanently put him in the nuthouse or outhouse—one. He jumped up and hurried toward the bathroom.

Sandra lay in Jamie's bed, feeling the coolness of white sheets resting on her body. She absentmindedly played with her hair, listening to Jamie pass gas behind the closed door, followed by the flushing of the toilet. Sandra knew this was taking a silent toll on him. She had lightened her load somewhat by confiding in him about her secret. But for Jamie, the burden was heavy, would quickly wipe a smile off his face by the mere mention of her mama.

After a series of blasts and additional flushing of the toilet, Sandra heard the click of the latch, then Jamie's soft footsteps on carpet. She dropped her hand from her hair and sat upright, leaning her back against the oak headboard. "You okay?"

"I'm okay," he mumbled, avoiding Sandra's eyes, wiping his hands with a towel. He flung it on the chair where he had sat.

Sandra patted the side of the bed. "Come here, then."

Jamie sat down wearily and touched Sandra's face. "Listen…I…I…"

Sandra brushed his hand from her jaw. "Wait! Don't tell me. You're sick and tired of this craziness and you want out! Right?"

Jamie stared at Sandra for a moment; his words spewed with venom, "Hell, yeah, I'm sick and tired of this! But I don't want out. I want to put an end to this mess!" He stood up abruptly and walked toward the oak bureau, looking at Sandra's reflection in the mirror.

Her eyes met his through the looking glass, then traveled down the deep furrow of his muscular back, stopping at his tight behind clad in silk red briefs.

Jamie swiftly turned around. "You've been living with this craziness for some time! You're used to it. I'm not!"

Sandra snatched a handful of sheets, wrapping them around her upper body. She lunged toward Jamie, her legs folded beneath her on the mattress. "So you do think it's craziness, then!" she shot back. "You think I'm crazy! I knew it!"

Jamie slapped his forehead with both hands. "Oh my God. Now did I say you were crazy? Did I?" He dropped his hands to his sides. "Sandra, I'm just using your own words. You said craziness first!" Jamie pointed his finger at Sandra. "But let me ask you something, do you think you're crazy? Always talking about what I think! Are you telling yourself that you're crazy, like you're telling yourself that you're not beautiful? Huh? 'Cause if you are, you better start paying attention to what your own inner voice is saying to you, not just your mama's!" Jamie plopped onto the foot of the bed, massaging his temples. "Damn!"

Sandra looked at Jamie's back in silence, stunned by his truth. Finally, she stood up and walked over to Jamie, bending on her knees in front him. She touched his forearm. "You're right." Jamie removed his hands from his temples and rested them on Sandra's shoulders. He looked at her intently. "You will become what you think, Sandra. Don't try to transfer your feelings onto me. I don't think you're crazy." All of a sudden tears gleamed in Sandra's eyes. "Now don't cry," he said, hugging her closely. "It's going to be all right." Sandra pressed her face onto Jamie's bare chest, sobbing softly.

"Shhh. It's going to be all right." He patted Sandra's hair. "Hey!" he said softly, "Did I ever tell you that my Grandma was a spiritual woman?"

"No," Sandra said weakly.

"Well, she was. Not religious, there's a difference, but spiritual. My Grandma was Cherokee, you know. That's where Janet and I inherited this reddish-brown skin and straight hair. When we used to visit my Grandma, she sat in her easy chair, with a black shawl wrapped around her shoulders, and two thick braids pinned on top her head. She always spoke to Janet and I like we were adults, made us feel grown. We loved her for that. So when she spoke, we listened.

"After my Grandfather died, Grandma said she would wear a black shawl until the day they met again. She had a whole wardrobe of black shawls, I tell you. She was never caught without a black shawl, even went to bed with one." Jamie chuckled softly, then kissed the crown of Sandra's head. "One night," he whispered, with the excitement of a child telling a fairy-tale, "Grandma was real sick, and she told me to sit on her bed and hold her hand. She told me her life with my Grandfather was not over, that their lives together hadn't ended just because he was dead, no, that sometimes he appeared to her in dreams, resuming unfinished dialogue."

Sandra suddenly raised her head from Jamie's chest, wiping her tears with her wrists. "Really?"

"Yeah, really," he said softly. "But when she told me this, Sandra," he voice rose, "I swear to God I thought it was an old lady's fantasy. Only lately—since I've been talking with you—I've come to realize that Grandma truly believed it, wholeheartedly, to the day she died. Listen," Jamie held Sandra's face, "when was the last time you visited your mother's grave?"

"A little after my birthday. Why?"

"Well, visit her tomorrow. Ask her if she wants to tell you something, maybe there's unfinished dialogue."

Sandra blinked. "Well...I...could..."

"Tomorrow. I'll come with you if you want."

Sandra looked at Jamie for a moment, then nodded.

Jamie yawned and stood up, pulling Sandra toward him. "Let's go to bed now. I'm tired." He turned off the light and guided Sandra to her side of the bed.

Ten minutes later, she whispered, "Jamie, you sleep?"

"Almost," he whispered back. "What is it?"

"I can't sleep. Can you put me to sleep?"

Jamie smiled faintly. "Sure." He reached over with familiarity and kissed her deeply, causing the curve of her spine to raise from the bed. Jamie's tongue then trailed to her navel, kissing her stomach, soft, feathery kisses.

CHAPTER 17
DOUBTS

When Reverend Dexter had arrived in Cambridge, he told people that his wife was dead, because to Reverend Dexter, Pauline was dead. He hadn't seen her in years, but knew one day he would need to find her. Then he told Sandra the truth. Well, he almost told Sandra the truth—he wasn't divorced, but separated, which was like being divorced, wasn't it? He had to admit that the burden was partially lifted when he told Sandra the half-truth. He didn't like living a lie. It just seemed more appropriate to tell people that a young reverend had lost his wife to breast cancer rather than to another man, and being a mere man himself, his lie was more palatable. He needed to tell someone, other than Camille, about Pauline. And Sandra had reminded him so much of Pauline—this he hadn't planned on. Sandra had taken him by surprise, had rattled old feelings inside him like dry bones. This did not mean he had romantic ideas about Sandra, he reasoned. It was more like dry bones beginning to form flesh—feelings—he once had for Pauline.

Now events were getting tangled. He had worked hard trying to gain Sandra's trust, but now she wouldn't talk to him. He hadn't planned on this either. This would push things back. Camille, who was normally patient, was growing impatient, not understanding why one thing had to do with the other. She had the engagement ring, and they'd made a vow not to touch each other until their wedding night, but it became increasingly hard to keep this promise—well, at least for Camille. She wanted to wear her engagement ring, tell people she would be Mrs. Dexter. Yet to Camille, it appeared that he could wait forever, and now he was nervous about meeting Pauline—did he have doubts?

Doubts. Reverend Dexter pressed his forehead against the window, leaving a smudge on the glass. There was one thing he did not doubt: Sandra was changing. The last time he saw her, she was looking pretty good. He'd never seen

Sandra with make-up on before. Not that she had on a lot of make-up. It was just right, accentuating her almond eyes and full lips he had never noticed before. Her style of dress had an Afro-centric flair. A shawl made of Kente cloth casually lay on her shoulder. Her earlobes glistened with hammered brass earrings that grazed her neck. Reverend Dexter didn't even know that it was Sandra. He was looking at another man, who was straining his neck, staring at the soft sway of Sandra's behind. Reverend Dexter didn't even know that she had a behind! It was just one week ago while strolling in a park. It was a late autumn afternoon. Sandra had said she'd taken a job at an African bookstore on Brattle Street. She'd been working there several weeks now, a good start for getting back into the retail business.

"Sandra, is that you?"

"Reverend Dex—I mean, Samuel. What a surprise."

He had immediately noticed the change, a change much deeper than her appearance. She had addressed him by his first name as if she had lost all reverence for him, but she was polite, though distant. Reverend Dexter searched for a trace of those soft-doe eyes, but they weren't there. He wanted to tell Sandra that he missed their discussions about dreams, visions, life. But before he could open his mouth, Sandra said her lunch hour was over. "Good-bye," she had said, in a tone of finality.

Reverend Dexter walked away from the window and sat down behind the gray metal desk in the administrative office of God's Grace Community Center. He leaned in his chair, with its back against the wall, and folded his hands behind his head. Soon Sara and Ron would be in the office to discuss the after school agenda for boys and girls ages fifteen through eighteen. Reverend Dexter wanted a strong agenda, something that would give young people a sense of themselves. Now that Sandra was working in an African bookstore, perhaps it would be fruitful for him to pay a visit. He wanted to see what it had to offer. And maybe, just maybe, he'd convince her to teach African studies on Saturdays. She'd been to Africa. How could she deny the children?

The front legs of his chair suddenly hit the floor, the thought of children. He opened the desk drawer and pulled out a book. He thumbed through its pages, and the black-and-white photo of the little boy fell to the floor. He picked it up, recalling that his mother had never taken pictures of him as a child. She was much too busy eking out an income by working two jobs. She would come home, with her familiar tirade of how a woman's work is never done, then she'd shuck peas, peel onions, scrub floors, and vigorously wash his clothes in the bathtub. Although his mother's love may have appeared thin to some, he knew, without a doubt, it was strong as catgut. After all, her love was strong enough for her spirit to rise from the casket, shaking her index finger, saying, "Boy! You better change your ugly ways 'cause God don't like ugly." Sure 'nough changed his life! That, and Pauline. Now his mind was on Pauline again. She wanted so much to have children. He remembered the day she had said: "All I know is that I really want to get married to a wonderful man, to have children—plenty of children—and be happy."

Reverend Dexter placed the picture between the pages of the book, then put the book back into the drawer. He rubbed his eyes and felt water, realizing that the water was his own tears. They never had children, and this is what hurt him. He wondered if the man Pauline had left him for had made her happy, would give her plenty of children now that they were getting married.

There was a knock at the door. It was Ron and Sara. "Is this a good time?" asked Ron.

"Sure, sure," said Reverend Dexter. He sat upright in his chair, quickly reaching for a tissue. "Is this allergy season? Because my eyes are killing me!"

The busiest hours at ART N FACTS were between 3:00 and 7:00 PM. So around 1:00 in the afternoon, Winston approached Sandra.

"I don't know about that, Winston!"

He walked behind the counter where Sandra was standing. "Listen, why don't you just think about it? That's all I'm asking. You don't have to develop new material."

"I know...but..."

"But what?" Winston looked Sandra in the eyes. "Listen to me!" He placed a hand on Sandra's shoulder. "Meridian and I raised three fine young women. From time to time, I give them a pep talk when they are in doubt—doesn't matter what it is. I first ask them, 'What are you afraid of?' After they have clearly define what they are afraid of, I then ask, 'Do you want to conquer your fear?' Now if—"

"Winston! You don't understand."

"Let me finish!" He shook his index finger at Sandra. "Please. Give an old man his due."

Sandra cracked a faint smile. "Well, okay."

"Much oblige. Now, Sandra," Winston held both her shoulders this time, "what do you fear? All I'm asking is that you read your mother's poetry on Zora's night. How befitting that would be! You would be commemorating her spirit like Zora's. So what do you fear?"

Sandra looked into his eyes.

"Well?"

"Listen, I'm knowledgeable about Africa. That's it. I don't know how to deliver a poem. And in front of those bright people, too! Even Harvard professors stop in on Zora's night."

"Aaah! I see." Winston dropped his arms to his sides. "I see." He walked around in small circles, looking down at the wooden planks, with his hands clasped behind his back. "Sounds like a very bad case of no confidence to me. You're knowledgeable about Africa. That's it." Winston stopped circling and stood directly in front of Sandra, grabbing both her shoulders again. "Then remember the African griot. Be the keeper of your mother's history! Your history!" With that said, he walked away. Sandra heard him address a customer: "Good afternoon, young lady, may I be of some service?"

Sandra was a statute, frozen by Winston's words. Finally, she walked over to the shipment of new books that had arrived that morning, placing a few of them on the shelf. Her mind drifted toward Jamie and their visit to Mama's grave, which she thought would have provided all the answers to her problems. Jamie had evoked in her nothing short of the miraculous, so she thought that perhaps if she understood the reason behind Mama's voice that somehow she'd understand the reason why she was still here.

As Jamie had instructed, she knelt down in front Mama's grave, eyes shut tight as if she were making a wish, but nothing. Absolutely nothing had happened. No revelation. No epiphany. Nothing. So, she waited. No poof, then the summoning of spirits. No ominous skies. No bolts of lighting. No rumbling voice from above. Nothing. Then, "This is ridiculous!" she said. She opened her eyes and looked up at Jamie, who was standing over her like a sentinel. She shook her head sideways and said, "Nothing."

"Nothing?"

"No!"

"Concentrate."

She closed her eyes again, cursing him silently. This act had nothing to do with her but him, she realized. He had to solve this mystery—and quick! But you know what? This had to do with her, plain and simple, she thought. She appreciated the help and all, but right there and then, on aching knees, she had concluded that she would have to do this alone, the only way. The snap of a twig made her open her eyes.

"Sorry," Jamie whispered and pointed a few feet away. "I'll be over there."

"Don't bother," she said, attempting to get up.

"What are you doing?"

"Getting up! That's what! " She struggled to her feet.

"But you can't—"

"Can't nothing! Help me up. I'm damn near crippled because of this!" She grabbed Jamie's hand, and as soon as she brushed off her knees, she saw it. "Oh my God." She covered her opened mouth. "What, Sandra, what?" She walked slowly and rigidly passed Jamie, toward the tombstone not far away from Mama's, and etched in gray letters was the name Ursula McKeon.

"Ursula!"

"You knew her?"

"No!...not...really...I mean...well...yes...yes!" Sandra rubbed her brow fiercely.

"Your mother's friend?"

Sandra was wild-eyed. "Probably!...Yesss."

How could she begin to tell Jamie about Ursula? He wouldn't believe her, anyway. Who would? Sandra looked at Jamie, dumbstruck, searching for the whys and hows, but she didn't know. All she knew was that while she waited for a bolt of lightening to strike—some sign—a piece of the mystery had revealed itself subtly, subtly as the day Ursula had sat next to her on the bench, old as dirt and appearing out of nowhere. Sandra hadn't found out the reason for Mama's voice, but she learned one thing: nothing, absolutely nothing, was coincidental in her life anymore. Everything that had happened to her and all the people she'd met along the way—even some wizened woman she had long since forgotten— were for a reason. There had to be! According to her tombstone, Ursula had died the day after they'd met. Mission accomplished it seemed. Sandra had held her head in her hands, trembling.

She was silent on her way back home, straining her memory, remembering fragments of Ursula's words: "Someone dear has died. No. No. More than one, but dear." Sandra squeezed her eyes. "Stop searching for life's answers and let them unfold!" Ursula had said. She had said this right after Sandra had told her everything, about Daddy and even Mama's voice. Yeah. Ursula had said, "Everything is revealed in due time. Take courage. Know that ya have a guardian angel." Sandra had opened her eyes. Guardian angel? There was a reason why she had met Libby too, for it was Libby who had first spoken of her guardian angel.

Several books fell to the floor. Winston looked up: "Are you okay?"

Sandra nodded. "Just slipped from my hands." She picked up the books, then stood up. Just slipped...from...my...mind, she thought. Sandra stared at Winston as if she were now seeing him for the first time. Of all the stores she could have walked into, why did she walk into his? She wasn't even looking for a store that day. But there it was, and she walked in asking for a job, surprising even herself. Coincidental? No. No. She was supposed to meet this man.

Winston looked up from his paperwork. "Are you sure you're okay? Look like you've seen a ghost." He chuckled.

Sandra draped her fingertips over her mouth, still staring at Winston, with squinted eyes. And how many bookstores...how many bookstores were there where poetry was recited every Friday and Saturday nights?

"Earth to Sandra."

That Mama just happened to have poetry that needed to be voiced?

"Sandra?"

Sandra snapped out of her trance. "Winston, I'll do it. I'll conquer my fear!"

Camille and Reverend Dexter were in the administrative office late in the day when Lilly knocked on the door. They looked up simultaneously. Reverend Dexter stood up.

"Why, Sister Johnson! What brings you here?"

"Don't mean to disturb you none, but I need to talk to you, " she whispered.

Camille quickly gathered her papers. "We can finish this later, Pastor Samuel." She nodded at Lilly then left the room.

"Sit down. Is there something wrong?" Reverend Dexter's forehead wrinkled as he sat in his seat.

Lilly sat down, neatly tucking her flowered dress beneath her. She reached into her handbag and pulled out the picture of the little boy, placing it on the gray metal desk.

"Where did you get that?"

"Is it true, Reverend Dexter?"

"Where did you get that?"

"Is it true?"

He reached into the desk drawer and pulled out the book. He thumbed through its pages, placing the identical picture next to the one on the desk, side by side.

"It is true." Lilly slumped in her seat.

Reverend Dexter shot up and walked toward the window. He looked through the slats of the blinds, folding his arms across his chest.

Lilly looked at the vertical streak of wetness beginning to form at the back of his beige shirt.

"My Uncle Troy was a hard man, man of discipline. He taught me a lot about discipline." Reverend Dexter paused, looking down at the floor, then back to the window. "There was blood everywhere."

Lilly was confused, rubbing her chin. She had no idea what Reverend Dexter was talking about, but thought she should ride it out to see where it led.

"He was standing in the middle of the street in front of the house. He was reminding me about some errand to do. He walked to his car, and out of no where a van hit him, throwing him in the air. He hit the ground—it sounded like a slab of meat thrown on a countertop. The car sped off. The sound filled my ears, then it was quiet. I was too shocked to say anything, and there was blood everywhere. One of Uncle Troy's legs was pinned underneath his back like there wasn't any bone in it. One of his shoes was missing. And I thought, a man has got to be hit pretty hard to knock off his shoe. Later, I asked myself, 'Why did a good man like Uncle Troy have to die like that?' He didn't die right away, though. He lasted three days in pain and agony." Reverend Dexter shook his head. "But Uncle Troy was a godly man. He believed in keeping his business in order—more ways than one. The insurance was paid up. Plot was already chosen. Funeral home already picked out." Reverend Dexter slipped both hands into his front pockets. The sound of chinking coins filled the room. He shifted his weight from one foot to the other, his back still towards Lilly.

"After Uncle Troy was buried, his wife had given me that picture. She said my uncle had been meaning to give it to me for a long time. They'd visited my mother once, and took that picture of me. Made two copies. Sent one to my mother since they did not see any baby pictures of me around the apartment. Then years later, my father-in-law, Pastor Avery, and a very good friend of Uncle Troy, told me that he knew a man named Reverend Hamilton. He'd met Reverend Hamilton at a National Baptist convention decades ago. He'd heard that Reverend Hamilton was ill.

"Now up until this point, my father-in-law never mentioned anything about

Reverend Hamilton before, but he said it was time to break his promise he had made to Uncle Troy—now that he was dead and all. Uncle Troy had told him Reverend Hamilton was my father, and my father-in-law said I had a right to know. So he called Reverend Hamilton and told him about me, saying he should recommend me as associate pastor. My father-in-law had also written Mount Baptist Church, recommending me for the position as well. He urged other pastors to do the same. Then he told Reverend Hamilton to set things straight before he met the Lord."

"But why didn't you just tell us? Sandra and me!"

Reverend Dexter quickly turned around, startled. "Why didn't I just tell you? Good question." He looked to the ceiling, then walked toward Lilly. "I don't know. It's hard to spring that kind of information on people. And I guess that, well, deep down inside, I wanted people to get to know me first. I was planning to tell Sandra, but events changed for the worst. Anyway, I needed to know the truth initially. I worked with Reverend Hamilton for a while way before I even had a discussion with him about me, my mother. Reverend Hamilton confirmed it when I handed this picture to him. He recognized it immediately. His eyes confirmed that I was his son. I was his son." Reverend Dexter suddenly looked at Lilly. "That copy of the picture belongs to Reverend Hamilton, doesn't it?"

"Yes, Sandy found it in his closet." Lilly flipped the picture over.

"That's my mother's handwriting! She must have sent her copy to him...and...and he kept it all these years." Reverend Dexter sat down, overwhelmed with emotion. He covered his eyes.

"Trudy would have been mighty proud of you. Yes, Lord. Mighty proud."

"Thanks."

"You know, somebody told me Trudy's last name was Langston."

Reverend Dexter wiped his eyes with the back of his hands. "It was. My mother was married before, but her maiden name was Dexter. But I don't understand something. How did you know this was me?"

Lilly did not respond.

"Tell me. Please. As God is my witness, I will not say a thing." His eyes pleaded.

She looked down at her lap. "Sister Adele told me."

"Sister Adele? Sister Adele Thurman?"

"Yes."

"But how would she know?" Reverend Dexter no longer looked like a mournful little boy, but a concerned grown man. His shoulders now assumed a straight position.

"Well, Sister Adele has a niece who is friends with Sister Camille."

"Are you saying that Sister Camille told Adele's niece?" He leaned forward. His eyes sunk below the angry cliff of his brow. The black kid from Harlem was rising.

"Yes, yes, I believe so, according to Adele."

How did things get so disjointed? Reverend Dexter asked himself after he had escorted Lilly outside. He walked back to the office and sat down in a daze. Why would Camille do such a thing? Was this her way of pushing things along, because he was dragging his feet? Didn't she understand that he needed time to establish a relationship with Sandra before he told her the truth? Apparently, not! Camille was weary of their personal life being put on hold—that's all that mattered to her. Yeah, but she had to know that this would get back to him! Maybe she didn't care? She wasn't spreading any lies, only the truth, and the truth will set you free.

Camille stuck her head in the doorway, "Listen. I need to do a couple of errands. Are we through for today?"

"Yes. We're through. You've done enough for today."

CHAPTER 18
AFFIRMATIONS

Lilly kneaded dough with the heels of her hands as expertly as kneading someone's back. Christmas was upon them, the best time of the year for Lilly, delivering pleasant thoughts to her mind like the three kings bearing gifts. She smiled, thinking of Reverend Dexter consuming large quantities of her sweet potato pie he loved so much. Over the past month, he'd become the son she never had, and still Sandra hadn't embraced him as a brother.

Lilly wiped her hands on her apron and walked over to the kitchen sink, peering outside the window. It was dark, and the Christmas bulbs on their hedges and windows glowed white and constant like the North Star. The flickering colored lights on the house across the street reminded her of a sign on a cheap motel. Less is better, she thought, adjusting her hairnet with her wrist. She rinsed her hands, then reached for the tiny glass of cordial on the counter. She turned her back toward the window and leaned against the sink. Very rarely had alcohol touched her lips, but there was much food to cook, so a little cordial and Christmas music made the task pleasurable: "Chestnuts roastin' on an open fire…" Lilly's voice stabbed the air that was laden with the aroma of cloves and sweet ham. She took a sip of cordial. Blackberry cordial. The kind Hyacinth used to drink.

"Hyacinth," she said softly. They had so much fun together during this time of year, wrapping presents, trimming the tree, stuffing the stockings hung by the fireside. Both enjoyed an old-fashioned Christmas. Two women who had grown up differently, but who'd grown to love each other. The difference in the way they'd grown up manifested itself in the simplest ways, especially in the kitchen. Put an onion before Hyacinth, and she'd sever the skin with a knife, then delicately remove the transparent layers, as if she were plucking a daisy. Now Lilly tore the skin with the calluses on her capable hands, shucked each onion like ears of corn, one after the other in rhythmic speed, then look at her three peeled onions to Hyacinth's one and shake her head, saying, "Lord. Lord."

The calluses on Lilly's hands were her protective skin, allowing her to hold pain like children. Yet Lilly did not have children, and questioned whether she would've been able to bear the loss of a child she'd loved and reared. Hyacinth couldn't—knew that she wouldn't. Lilly remembered how Hyacinth had grabbed the hem of her skirt one day, a few weeks before Christmas:

"Lilly, promise me you'll look after Sandra when I'm gone."

"Now where you going? Talking 'bout when you gone."

"I'm not going to see this Christmas. Promise me, Lilly."

"Now why you talking that way? The doctors say you going to be just fine. Your heart is a little weak right now. That's all."

"My heart is broken. Promise me."

So Lilly made her promise that she'd look after Sandra, had given her word to Hyacinth, serious as a blood oath. After Hyacinth's death, Lilly had tossed and turned many nights, like all mothers, worrying about the welfare of her child. When the tossing and turning became a full-time job, and Lilly's heavy lids wailed for some shuteye, she handed the matter over to the Lord, and slept straight through what could've been many sleepless nights, not even waking up to empty her bladder. Lilly kept Sandra in her prayers: prayed for her happiness, her health, for her soundness of mind, prayed that Sandra would walk into the middle of the circle—their newly-formed family circle—to meet her half-brother halfway. She envisioned how he'd walk toward Sandra too, both meeting full circle: their first encounter, their numerous discussions, misunderstanding, falling out, making up, and then their love. Full circle. This was Lilly's prayer.

Lilly placed the glass on the counter and walked toward the butcher block in the middle of the kitchen. She sprinkled flour on it and flattened out the dough for the pie's crust with the rolling pin. "And so it's been said, many times, many ways, Merry Christmas to you…Merry Christmas, Hyacinth. I kept my word. Always been a woman of my word."

Even on mornings when Sandra was not feeling up to it, she recited her daily affirmation: "I am unique. I am worthy. I am reaching toward wholeness." Each word was a brick, slowly building the belief in herself. Sandra had remembered that the book was not perfectly aligned on the shelf like all the others. It seemed to tiptoe out of place, determined to be noticed. Sandra had walked over to the bookcase, about to push it back in line, but the two words within the title captured her attention: Love Affirmations. She quickly looked around. Winston's subtle way of communicating some profundity, no doubt, but he was nowhere in sight. Sandra thumbed through its pages, deciding that she would buy it—her Christmas present in advance.

After reading a quarter of the book later that day, she was inspired to write down her own affirmation. It came to her differently at first: "I will be worthy." She cocked her head, then hunched over the pad, scratching out the sentence. She rewrote: I am worthy. Worthy of what? she had asked herself. Worthy of self-love, her inner voice had dared to reply.

After her morning recitation, Sandra got up from her knees and stretched elaborately. She sat down on her bed and yawned, water filling her eyes. She was slow to move this Christmas morning, plunging on her back, looking at the ceiling, thinking that a month ago her inner voice had also dared her to take a stand at the Poet's Corner—the moveable platform set in the middle of the floor at ART N FACTS during Zora's night.

"So, Jamie, you're coming, right?"

"I wouldn't miss your debut for the world, Maya Angelou."

"Maya Angelou! Huh, I wish."

"You afraid?"

"A little." Silence. "A lot."

"You can always back out."

"I know, but I don't want to."

"I'm glad you said that. See you 'round nine."

The rich aroma of freshly brewed coffee permeated ART N FACTS when Jamie had arrived that night. The poetry reading hadn't started yet, and people were standing around, engaged in conversation. There were scruffy Harvard students wearing dingy t-shirts, worn jeans, and rundown boots, but their perfect teeth, sturdy squared jaws, and sanguine complexions undermined their seeming poverty. Bearded literature professors, who were clothed in tweed jackets, leaned against the walls, holding the night's agenda rolled up in their hands. And women belonging to lesbian activists groups huddled together, mannish looking, with severe crew cuts. Jamie spotted Sandra in a far corner of the room under the gleam of track lighting, talking to a circle of young women. He raised his arm high above the crowd and waved, and she smiled radiantly. He said she looked like a poet: head wrapped in African-print cloth, a free-flowing black dress accentuating her tribal-looking jewelry, and a thick leather belt hung low around her waist. Sandra walked over and kissed him, then whispered,

"Glad you're here."

Some of the poets were very good, Jamie had thought. But of course, he was partial to Sandra. The place was packed when it was her turn to stand behind the podium. There weren't anymore empty seats, and so a few young women sat on the wooden floor, cross-legged, chins resting in their palms. Sandra's voice quavered in the beginning, but that was to be expected. She recited two of her mother's poems, which were received with gratitude. Then she surprised even Jamie.

She looked directly at the audience. "This last poem I'm about to recite is my own, first one I've ever written." She tucked her lips into her mouth and looked up at the indigo floodlight shining on her. Her eyes returned to the audience. "One night, I was thinking about my mother—who as you know is gone now—and about a woman who is a dear mother to me. Her name is Lilly Johnson. I thought long and hard about their lives, the hardships, like cold winters, that they've endured, the cold winters that many women have endured. As I struggle through my own winter, many times tired and weary, I hope to be as strong. The title of my poem is 'In the Winter of Her Season.'" She took a deep breath, fighting back tears. Jamie leaned forward in his chair, knowing that this was a big step for her.

She cleared her throat. "The fragrance of a true—" Her voice cracked. She stopped, placing a hand on her chest. "Excuse me. I'm sorry." The room was quiet, all eyes on her. She hesitated, then looked at Jamie.

He nodded, mouthing the words, "Go on, you can do it." Her head dropped toward the piece of paper and she began in a strong clear voice.

The fragrance of a true woman
comes not from the essence of a bottle.
But of a flowering soul, boldly withstanding
gusty movements of the wind,
storms,
and downpour of torrential rain
upon her open field.
And seemingly, the earth's elements
are all too cruel.
But yet, they are life sustaining.
For she has arisen from the winter of her season,
gathering a distinct knowledge as her spirit

unfolds into a defiant blossom.
Truly, a lesson has been learned of life, endurance, of livelihood.
So, she asks not for the lack of the earth's elements, but that
her seeds of aspirations be abundant
with the moistness of her tears
and the warmth of an undying sun.

Sandra looked up from the podium with moist eyes. "Thank you," she whispered, and Winston rushed over to hug her, saying, "Give her a big hand. A big hand!" Everyone stood up, clapping for what seemed like hours.

And even now, the memory moistened her eyes. Sandra stood up and slipped into her plaid flannel robe, then bent down on her knees and looked under the brass bed, pulling out several gifts for Lilly. She dared not put the presents under the Christmas tree downstairs, for Lilly had a tendency to snoop! The other gifts under the tree were safe. They were clearly labeled: Terrence, Maureen, Janet, Jamie, and Carl. Sandra brought a Fisher Price See 'n Say for Terrence, a black Barbie Doll for Maureen, a gift certificate to a health spa for Janet, a chrome pendulum paperweight for Carl's desk at home, and a gold watch for Jamie. Sandra planned to say to Jamie, "Now you will know the exact time when I'll awake you from sound sleep." He would get a chuckle out of it, she was sure, trying his best to be a good sport. He'd stopped complaining whenever she'd grabbed his arm in the middle of the night or wee hours of the morning following the sound of Mama's voice that even jolted Sandra out of her own sleep—and still, nothing changed in this regard.

Yet everything else had changed. She and Jamie had drawn closer, understood each other better. Now Lawrence and Rita were talking about college. "College?" Sandra was shocked when Gee had told her the news a few weeks back. Sandra had called and asked Gee what should she send the kids for Christmas.

"Money. They're grown, and it's difficult to buy anything for either of them. Trust me on this one!" She laughed. She sounded good, the scars of the past clearly mended. She was even dating now. "His name is Frank. He's good to me and the kids." Gee said. "But no one, no one will ever take the place of Jimmy!"

Sandra's heart understood what Gee had meant. For even though she loved Lilly as a mama, she wasn't Mama. And her heart ached, especially around this time of year. Mama's death had ended the holiday mood forever, but she kept up a good face for Lilly. Lilly often reminded Sandra that the Lord may have taken away Jimmy, but he'd given her another brother. So next time, Sandra planned on saying, "But no one, no one will ever take the place of Jimmy!"

As for Daddy, Sandra barely thought of him, and fought hard not to think of his illegitimate son, who was now her brother. It was harder to look him in the eye, never mind to embrace him. When Lilly first handed Sandra the news, she kept herself in isolation for days. She hadn't gone to work, hadn't seen Jamie. Sandra was certain her isolation was an attempt to shut the door in the face of the truth. But then she let the truth in—or rather the truth barged in—deep from the unconscious. Out of the blue, she remembered the daydreams she had, about making good lovin' to Reverend Dexter, the man who was now her brother. Damn! She felt foolish, even more so for thinking that he had feelings for her. Well, he may have had feelings for her, but not the kind she'd thought. She remembered the times they'd spent together, the time he'd cooked for her. She felt stupid now, stupid since she'd been ignoring him all this time, thinking that he was trying to pull a fast one. How does one start anew? She didn't know, especially with embarrassment staring her in the face, shame even.

But after the truth had sunk in, it became apparent why Reverend Dexter was so interested in her father, recalling a conversation they once had:

"Sandra, what…what…what type of relationship did you have with your father? What was he like when you were growing up? Was he a good father?"

"My father? What was he like when I was growing up? Oh, I don't know. He was a good father, I suppose."

"What do you mean, you don't know? What was he like?"

He could only imagine growing up in the Hamilton household, and he needed Sandra to sketch in the details. Now it was clear to Sandra what Enid had meant: "Ask him about his mama!" Oh, Enid knew about Trudy, but she would never admit Reverend Dexter was actually her brother's son, her nephew. But she sensed it, watched every move he made, probably saw the resemblance that nobody else saw. Asked him with suspicion, "Where are you from?" And being Enid, she could only believe that this long lost son was after money, forget about the inconsequential things, like love and a sense of belonging. It had to be money. That's the way Enid thought!

Sandra shook her head, then placed the gifts underneath her arm and stepped into the hallway. Cinnamon, nutmeg, and brown sugar hung in the air like Christmas ornaments. She slowly walked downstairs, brushing her fingertips against the tinsel that was coiled around the banister like a snake. Lilly loved decorating. She'd placed poinsettias on the mantelpiece in the living room, a wreath with a red bow on their front door, and Christmas bulbs on the windows and the hedges outside. She even convinced Sandra to help her decorate the Christmas tree. This was a surprise to Sandra since she hadn't decorated a Christmas tree in years; in New York, she always celebrated Kwanzaa. But Sandra had to admit it was fun watching Lilly rearrange the ornaments over and over until they were just right.

Sandra placed Lilly's gifts underneath the tree and walked into the kitchen when she heard the clanging of pots and pans. Lilly was moving briskly, lifting up lids from pots, opening and closing the oven. Sandra smiled, looking at Lilly's apron with pictures of mistletoe. Her hairnet was on her head, her hair in rows of curls as if she'd just taken out the rollers.

"You're still at it?"

Lilly quickly turned around to face Sandra, then looked back at the stove. "Can't let these collard greens burn!" She knocked a large spoon on the edge of the open pot, lowered the range, and placed the lid back on top. She turned to face Sandra again, laying the spoon in the sink.

"And yes, I'm still at it! Merry Christmas, baby." She walked toward Sandra and hugged her.

"Merry Christmas to you, too." Sandra hugged Lilly back, swaying side to side.

"I'm almost finished, except for the turkey and greens." Lilly sat down at the table.

Sandra followed her. "Who are you inviting for dinner, Lilly, the United States Army?"

Lilly laughed. "No, baby. Just several ladies from church, Uncle Rufus, Reverend Dexter, you." Lilly stared at Sandra. "I'd like to see you at the dinner table, baby. It would mean so much to me, plus you got to face him sooner or later. Just ain't right! He's blood."

Sandra stared at the tabletop.

Lilly placed her hand on Sandra's. "Please, baby. It's Christmas. Do it for me."

Silence.

"Please, baby."

More silence.

Then: "So, what's on the menu?" Sandra said softly.

Lilly scratched off the wrapping paper like a cat in a litter box.

"Boy! Lilly!"

"You know I get excited when it comes to opening presents, barely slept a wink last night."

Sandra laughed. "That's why I kept your presents underneath my bed!"

Lilly held up the black felt hat, with a feather stuck in its band. "My, my. Now this is something!" She examined it carefully.

"You like it?" Sandra held her hands to her mouth.

"Like it? Love it! I'm going to look good this Sunday in church! Wait 'til Lucinda sees this. Um uh." Lilly placed the hat back into the box and put it near her feet. She rubbed her hands, waiting for Sandra to place the next present on her lap.

Lilly shot up, placing the black coat with mink collar and cuffs against her body. "Oh! Sandra!" She placed the coat on the couch and quickly pulled out a tissue from the pocket of her apron. "It's beautiful!" She sat down again, dabbing her eyes.

"I'm glad you like it."

"Love it. Come over here and sit next to me." Lilly patted the couch.

Sandra sat down.

Lilly kissed her on the cheek and placed a box on her lap. "Hope you like it, baby. I was waiting for the right time to give it to you."

Sandra opened up the box and attempted to say something, but couldn't. She cleared her throat and tried again. "Where did you—" She placed a hand to her mouth, and the black-and-white pictures in the photo album became blurry.

"The real treasure was in your mama's closet."

There was silence. The tick of the grandfather clock in the hallway permeated the living room.

Sandra wiped her tears with her palms.

Lilly leaned over to hug her, pressing Sandra against her ample bosom. She wiped Sandra's eyes with the tissue she'd pulled from her apron. "Bet you didn't know about these pictures, huh? Well, one day I was cleaning your mama's closet, and there they were. The idea came to me a long time ago, but I was waiting for the right time. Your mama loved you more than you'll ever know. Although, " Lilly paused, "at times you may not have thought so."

Sandra lifted her head from Lilly's bosom. "I just wish I had more time with Mama, you know? Just when we were getting to know one another…"

"I know, baby, I know. Who knows why things happen the way they do? Only God knows. But I tell you one thing, your mama wanted the best for you…opportunities she never had. She did the best she could. Her life was easy in some ways—had everything she wanted—but at the same time, it wasn't easy."

Sandra looked closely at a picture under the clear sheet of plastic. Her mother, young and vibrant, was smiling at the camera. She held Sandra butt-naked as a baby in her arms. A towel was thrown over her mother's shoulder, as if she had just given Sandra a bath. "God! She looks so happy, doesn't she, Lilly?"

"Yes. She does."

"I wish I had memories of the good times. The early years, you know? I mostly remember when things turned sour between us. When I was twelve years old, Mama turned cold."

Lilly kissed Sandra on the forehead. "I know, baby. You told me. I know. Maybe that's why you hear her voice, 'cause you miss her so. You knew the last thing on her lips was your name."

Sandra rested her head on Lilly's shoulder. "Could be," she said softly, not certain of anything anymore, not when it came to Mama.

Janet opened the front door with her hands on her hips. Her head then disappeared behind the door, stretching her neck: "Hey! Carl! Look who's here—a female Santa Claus. Black one, too!"

"Oh! Janet, please! Let me in. It's cold out here!"

"Maybe," Janet said, wagging her head.

"Maybe?" Sandra balled a fist. "You want some of this?"

"You wouldn't want to do that to your future sister-in-law, now would ya?"

"Don't try me!" Sandra pushed the door open and barged in.

They laughed.

"Where's that wretched brother of mine?" Janet asked, closing the door.

"He'll be here later."

"Hey! Hey! Hey! Merry Christmas!" Carl kissed Sandra on the cheek. "Let me take these bags from you. Give me your coat."

Sandra stood in the foyer, rubbing her hands. She glanced at Janet. "Sure is cold."

Janet could always decorate a Christmas tree, Sandra thought, as she sat in the living room. Sandra was pleased that they loved the presents she'd given them. Even Terrence seemed pleased, who was now walking!

"Here!" Janet said breathlessly. She ran into the next room for Sandra's gift, then hurried back into the living room, and dropped it onto Sandra's lap. Whatever it was, it was flat, large and square, but not heavy.

"I had to keep it in my bedroom. Nothing's safe anymore with him roaming around."

Their heads swiveled toward Terrence, who now had a Christmas tree ornament in his mouth, the See 'n Say thrown to the side.

"Terrence!"

Terrence jumped, dropping the cherry red ball. He was stunned, his mouth forming a wide circle, emitting a long cry.

Carl, sitting in his easy chair, looked up from his pendulum paperweight. "You scared him, honey."

"You're supposed to be watching him, Carl!"

"Me?"

"Yeah, you!"

Terrence ran to Carl, hugging his knees, placing his head onto his father's lap. "Shhh," Carl said, raking his fingers through Terrence's mass of curls. "It's all right."

Terrence's wail grew louder.

Janet cupped her ears.

Sandra looked curiously at her gift.

"My God! This place sounds like a madhouse. Maureen! Turn down that TV!"

Maureen was engrossed with the bendable legs of her Barbie Doll. "Okay, Ma," she whined, annoyed at the interruption.

Janet suddenly grabbed Sandra's elbow, practically pulling her off her seat. "Let's go into my bedroom."

Sandra held onto her present to keep it from falling off her lap. "Okay! Wait a minute, Janet!"

The bedroom was oppressively quiet. Sandra sat down on the rose-colored quilt, making note of their footprints in the plush, matching-colored carpet.

Janet sat down, too. Her hands moved before her as if she were negotiating a deal. "Now! You can tell me if you don't like it."

Sandra shrugged. "Okay." She proceeded to open her gift.

"Wait!"

"What, Janet?"

"Remember when we were kids?"

"No!"

"Sandra!"

"Of course I do! Can I open my present now?"

"In a minute." Janet placed her splayed fingers on top Sandra's gift.

"Sometimes I remember when we were kids, especially when I look at Maureen, and I reminisce when we were that age. Walking hand in hand to school, spindly legs and all. Remember?" Janet clasped her hands between her thighs and looked off into space, transported back in time. "Yeah. Time sure flies." Janet laughed to herself, shaking her head. She suddenly looked at Sandra. "Okay! Open up!"

Sandra removed the wrapping paper, gazing down an oil painting of Janet and herself at Sandra's tenth birthday party, their arms wrapped around each other's shoulder. Janet's hair silky smooth, and Sandra's, well, a mess.

"I got the picture from my mother and took it to a friend who does portraits. Like it?"

Sandra brought the painting close to her face, analyzing the perfect brush strokes, her wonderful childhood immortalized, false as it was. She placed the painting on her lap, silent.

"Hope you like the frame. It's cherry wood. I searched all over for that frame, almost drove Carl crazy! He can tell you! I wanted everything to be just perf— What's wrong?"

Sandra cradled her face in her hand.

"Don't you like it?"

Sandra lifted her face and rested her hand on her mouth. She looked at Janet. "I love it," she whispered.

Janet traced her fingertips alongside the picture frame. "Those were some happy times, carefree."

"Not always," Sandra said coldly.

"Not always? What did we have to worry about then? Nothing but wonder if we'd win our fights with the boys." Janet giggled, but stopped abruptly, looking at the seriousness on Sandra's face.

Sandra placed the picture on the bed and stood up and walked toward the window. Janet's next door neighbors had just finished loading their car with presents, slammed the trunk, then rushed to their front seats, the cold dictating the briskness of their movements. They sat in the car for a while before driving off. "Janet," Sandra said softly, still peering outside the window. "You've known me practically all my life, but you don't know me."

Janet stood up and slapped her thighs. "There you go again, complicating things! Know you, but don't know you?" She walked toward the window.

Sandra spun around. "If you say I complicate things one more time, Janet, I swear I'll scream! Sometimes things just get complicated!"

Janet stepped back. "What's wrong with you?" She walked backward, still facing Sandra, and sat down on the bed again, puzzled.

Sandra advanced toward her. "I'm not the person you think you grew up with! That's what's wrong! Our childhood friendship was a farce, Janet! Carefree, you say? At twelve I had to deal with my father touching me!"

"What?" Janet jumped up.

"I was battling alcoholism in grade school. No! It wasn't carefree. Maybe for you, not for me! And you need to know this!"

"Your father? Reverend Hamilton? My God. Oh my God." Janet was on the verge of tears. She cupped her mouth, then dropped her hand to her side. "I can't imagine—" She pressed her palms to her temples and walked in small circles, the full brunt of Sandra's words sinking in. "That's like...that's like if Carl molested...touched Maureen...I can't imagine." Janet suddenly looked at Sandra. "Does Jamie know this?"

Sandra nodded.

"Well, why didn't you tell me?"

"I'm telling you now, Janet!"

Janet burst into tears, nearly collapsing on Sandra's shoulder. "I'm so sorry. I'm so sorry."

"I know. I know," Sandra said, stroking Janet's silky smooth hair.

"You've certainly outdone yourself, Sister Lilly. The dinner was ex-cel-lent!" Reverend Dexter said, smiling.

There! Sandra saw it again. His smile was a lot like Jimmy's. She hadn't noticed it before.

"Thank you." Lilly beamed across the living room.

Her Christmas dinner turned out well, and the ladies from church and Uncle Rufus left satisfied. Reverend Dexter sat in his father's wingback chair. Lilly and Sandra were on the couch.

And his cleft chin, just like Daddy's. Those big eyes must be his mother's.

Reverend Dexter rubbed his lap, looking at the shadow of the lit Christmas tree high upon the wall. He glanced at Sandra. "Wasn't dinner great?"

"I'm sorry. Excuse me?" She sat upright.

"Dinner was great, wasn't it?"

"Oh, yes! We know that our Lilly is a wonderful cook!" Sandra patted Lilly on the back.

Lilly beamed again. She stood up: "Well! Anybody want more sweet potato pie?"

"You know I do," Reverend Dexter said.

"I'll have another piece later."

The air was uneasy after Lilly left the room. Reverend Dexter glanced at Sandra, then moved around in his seat, repeatedly rubbing the armrests. The ease that he and Sandra once shared was apparently gone. He thought of something to say, nothing that sounded too rehearsed, but came up empty.

Sandra looked at her fingernails for the fourth time, at the flames of the fire, the way it cast its glow around the room. In any other situation, the room's setting would have been romantic: a cozy fire, the white lights of the Christmas tree, the clean smell of pine, soft music, dim lights. What was taking Lilly so long to cut a few pieces of pie? She moved back to her finger again, nervously nibbling on a hangnail. Finally, she couldn't take it anymore. She deposited the dead skin from the side of her mouth and said, "That was Daddy's favorite chair."

Reverend Dexter looked up from his lap. "Was it?" He touched an armrest.

"Yep. That's an old chair. Nobody could sit in that chair—unless, of course, you wanted your head bitten off."

Reverend Dexter laughed heartily, then turned serious. "I can't believe he's gone."

"I can't believe my whole family is gone, and I'm still here." Sandra looked at her hands again. "Why? I have no idea," she said to herself.

There was rustling outside the doorway, and Sandra's head turned in its direction, certain it was Lilly.

Reverend Dexter leaned forward in his chair and said thoughtfully, "Well, nobody has the mind of God, but I'd like to take the liberty to speculate. Maybe there are things that God wants to reveal to you…lessons you haven't learned yet. That's why you're here. He does have a purpose for your life, Sandra. For everyone."

Purpose? Sandra's mind surrounded the word like an angry crowd. What purpose? Her life didn't even seem to have a pattern—well, at least not one that made sense to her—never mind a purpose. Sandra shook her head and heard herself say aloud, "Purpose. Yeah, right."

Reverend Dexter sat back in his chair and looked at her pointedly. "You do."

He had said this with so much confidence it made Sandra laugh. She waved her hand. "Yeah. Okay."

"Don't believe me, huh?" He rested his elbow on an armrest, his fist nestled beneath his jawbone.

Sandra sighed. "Listen, if you knew all the crazy stuff I'd been through, you wouldn't be saying that. Purpose implies a clear direction. See, that's not my life, never been."

"But it's the life that God wants for you."

"Oh, please! God. I already told you how I felt about him."

"You believed in him once, when you were little. I remember." Reverend Dexter leaned forward in his chair, making a steeple with his hands.

"Once! And long ago!" Sandra folded her hands across her chest.

"Why are you so angry?"

"I'm not angry."

Reverend Dexter sat back in his chair again. "You're right. I don't know all that you've been through."

"You can say that again!"

He looked at Sandra for a moment. "But just because darkness comes our way, doesn't mean that God has abandoned us...or that He caused it."

"But he allows it! He allows it!"

Reverend Dexter stood up and walked toward Sandra, but stopped, startled by the glistening fierceness in Sandra's eyes. He plunged his hands deep into his pockets, standing in the middle of the room. His head dropped toward his shoes. "Well," he finally said, "God still loves you." He looked at Sandra. "I don't know what turned you away from the Lord. But He's still near you, with outstretched hands, saying, 'Come...you've run a long race.'"

Sandra immediately remembered the faceless man in her dreams. "What did you say?"

Reverend Dexter frowned. "I said, God says, 'Come. You've run a long race.'"

Sandra scratched her head. "That's what I thought."

CHAPTER 19
FORGIVENESS

Jamie folded the letter and handed it back to Sandra. They sat on the bench in her backyard, shoulder to shoulder.

"I don't know why she wants me as guest speaker," Sandra said. "I gave Lindsay hell when I was at Haven."

Jamie shrugged. "Yeah, but you said Gee had told her of your progress. You've been off the grape for a while."

Sandra burst into laughter. "The grape?" She placed the letter beneath her lap, shaking her head. "The grape. Funny."

It was August 1993, the thick of the summer, end of the brutal winter.

Jamie winked and made a clicking sound from the back of his cheek. "The grrrape." It sounded like a low resounding belch.

"You're sick. You know that?" Sandra leaned closer to his face, eyebrows raised.

Jamie smiled and kissed her forehead. "That's what they tell me. So, are you going to California?"

Sandra raised one shoulder, then let it drop. "I don't know."

Jamie squeezed her denim-clad thigh, and the gleam of the sun bounced off his gold watch, causing Sandra to squint. She immediately touched her necklace he'd given her for Christmas, a gold half heart, with broken jagged edges. She remembered how Jamie had strung the other half along his gold chain and slipped it over his head, then patted his chest, saying, "This is my half. Together we're whole." Sandra shifted on the bench. No one likes to be broken, she thought, slipping her hand into Jamie's, their fingers interlocking. She raised his hand and kissed his knuckles, thinking about her darker days at Haven, about Libby, Burly, and all the others striving for wholeness.

One day—seemingly out of the blue—it occurred to Sandra that there was a sudden change within her, like the sudden change in the direction of the wind. Of course, she knew that it wasn't sudden, but only felt that way. It was a process really, happening moment by moment. Her ongoing conversations with her brother about God and one's purpose were beginning to produce results, as well as her daily affirmation. It wasn't simply a recitation anymore, but now conviction. "I can't" gave way to "I can." "I may" gave way to "I will." Each one defeated the other, like a prizefighter knocking his opponents outside the ring. Yes, from time to time, old doubts and fear still arose, and "I can't" tried to muscle its way back in, but these were the times when Sandra kept vigilance, understanding human frailty, knowing that life is a fight.

Other people besides Jamie saw the change in Sandra, too. Winston marveled of course. He marveled even more when Sandra inquired about the purchase of ART N FACTS. Sandra had been employed there for almost a year now, and knew that Winston and Meridian were more than ready to retire. Meridian was ecstatic. Not only did she and Winston get a buyer very quickly, but she also knew that Sandra would keep up the tradition of Langston's and Zora's nights. Sandra remembered the first time she had recited poetry. Many women had approached her, saying how much they were moved. Sandra could never abandon the tradition now. This was a way of sharing herself, allowing her mother's voice to be heard, appreciated. After all, that's what Zora's night was all about, wasn't it? Commemorating, sharing?

Reverend Dexter suggested that Sandra should reserve a section of the store for Christian publications. Of course, this was one of his ways of spreading the gospel, and Sandra obliged. She had to admit that it was also sound business advice—the larger the variety of books, the better people's needs would be served. Anyway, God's Grace Community Center had become ART N FACTS most faithful patrons over the past several months. Reverend Dexter brought many books for the after school cultural classes, and he'd finally convinced Sandra to teach African history on Saturday afternoons. Sandra enjoyed it more than she thought, and was even considering a second degree in education.

She also acted as a substitute counselor for girls between the ages of fifteen and eighteen—and she loved it. Some of the girls were tackling a host of problems, mostly stemming from low self-esteem. Even Reverend Dexter told Sandra she was most beneficial in this area. "Of course," she said one day. "I'm certainly an expert on low self-esteem." And being an expert on the matter, she couldn't ignore the shame scrawled on Karen Brown's face, a full-breasted fifteen-year-old, who walked with her eyes cast to the ground. Only once had

Karen looked directly into Sandra's eyes—then Sandra knew. She was careful not to project her own experiences onto the girls. Her objective was to share her experiences with them, to let them know she had overcome great odds, was still overcoming great odds. But that look of shame was too familiar for Sandra to ignore, and she approached Karen one afternoon.

Karen was sitting in the recreation room, hunched in a corner, eating potato chips. Sandra beckoned Karen to follow her to the back office. First, she talked generally about young ladies having the right to their own bodies, then delicately asked the question, "Karen...is...is someone touching you? I mean, without your consent?" Karen eyes remained cast to the floor, sitting quietly in a chair. Sandra looked at Karen's breasts bulging from the sides of her yellow tank top, bra straps showing, digging deeply into the skin of her shoulders. She had no business wearing that, Sandra thought—where was her mother, anyway?—deciding that she would talk to Karen about her dress later. One step at a time.

She was an attractive girl, though, a round face like a child's and a cleft chin shaped like a heart. But to Sandra, Karen appeared to hate the size of her breasts, drawing her shoulders inward to minimize their size. Yet still she wore a ribbed tank top! Sandra couldn't figure that one out. Silence. Sandra didn't know if the silence meant, yes, no, or simply Karen was much more shy than she'd initially thought. "Is it your boyfriend? Assuming that you have one." Still silence. Sandra took a bold stance, remembering her own feelings of guilt and shame: "Is it your father?" Karen's head bobbed up, tears beading at the corner of her eyes.

Karen's look of terror startled Sandra for a moment, for she had expected the same silence. Sandra slowly draped her fingertips over her mouth, realizing what was happening. She reached over to hug Karen, rubbing her back. Her shoulders and arms were surprisingly fragile to the touch. Sandra felt the tiny bones underneath her golden-brown skin. Karen wept, and a layer of sadness descended upon Sandra like a heavy blanket.

"I don't know about that," Reverend Dexter said. "That's a serious charge, Sandra! The man can go to jail! Did Karen actually say that?" He placed his hands behind his head, sitting behind his desk, eyebrows knitted together in concern.

"She didn't have to. I know." Sandra slumped onto a gray metal chair.

The afternoon sun shone on her face, and she shielded her eyes, as if engaged in a salute.

Reverend Dexter stood up and closed the blinds. He walked slowly around the room, hands on his hips, head down. The sound of his hard shoes pervaded the room. Suddenly, he stopped.

"Why are you so certain, Sandra?" He stood behind her.

Sandra did not turn to answer him: "Because I know. I've…"

"You what?"

"I've…I've…because I've been there!"

Silence. Dead silence. Sandra didn't even hear Reverend Dexter's breathing anymore. Finally, she heard his footsteps again. He grasped the chair next to her, pressing so hard that his knuckles turned white. At the corner of her eyes, she saw his hairy forearms below the rolled up shirt sleeves.

"I want to ask so many questions," he said softly, "but I'm not going to. What purpose will it serve? I'm so sorry, Sandra."

"I'm sorry, too. Boy, am I sorry. I carried that around for years. After a while, I got tired of carrying the load. So I buried it. But it still haunts me to this day— especially now." Sandra leaned forward, cradling her face in her hands. "Gets me so angry!"

Reverend Dexter sat next to her, resting a hand on Sandra's back. "Get rid of it, then."

"And how do you suppose I do that? What's done is done." Sandra wiped the tears from her eyes with the back of her hand, facing him.

"Forgiveness."

"Forgiveness?"

"Forgiveness."

"So what am I to tell Karen, huh? Forgive your father every time he molests you?"

"We'll deal with Karen later. Right now I'm talking about you. Yes. What's done is done—can't change that. But you can change the power that our father has over you. As long as these thoughts make you angry and overwhelmed, well, he still has power over you. Even though he's dead, been dead for almost a year now. Bury it once and for all. Forgive him. Let it go. If not, he'll keep molesting you until the day you die."

Tears streamed down Sandra's face, and she burst into a long wail. She shuddered hard, surprising Reverend Dexter. He hugged Sandra, pressing her head onto his shoulder, dabbing her eyes with his handkerchief. This was her grown baby brother, she thought. Wise in so many ways. A long period of time elapsed before she raised her head from his shoulder.

"Well, have you forgiven Camille?"

"What?"

"You heard me." Sandra nudged his side.

"Yes. Yes. I have."

"Must I soon prepare for a wedding, then?"

No answer.

"Well?"

"I've asked God for direction on that one."

"And?"

"Still waiting."

"But what if Camille can't wait?"

"Then I will be assured that she's not the one for me."

Sandra looked into Reverend Dexter's eyes.

"What?"

"I've really grown to love you, Samuel Ronald Dexter. I really mean it."

His eyes grew misty. "Give me my handkerchief, will you?"

It was the first anniversary of her father's death: September 10, 1993, a Sunday. This was a good time to go to her father's grave and bury the past, Sandra thought. What would she say when she reached his grave? She didn't know. She'd never forgiven anyone before. How do you forgive somebody?

"Just say I forgive you, and mean it," Reverend Dexter later told her. "Don't make things more complicated than they really need to be. And while you're at it, try to think of anyone else that you need to forgive. Throw it in the receptacle all at once." Sandra chuckled, shaking her head. Sam. She took another sip of coffee, sitting at the kitchen table. She wore an oversized white t-shirt, and her kinky curls stood on end. It was eleven o'clock in the morning, and the day had a gray overcast, dreary.

Who else did she need to forgive? Les, most certainly—although her feelings for him had turned from anger to pity. He didn't have power over her any more. Les eventually lost the house and business, which were means of quick cash now that he had a drug problem. Gee was even trying to convince Les to seek rehab, and with her unquenchable optimism, believed that Les could still defeat his problems, regardless of the cumulated ruin. That was Gee! Sandra thought. Her mind moved to Enid. These days, Enid was fighting a different kind of problem: multiple sclerosis. Enid couldn't harm a kitten even if she wanted to, but Sandra believed that she needed to forgive her, anyway. Life has a mysterious way of changing course, Sandra thought, and the old cliché, "What goes around comes around" became a testimony to her. She thought about Lindsay, about what she'd said years ago, "Do you think that alcohol is the root cause of your problem?" Sandra looked into her mug of coffee. Now she knew that alcohol was not the root cause of her pain, but her inability to forgive, to let go of the anger that was eating her insides. She decided that she would go to California. Yeah. Why not?

The sun made an appearance later in the day. Mount Auburn Cemetery was filled with family members visiting the dearly departed, and tour groups exploring its beautiful landscape and bird sanctuary. Other people simply came to view the tombstones of the famous people buried there. Sandra bent down on her knees and placed a dozen red roses with baby's breath on her mother's grave, a wreath of yellow carnations on her father's. Their tombstones stood side by side, as in life side by side, for better, for worse. She sat cross-legged in front of their graves, pulling the threads of her frayed jeans. She wore a red t-shirt knotted at the midriff, clogs, and her head was wrapped in African-print cloth.

It seemed like centuries ago since she seriously thought about killing her father. Kill. Now it seemed like a terrible thought. But truthfully, the thought had soaked her mind like a heavy downpour for years. Sandra remembered when she'd resolved to walk into her father's bedroom, fling open the window, wait, watch. She'd imagined that his hollow eyes would fly open, acknowledging the horror. She'd opened the door, pushing forward on the balls of her feet, a creak underfoot—no turning back, not even if she wanted to. Then the voice came. That voice was Mama's. And to this day Sandra still hadn't determined whether Mama's voice was real or imagined—she didn't have all the answers—but it prevented her from carrying out her act. Lilly said that Mama wanted her to have all the opportunities that she never had, and now Sandra was able to do just that: to live her life, be the person she was meant to be. Mama would've wanted it that way.

Sandra brushed a hand over her forehead. She couldn't imagine what her life would have been like if she'd actually done it. Probably in prison somewhere, far from ever reaching her true possibilities. Yes. Mama was her guardian angel. Sandra looked intently at her father's grave. "I forgive you, Daddy," she said softly. "Please forgive me." To her mother's tombstone, she simply said, "Thank you. Thank you."

Printed in the United States
31991LVS00005B/382-384